# I Came to Say Goodbye

## Caroline Overington

arrow books

Published by Arrow Books, 2013

2 4 6 8 10 9 7 5 3 1

Arrow Books
The Random House Group Limited
20 Vauxhall Bridge Road, London, SW1V 2SA

www.randomhousebooks.co.uk

Addresses for companies within The Random House Group Limited can
be found at: www.randomhouse.co.uk/offices.htm

The Random House Group Limited Reg. No. 954009

A CIP catalogue record for this book
is available from the British Library

ISBN 9780099584766

The Random House Group Limited supports the Forest Stewardship
Council® (FSC®), the leading international forest-certification organisation.
Our books carrying the FSC label are printed on FSC®-certified paper.
FSC is the only forest-certification scheme supported by the
leading environmental organisations, including Greenpeace.
Our paper procurement policy can be found at:
www.randomhouse.co.uk/environment

Printed and bound by CPI Group (UK) Ltd, Croydon, CR0 4YY

*For Jacqueline Samantha*
*and Steven John (Overingtons all)*

# FROM THE AUTHOR

I'm writing to you from Sydney, Australia, about issues that are important to me – and, I believe, to all of us around the world.

For the past seven years, I've been working as a journalist on a daily newspaper.

For better or worse, my round has been child neglect and child murder.

I can't say for certain how I ended up having to do this round, but I am proud to be able to say that I can still be shocked by what I've seen.

In almost every case I've had to cover, the killers have been the parents, or else what might be called 'the system' of dysfunction, and welfare, and drug and alcohol abuse and, sadly, mental illness.

Also in almost every case, good people have tried to intervene to save the child's life.

It is still shocking to me that those of us who live in rich countries like Great Britain, like sunny Australia, in the US, and all around the Western world, still manage to fail the smallest and most vulnerable amongst us.

I will never forget the police officers, the nurses, the doctors and others who have had to pick up the pieces in these cases.

I will never forget the many grandparents, including those still fighting for justice today.

Part of the reason I started to write books was to honour these people in ways I couldn›t in the newspaper. I dedicate my work to them.

Yours,
Caroline Overington

# Prologue

It was four o'clock in the morning. The car park outside Sydney Children's Hospital was quiet. A 27-year-old woman, dressed only in a dressing-gown and slippers, pushed through the front revolving door.

Security staff would later say they thought she was a new mother, returning to her child's bedside – and in a way, she was.

The woman walked past the nurses' station, where a lone matron sat in dim light, playing laptop Solitaire. She walked past Joeys – the room where pink and puckered babies lay row by row in perspex tubs – and into Pandas, where six infants – not newborns but babies under the age of one – lay sleeping in hospital cots.

The woman paused at the door for a moment, as though

scanning the children. She then walked directly across the room, where a gorgeous baby girl had kicked herself free of her blankets. She was laying face down, the way babies sometimes do, her right cheek flat to the white sheet, her knees up under her chest. The white towelling of her nappy was brilliant against her dark skin.

The woman took a green, nylon shopping bag from the pocket of her nightie. It was one of those ones that had *Woolworths, the Fresh Food People* written across the side. She put the bag on the floor and lifted the baby girl from the cot.

The infant stirred, but she did not wake. The woman placed her gently in the bottom of the shopping bag, under a clown blanket she had taken from the cot. She stood, and looked around. There was a toy giraffe on the windowsill. The woman put that in the bag with the baby, too. Then she walked back down the corridor, past the matron at her laptop, through the front door and back into the hospital car park.

There is CCTV footage of what happened next, and most Australians would have seen it, either on the internet or the evening news.

The woman walked across the car park towards an old Corolla. She put the shopping bag on the ground, and opened the car's rear door. She lifted the giraffe and the blanket out of the bag and dropped both by the wheels of the car.

For one long moment, she held the child gently against her breast. She put her nose against the rusty curls on the top of the girl's head, and with her eyes closed, she smelled her.

She clipped the infant into the baby capsule, and got behind the wheel of the Corolla. She drove towards the exit barrier and put her ticket in the box. The barrier opened and the woman drove forward, turning left at the lights, towards Parramatta Road.

That is where the CCTV footage ends. It isn't where the story ends, however. It's not even where the story starts.

# PART ONE

# Chapter 1

## Med Atley

I WAS OUT ON THE TRACTOR when a woman phoned to say I'd
have to go into the cop shop and make a formal statement.
I'd turned off the engine to take the call on the mobile and
straightaway wished I hadn't.

I told her. I said, 'I'm not sure I can do that.'

She told me, 'You don't really have a choice, Mr Atley.
The case is coming up. The judge wants statements from
witnesses. We also need your signature.'

I told her, 'I didn't witness anything.'

The woman, she said, 'We're not suggesting that you did.
It's more that the judge has got to make a decision. It's your
grandchild we're talking about.'

I said, 'I know what it's about.'

The woman said, 'Mr Atley, if you don't make a statement, the judge will call you in, and you'll have to do it on the stand. It's not something you've really got a choice about.'

I said, 'It was still a free country last time I checked.'

I put the phone back in my pocket. The next day, a bloke from the local police station, a fellow I knew, put his head through the open flyscreen, into my kitchen. He said, 'Med, you there?'

I'd been making coffee. I held up the cup, meaning, 'Can I get you one?' He nodded.

I said, 'Mate, I appreciate you making the house call, but I know what this is about. I already had a girl on the blower yesterday.'

He said, 'Well, are you going to make the statement, Med? Because if you don't, they'll only subpoena you, which means you'll have to go in, and take the stand.'

I said, 'I realise that. I'm just not sure what I'm going to say.'

He said, 'Get yourself a lawyer then.'

I said, 'You don't think lawyers have got quite enough of the Atley money?'

He said, 'Then do it yourself, but make sure you do it, Med. You've got a grandchild out there. Decisions are being made.'

I said, 'I'm grateful for the reminder.'

Later that night, I went out onto the porch. It was dark all around. I flicked the switch on the outdoor light. Not for the first time, I thought, 'How do the moths get inside the lightshade?'

There's an old table on the porch. I bought it for my wife back in 1974. It was the thing to have in those days. It had a formica surface, so cups didn't leave a ring. I pulled up a chair, the only one left now from the set of four. Those chairs, that marriage, it's all gone.

I sat for a while, doing nothing.

The dog saw me come out. She got up off her hessian bed, wandered over, wagged her tail. I bent down, gave her a bit of a rub along the spine with my knuckles. Her back leg kicked.

I said, 'Alright, old girl?'

Kick, kick, kick.

I said, 'Okay, old girl. Let's see what we can do.'

I had before me a pad of white paper. It wasn't anything fancy. I bought it from the newsagent. It was one of those lined pads with the pink gum across the top to hold the pages together. I had my old man's Parker pen with me. I twisted the barrel and the nib came down.

The first words I wrote were, 'Well, let me warn you now, Your Honour, this isn't going to be Shakespeare.'

I wrote, 'I can see you've got a problem here that you need to solve. You've got a grandchild of mine and you're trying to figure out what to do.'

I wrote, 'Police here have explained to me that you need a little background.'

I wrote, 'It occurs to me that there's a half-dozen experts out there, maybe more, who will be giving you their version of my family history. They'll tell you what they think we are – kidnappers, child abusers, you name it. I've got no problem with that. Every man is entitled to his opinion.'

I wrote, 'What I'm going to put down, it's not going to be a theory, and it's not just my point of view. It's more going to be the nuts and bolts of what's gone on over the past four years.'

I wrote, 'My mate in the police force here, he says I ought to get a lawyer to help me get it right, but bugger that, I'm perfectly capable of putting down what I think.'

I wrote, 'There's been plenty of lawyers caught up in this mess already, and mostly what they've done is lighten our wallets.'

I wrote, 'Much of what I'm going to tell you I haven't said out loud to anyone before. It's not going to be easy for me. Parts of it, I might even have to get my oldest daughter, Kat, to write down for me.'

I can promise you this, though, Your Honour. Everything I put down here – every word of it – is going to be true.

# Chapter 2

I WANT TO GET SOMETHING STRAIGHT off the bat, Your Honour. My name, it's Med. Not Ned. *Med*. It's short for Meredith.

Now, don't bother telling me that Meredith is a girl's name. It's a boy's name, or at least, it was, when I was born, and I ought to know. I've been asked about it often enough – every day, practically, since I was old enough to talk.

People say, 'Ned?' and I say, 'Med' and they say, 'Med, with an M?' and I say, 'Med, short for Meredith' and they say, '*Meredith*? Your name's Meredith?' like I might say, 'Nah, just kidding' and I say, 'That's right. Meredith' and they say, 'But Meredith's a girl's name' like I might say, 'Hey, hang on. You're right, and I wonder why my mother didn't think of that.'

It's not a girl's name. It's a boy's name, just like Kelly is a boy's name, and I ought to know, because I've got a brother

Kelly, and a brother Lindsay, who is known to us as Lin, and a brother Vivien, who is known to us as Viv. When I tell people that, they say, 'Seems like your mum wanted a girl' but we had girls. We had Patricia, known as Trisha, and we've got Edna, known as Ed.

Even so, there are times when I announce myself as Med – no, not *Ned*, but Med, short for Meredith – and I can see people thinking, maybe he's had a sex change? If I'd had a sex change, I'd want my money back. They'd have done a pretty poor job of making me look like a woman. I'm not a big guy. I'm five-feet-four-inches tall, and I've got a beer belly, and a bald head.

I've also got a fairly big beard. Sometimes I think that's why people keep thinking I'm saying 'Ned' when I'm saying 'Med'. They hear Ned, because they are thinking 'Ned Kelly'. I suppose that's fair enough. That is the kind of beard I've got. A bit shorter, a bit neater, but yeah, pretty close to that. My youngest daughter, when she was little, she always reckoned I looked like a garden gnome. She had in mind the one that holds a fishing line over the pond in what was her grandma's garden. I had to tell her, 'That can't be me. That's Grumpy from the Seven Dwarfs.' It made no difference to her. She still said it looked like me, and I suppose that's fair enough. I'm not saying I'm grumpy. I am saying I'm not normally the one that keeps the party alive.

Anyway, the long and the short of it is, my first name is Med, and my last name is Atley, and if this is the year 2009, then I'm 59 years old, because I was born in 1950, the fourth of eight kids.

# I CAME TO SAY GOODBYE

This probably won't count for much in terms of the matter at hand, but for the record, my old man, Jack Atley, served in World War II. He was a cook. I'm not a bad one. Like most blokes in those days, he had a bride picked out before he shipped out. Her name was Catherine Mary McCarthy, and she was from the little town of Forster, on the NSW Central Coast, and he married her in 1946.

The house I grew up in still stands. It's a two-bedroom weatherboard. It used to have a loo at the end of the back porch but Dad put up some wood one winter to bring the loo indoors. Two bedrooms might not sound like a lot but it was enough for us.

People say to me now, 'Oh, are you from Forster? I know that area.' What they mean is, they know it now. They know the McDonald's on the freeway and the Coles and the Kmart on the outskirts of town that were not there when I was a boy. They know the Pirate's Cove caravan park, and Moby's Retreat, down at Blueys, where a two-bedroom fibro beach shack will set you back $700,000, and that's if you can find one that hasn't been bulldozed to make way for some units. They don't mean Forster as I remember it, farmland and fishing boats.

There were three schools in town, the State, the Catholic and the Church of England. Mum was Catholic – her name was Catherine Mary. What else was she going to be? – so us boys, we went to St Charles, and the girls, they went to St Clare's.

Of the eight of us, there's six left. Greg, who was Daryl's twin, died when he was five. Nobody explained what happened. All we knew was he had fits. Today, we'd say epilepsy. Greg's buried at the lawn cemetery in Tuncurry. I'll be honest and say I don't really remember him. There is a photograph. He looks like Daryl, only a good head taller. Funny that he was the one who didn't make it.

'The other Atley that is gone is my sister, Trish. She got the big C – cancer – in the breast, before she was even married. She fought it off, and had two children. When it came back the second time, it was in the bone. She wasn't old, only 47, when she died. That was just a few years back. She went to the crematorium. She had two teenage kids. I tried to talk to them at the funeral. It wasn't much use.

After school the girls went into a typing pool. Daryl, Lin and me, we were apprenticed out as labourers to blokes that Dad knew in town. This was the late 1960s. There were triple-fronted brick veneers – the orange ones, with venetian blinds – going up on subdivisions. That's what we built.

Dad's dead now. Like Trish, he got cancer. Last time I saw him was on the cancer ward, with his head back, and a hole in his throat. He wrote a note for us. It said: 'I'd kill for a smoke.'

Mum's still alive. She's 87, and the hearing has just about gone, and she's starting to forget who goes where. She might think my eldest is one of her own, if you see what I mean.

Until a few years ago, she was still living in the house where she'd lived with my old man. Then one night she fell on the way to the loo and it was morning before Edna went around and found her, still cheerful.

'Don't worry about me!' she said, when Edna was helping

her up. 'I was fine. I just lay down and had a bit of a sleep. No point fussing!'

I didn't think Mum would want to go into an old people's home. I know I wouldn't. But when Edna put it to her: 'Why don't we find a place for you, Mum? Somewhere nice and closer to town?', Mum said alright.

She's been there a few years now. The smell's not great, but the place isn't bad. They have a fake fire and some budgerigars. Mid-morning, the nurses push all the old ducks down the corridors in their mobile beds and crank them up, so they can watch TV.

I should say I've protected Mum from what's gone on with my lot. I didn't take her to the funeral, for example.

But anyway, let me get back to Forster. I left school at age 15, and Kelly did the same. We laboured, and in 1969 Kelly's number came up for Vietnam.

I was a bit surprised by that. What were the odds? For country kids, apparently the odds weren't bad. Next thing we know Kelly got a letter saying, well, on this day in July, you've got to get on the Army truck, and it's going to take you to Puckapunyal, State of Victoria, for your basic training.

Well, Kelly wasn't the type to join a protest movement. That was for hippy types, in the cities. He took the call-up in his stride, and did the six weeks basic training with no complaints. When he came home in uniform, he looked like a man.

A month before he was due to ship out, we went to a dance at the Tuncurry Dance Hall, which I suppose was a

11

bit old-fashioned, even then. I mean, this was post-Beatles. But anyway, he met a girl called Pat. I'm a fool, obviously, but if I close my eyes I can still see her as she looked that night. She had a crochet dress that stopped above the knee and white boots and at some point in the evening she went outside and climbed up on the bonnet of Kelly's car to have a smoke and waved her arms above her head.

Kelly said he wanted her number but she lived in a women's boarding house and wasn't allowed to take calls from men. He could drive up on a Sunday and stop in for tea though.

Well, Kelly did that once. He stopped for tea.

The next night, he told me, Pat came out the window. She did that two nights in a row.

What happened between Pat and Kelly on those two nights, Your Honour, I do not know. I have not asked. My idea has always been, Pat was raised by the Sisters of Mercy, so probably it was nothing.

In any case, Kelly went to Vietnam and Pat wrote to him and for a while there Kelly wrote back, but then the letters stopped coming.

Edna told her not to worry. Maybe it was hard to get mail out of Saigon? Vietnam was a place that none of us knew much about. Then he did write but not to Pat. He wrote to me. It wasn't a letter so much as a card, and it had only one line on it. It said, *'They're all the same.'*

Mum picked it up from the letterbox. She didn't get what it meant, and probably Edna didn't either.

Mum puzzled over it for a while, and put it on the mantelpiece. That's what you did with cards from boys who were overseas. I took it straight down again and took it to my room. I put it under a book on my desk.

The next day, or the day after, Pat came to see Edna. Mum went straight to the mantle and said, 'Where's that card from Kelly?' and Pat said, 'Kelly sent a card?' and Mum said, 'It came yesterday. What have you done with the card, Med?'

There haven't been many times in my life when I've wanted to lie to my mother, but that was one of them. I wanted to say I'd lost it or I didn't know what happened to it.

Instead, I went to get it.

I handed it to Mum, who handed it to Pat. She said, 'I don't know what it means.'

Pat turned it over. I could see her reading it. *They're all the same.*

She said, 'They're all the same? What does that mean, Med?'

At first I said, 'Don't worry about it' but I think I always knew I was going to tell her.

Pat said, 'You know what it means, don't you, Med? What does it mean? "They're all the same?" What's all the same?'

Like a big goose, I said, 'The girls are.'

Pat still didn't get what I meant. That was awkward. She said, 'The girls are what?' and 'What girls?'

I said, 'The China girls. They are the same.'

She still didn't get it. I thought she'd get it straight-away. I felt embarrassed now, to be the only one who knew. I said, 'When Kelly was at Puckapunyal, the other blokes had told him that China girls were different. They were built sideways down there, like their eyes.' The way Pat was looking at me, I've never forgotten it. Her eyes were like saucers. I said, 'Kelly told me he was going to find out.'

The card – the card from Kelly to me – what it was saying was that it's not true. China girls, they are built like other girls.

'They're all the same.' Thinking back now, I still can't believe I had the nerve to say that. What did I think Pat would do?

She left before Edna came back with the tray. She said, 'What did you say to her, Med?'

I didn't tell Edna. I was starting to think that maybe it had been a mistake to tell Pat. Then again, what I've learnt over my life is that people don't do things by mistake. We know what we're doing, whether we admit that or not.

The next time I saw Pat, she did her best to ignore me. But after half an hour or so, she came over and said, 'Let's go and have a smoke.'

'We went outside, not so much to smoke – you could smoke anywhere in those days – more to be alone. Pat said, 'Let's share a bottle of beer.' Where she got the beer, I don't know. She was only 17.

Next thing, she was pregnant.

You might think that happened fast, Your Honour. I suppose it did, but remember the era. You couldn't get a condom unless you went into the chemist and asked for one. Forster was a small town. People knew each other, from the fishing boats, the club, the co-op. There was a fair chance the chemist would have known my dad. Dad was in Rotary. The chemist might have told him, 'Your son came in for a French letter.' I might have been able to handle that but what if Dad told Mum?

Anyway, I didn't think we needed a French letter. Kelly told me, with some girls, you just asked, when was your last period? If it was a week ago, or less than that, you were good to go. Or else you could ask them, do you have a cap? Some of them had their own caps.

Also, Kelly said virgins wouldn't fall pregnant the first time. Pat was obviously a virgin. That's what I thought, anyway. So we did it, and Pat fell in.

Straightaway I told her, 'I'll marry you.' She looked at me like that might not have been what she was waiting to hear, but what else was I supposed to say? There were abortions in 1970, but not the kind you'd want to have. We sat on the news for a bit, and then Pat was four months along, and we told my folks.

Pat had no folks to tell. I better explain why that was. Pat was raised in a baby home, and the strange thing is, she wasn't an orphan. Pat had a mother. She had a father too. Her old man, like my old man, had been in the Army, and when he'd come out, he turned to drink, and that was the start of Pat's troubles.

Pat could remember her old man going out in the morning in a felt hat, and coming home late at night, with the same hat folded into his fist, and her Mum would get thrashed, and she'd have to run and hide.

Now, Pat was born after me – 1953 – and the way she remembered it, she was five, maybe six, when her mother took a suitcase, and took Pat, and went to Central railway station in Sydney, planning to get the train to Melbourne but of course, they had no money. A woman in a Salvation Army hat came up and said, 'Can I help you?' and Pat's mum, she said, 'I've left my husband' and the woman said, 'Well, why don't you go right back to him?' and Pat's mum, she said, 'I'd just as soon throw myself under the train.'

The lady from the Salvation Army, she said, 'Do you have somewhere to go?' and Pat's mum, she said, 'My sister's in Melbourne but I haven't got the fare' and the lady from the Salvos said, 'Come with me instead' and Pat's mum, and Pat, they went off with this lady, who got work for Pat's mum in the vinegar factory, and took Pat to the baby's home where nuns would take care of her.

The arrangement wasn't supposed to be permanent. Pat's mum was supposed to come back for Pat but she never came back, and at age six, Pat moved from the baby home to Belmont, the School for Girls, across the road from the School for Boys. I knew those homes. Everyone did.

They were where they put kids when their parents didn't want them anymore. Everyone's parents kept that story going. I clearly recall, Your Honour, every time my old man drove me past Belmont – that's what we called it, Belmont – I'd say, 'What's that home for again?' and my old man would say, 'That's where they send the bad kids' and I'd say, 'Who sends them?' and he'd say, 'The police come and take you away' and I'd say, 'I'd run away!' and he'd say, 'They run after you, and can catch you.'

The way I understand it, Pat wasn't the only kid in there that had parents. Some people did drop their kids there, and not come back. It wasn't that uncommon. She told me she could have been adopted out and one time she nearly was. At age seven, or maybe eight, the nuns who ran the home, they told her, 'We'll be putting on a show this afternoon, and you'll be Little Miss Muffet, and if you do it right, some parents who come for the show, they might take you home.'

Pat went behind the curtain, and then she came out, and she put on her show, a tap dance and a song, and one set of parents, they said, 'Alright, we'll take the brown-haired one' and that was Pat.

One of the nuns, she gave Pat a cardboard suitcase and said, 'Put your Bible in here, and your coat too, and remember your manners, and you now have a new mum and dad', but instead of being grateful, Pat bit that nun on the hand and ended up getting hit with a spoon.

At age 15, Pat got moved from Belmont to the Parramatta Training School, and there she got taught to sew and then to type, and at 16, they got her a place in the typing pool at Newcastle, at the coal works, and with that job came a room and board in a boarding house.

The boarding house closed its doors at 8 pm, except on Fridays when the girls that had turned 17 could stay out until 10 pm, and that's how, on that Friday night in July in 1969, Pat was at the dance hall, where she met Kelly, and then me, and not long after, she got pregnant.

In any case, we got hurried into St Mary Star of the Sea at Forster, and tied the knot, Pat in a blue suit, and me in something I'd worn to Edna's wedding. The reception, we had at the reccie at Smiths Lake. We got a keg. I reckon my brothers drank most of it.

For the record, Kelly wasn't there. Kelly was still away.

Our first two kids – Karen and Paul – were born a year apart, and I mean that when I say it. Karen – we called her Kat, like after Pat – was born September 14, 1970, and Paul – who is Blue Paul, or else just Blue, on account of him being a carrot top – was born September 13, 1971.

I used to get ribbed about it. My old man, he said, 'What, are you only getting it once a year?' I didn't laugh. It wasn't that far from the truth. Pat and me, we were pretty much exhausted. I mean, what did we know about babies before they came along? Me, not a thing. Pat, being raised in the baby home, she knew a bit more – how to put on a nappy without getting the pin stuck in the baby – but the fatigue, I can tell you, it wore me down.

As for what Kelly made of it, well, he came back from Vietnam the year after Kat was born, already knowing, by letter from Mum, that Pat and me had got married and had a baby, with another on the way.

He came by the place we were living, bringing a Zippo lighter he couldn't stop flicking. There was a smell of gas about him. He looked bigger than I'd remembered. He wore army boots. His skin was freckled from the sun. I don't remember whether he phoned to say, 'I'm coming by.' I do remember that Pat was there, on the lounge, nursing Kat, when Kelly came through the flyscreen.

The first thing he said was, 'Hey, you've got a blood nut!' because Kat, like Blue, she's a redhead. He said, 'I'm happy for you, Pat.'

'I watched them going at it. Watched it like a hawk. Pat got up from the lounge, struggled up, because she had Blue on board, and Kat on the breast, until she looked right at Kelly and said, 'Don't say that again' and she walked out of the room.

We heard a door close, and that was it. Pat had gone into a bedroom. She didn't come out until Kelly was gone.

After he was gone, I went into the bedroom. I said, 'What was all that about, Pat?' To myself, I was thinking she was mad at him for doing what he did with those girls in Vietnam. Pat said, 'I don't want him in the house, Med' and I said, 'Well, come on, Pat, we're brothers' but what did that mean to Pat? She had no brothers.

I can't say for certain whether Kelly came by the house again after that. Not while Pat was still there, I mean.

I know we saw him, but maybe it was only at the family things, where we'd both just happen to be. I can tell you he did get married. His wife was a funny lady, a real riot. She had dyed hair and a shiny red belt she wore all the time. She told everybody, 'My name is Dorothy, but friends call me Bunny so you call me Bunny.' Pat never called her Bunny. She called her Dot. I remember once, the three of us – Kelly, Bunny and me – were having beers. He tapped me on

19

the chest, his cigarette between his fingers. He blew smoke out the corner of his mouth. He said, 'This man here stole my woman. I was off at war and he stole my woman.'

Bunny didn't freeze the way Pat would have frozen. She threw back her head and she laughed. We both knew I never could have stolen a woman off Kelly. Not one he wanted, anyway.

Now, if Pat was writing the part that's coming up – the part about our married life – it would come out differently. Pat would tell you that our marriage wasn't a happy one. I don't agree. I know that's strange – how can a man be divorced and say he had a happy marriage? – but that's the way it was for me.

Pat would tell you the problems started in year dot. She didn't like the place I bought us to live in. Most women, when you bought them a house, were pleased about it, plus Pat was the one who said we had to get a place of our own. That was a pretty extravagant idea in Forster in 1970.

People in those days did not rent the way they do now. They stayed with their folks until they could get a little cash together. But my old man, who liked Pat, said, 'I know of a place you two lovebirds might be able to afford, if I sling a little your way.' He drove me out to that place. It was not too far from where I'd been raised. It had a weatherboard house on it. It's the place I'm writing to you from right now.

Dad drove me back into town. We went to the Commonwealth Bank and spoke to the manager. The old man explained that I was married and employed, and about to have a baby. He had been with that bank 30 years. The deal was done that afternoon. We could move in before the baby was born if we'd felt like it. I didn't have to ask Pat about the mortgage. This was a time when you didn't need a woman's signature. I drove out to the boarding house to tell Pat what I'd done. I thought maybe she would jump into my arms. I'd seen a woman do that once before, maybe on TV.

What she said instead was, 'Did you think to ask me where I wanted to live, Med?'

I said, 'Where else is there?' I wasn't trying to be smart. Where else was there? I had never been of the mind to venture into Sydney. Newcastle was a bit too busy for me. I said, 'It's a good block, Pat. It's bush, but it's part-cleared.'

But Pat, she said, 'And why would you think I want to live in the bush? I don't want to live in the bush, and I don't even know what a part-cleared is.'

I thought, What is she on about? and she told me. She wanted to live in town, if not in Newcastle, then at least in Forster, on a quarter-acre block up close to a neighbour.

I said, 'Why would you want that, Pat? Living one on top of the other? Out where we'll be, we've got a bit of space.'

Pat said, 'I'm planning on going back to my old job once I have this baby, Med. I'm going to need to be in town.'

I cannot tell you what a radical idea that was, Your Honour. I might even have laughed at Pat when she said it. Girls now, they have babies and go off back to work but this was before that idea had taken hold. Pat was married. There was no reason for her to work.

I said, 'Do they take married women at the typing pool?'

Well, she had no idea. Big companies generally didn't take married women. Even if they did, what did she plan to do with the baby she was carrying?

Pat said, 'They have crèche in the church hall.'

Well, I knew that. I knew there was a crèche in the church hall. It was for kids whose parents had no money, or women who had no husbands. I said to Pat, 'I won't have my child in the church hall with the kids from broken homes.'

When I told Edna what Pat had said, Edna agreed with me. She called Pat to say, 'Med might not be making a lot now, but he will make more in the future. In the meantime, there are ways to economise.' She told Pat, 'I can show you how to make a cut of meat go a bit further.'

Pat was cross with me that night. She said, 'You talked to Edna about this?'

I was confused. I said, 'Have you and Edna had a fight?' but Pat wouldn't say. She said, 'I don't want you running to Edna with what goes on in this marriage, Med.' I told Edna that, and Edna thought Pat was being strange because she was raised at Belmont. She said, 'Poor thing doesn't know what a family is. It'll be different when the children come.'

Well, Edna was right about that. I thought Pat would be happy when Kat arrived. All ladies want a baby, don't they? Edna would have killed for a little girl (by then, she had two boys). She would have made clothes and dressed them up and put patent shoes on them and showed them off.

Pat was not that type of woman. I know she made a phone call to the company where she used to work. A friend from the Shire, he told me about it. She wanted to know if she could have the old job back. She mentioned the church hall crèche to them. They told her they did not take married women. It wasn't true; they did, but only if they had no children, or if the children were older, and in school. This bloke thought what Pat was asking to do – take a job, and put little Kat in the church crèche – was strange. The bloke at the Shire asked me if everything was alright at home.

Not that it mattered. Three months after Kat was born, Pat was pregnant again. The old man ribbed me about it. 'You kids are like rabbits,' he said. I let him rib me. There was no need to say I'd had just one go at Pat, and then it had shut down again, and that Pat must have been one of those ladies that got pregnant at the drop of a hat.

With the second child on the way, I went up to the Newcastle Shire, and asked the bloke there to take me on. That was Pat's idea. She wanted me to have a job that paid a wage, one that came to me in an envelope, with some union protection.

She said, 'If you stay out on your own, you've got no protection in the down times. You want a job for life. If you can't get into the bank, go to the Shire. If you work your way up, you could get a manager's job.'

I suppose that was the first sign she wasn't all that happy with who she'd married. I didn't want a desk job. I'd been happy on the building sites. I liked to be outdoors.

There were other signs that we weren't matched. First up, Pat couldn't stop saying that we lived like bush cockies. What she meant was, we had a weatherboard house and everybody she was coming to know, from the local shops, were in brick veneer houses on the new estates outside Forster.

I said, 'That's all very well, Pat, but it's mortgage hill. Those people are paying out half of what they earn to live up there.'

Pat didn't see things like that. She saw that they had – mod cons, she called them – what we didn't. She wanted a kitchen with lino. She wanted a carpet sweeper. She wanted town water. We were still on tanks.

She told me, 'I run the bath for the kids, and the leaves get in the tub.'

I'd loved that as a kid. A slimy leaf in the tub, maybe with a bug on it to examine. I said, 'I can hardly force the shire to get town water on' but Pat, she still blamed me.

I did my best to smarten up the place, to get Pat smiling. We were first in the Shire, almost, to get the Hills Hoist. I phoned up Daryl and asked for his help, putting it up. We put it out in the back paddock where it could really spin and get the clothes dry. I thought we'd done Pat a favour, but Pat, when she saw it, she said, 'It's too far from the house.'

I thought, how can it be too far from the house? But then I saw her once, running out to get the sheets off the line, the rain exploding in the dust around her feet, and I thought, okay, fair enough, it probably is too far from the house, but we'd concreted it in, and it couldn't be moved.

It wasn't just the Hills Hoist she hated, though. She couldn't stand the heat under the corrugated iron roof. She wanted to know why we couldn't get a fan, but nobody had a fan. A fan was what people got if they were a bit soft. She wanted to know why we couldn't get cladding. People were getting cladding, like fake bricks, over fibro, but I said, 'No, let's just paint', and she said, 'Why paint? It peels and it fades and in five years you have to do it over again', the point being, I suppose, that people in town, in the brick veneers, they didn't have to paint. I got insulation for her instead; laid the batts myself.

She hated the isolation. She told me once, I look out the window, Med, and it's thistles, it's paddocks, and it's old cars that Daryl has dumped down by the fence. I said, well, plant something. Women like to garden, don't they? There were women around who took pride in gardens. They had roses, carnations, but Pat didn't want carnations. It wasn't the thistles she hated. It was being in a place that had thistles, if you see what I mean.

On one of those occasions when I tried to talk to Pat about what might make her happy, she said, 'If I hadn't got pregnant with Kat, I would have liked to travel' and I've got to tell you, that was a unique idea. Travel where? To do what?

Pat said, 'We don't even go into Sydney, to visit Bondi' but Bondi was, excuse my French, a shithole full of nothing but New Zealanders and turds floating in the water. Pat said, 'There's a ferry. We could take it to Manly.' I thought, what on earth would you want to go to Manly for? To go there, and then come back? Pat said, 'It's called sightseeing. It's a day out.' She said, 'I want a grown-up life, not picking up after kids all day.' I said, 'Well, phone up Edna' because Edna wasn't far away, and over time, she'd had three kids, all boys. Kat and Blue, they loved their cousins, and wasn't that what women liked to do, get together, talk about kids? But Pat, she said, 'Edna makes me want to bang my head on the kitchen table.'

She said, 'Why can't you leave me the car, so I can at least drive somewhere?' In those days, we had the Ford Falcon – the 500, bench seat in front – but it was too big for Pat to drive, and anyway, I had to take the Ford to work.

Pat said, 'Well, we could get a second car' and there were people doing that, getting second cars, one small one, a Japanese one, but Jap crap? I wouldn't have it in the drive, and in any case, we would have had to borrow, and aside from the mortgage, that wasn't something we believed in doing. I wasn't going to go to the bank to ask for a loan for a second car. The manager, he would have said, 'What makes you think you need one? Isn't one enough?' Beyond that, I wouldn't have taken a loan for a second car. My old man told me, you want something, you save up for it, or it will cost you more and be worth less. Pat was as good as me about it. I put her in charge of saving. She kept money in a tin. We saved up for what we needed. For Pat, that meant a washing machine. Another time, she bought a carpet sweeper.

Now, I don't want anyone to think that every day Pat spent with me out on the property at Forster was a day she'd rather have spent in hell. There were times when Pat seemed quite content. In '74, or maybe '75, she got into a cooking spell. She collected recipe cards. If you collected enough, you got a plastic box to put them in, with a lifting lid. She tried different things on the kids. She had Rice a Riso conquered,

and Ham Steaks and Pineapple. She bought four tall glasses
for desserts. She'd put pineapple rings and glazed cherries,
and tinned apricots and jelly in there, and serve it with long
spoons.

A bit later she got into sewing. She wanted a Janome and
she saved, and Dad chipped in, and she got one. Once a
fortnight she'd go to the haberdashery and pick up material,
folded over itself. The kids were banned from going near it.
She had pincushions and button jars and rows of cotton.
She'd use black-handled scissors to cut paper patterns and
pin them down, and then make dresses for Kat that tied at
the shoulder, and pants for Blue that he refused to wear.

If there was tension in the house at those times, it was
mostly over drink. Pat will tell you that I drank. I don't say
I didn't like a beer. I did. I still do. There was a time when
I was into home-brew. Most blokes were, around that time.
I had no problem with women drinking. Some companies
were starting to make wine. I wouldn't have minded if Pat
had had a moselle once in a while, but she didn't like the
taste of it.

I reckon her problem with my beer had more to do with
her old man, and how he'd liked to get drunk.

In any case, there were times when Pat seemed pretty
content. She'd been unhappy when the kids were really
little – so many buckets of nappies to soak, so many loads of
washing to do, all the usual complaints – but they grew like
weeds and were soon on their feet, and then off at school.

She did the school-mum thing for about a year. Taking
them there, picking them up, homework, dinner on the

table. Then she announced that she'd had enough of being at home. She was going back to work.

She said, 'Times have changed, Med. Plenty of married women are working. I'll take a college course during school hours. I'll get a qualification, then I'll get a job.'

I said, 'What job?'

She said, 'I haven't yet decided.'

I was curious. I said, 'What do you want to study?' Because to me, there was nothing worse than school.

She said, 'Arts.'

I thought she meant arts, like painting. Pat had never shown an interest in painting.

She said, 'Arts is not painting, Med. Arts is humanities. It means literature. It means history. I might even do women's studies.'

I thought that was funny. What was women's studies? I said, 'They have studies in how to be a woman? Do they have them for blokes too?' but she wasn't in a joking mood.

I said, 'Aren't you going to feel a bit of a goose, 28 years old, going to a college?' but she said there were a lot of women going back. There had been a story in the local paper about a 70-year-old woman getting her high school certificate. Pat said, 'I won't be the oldest.'

I said, 'And what about the cost, Pat?' but she'd done her homework on that, too. She said, 'It's free now, Med' and I had heard that. It was one of the things that Whitlam had done before they booted him out. He made the universities free.

I still had my doubts about it. Pat had a home to run. But

28

there was no stopping her. She said, 'I've done my time in this house, Med. I've been home every day for 8 years. Now I'm doing something for me.' That was radical.

She said, 'I don't care if I have to do it part-time. I don't care if I have to do it at night. I don't care if it takes me eight years to get a qualification and 10 years to get a job. I'm not waiting on you and the kids, hand and foot, for the rest of my life. I've got other plans.'

And so, for a couple of years, from about 1979 onwards, that's what Pat was doing. Three days a week she'd get the kids up and walk them to school, and then she'd walk to the station and get the train, and go into college, and take her classes. She made an arrangement with Mrs Cochrane down the road to collect the kids on those days, and then she'd swing by on her way home, pick them up, and bring them home for tea.

When all this started, I'd said something like, 'And who is going to make the tea?' And Pat had said, 'Well, Med, maybe you'll have to make your own' and at first I'd thought she was serious, but she still made the tea on college days. We just ate it a bit later and there was no more experimenting with the recipe cards. We had chops. We had baked beans. Some nights we just had eggs. Then she'd do the washing and ironing and folding. I had my own recliner in those days. I'd have my feet up and I'd say, 'Come put your feet up, Pat,' and she'd say, 'Is the washing going to do itself?' I learnt not to put my nose in.

At around 10 pm, when a normal person might be going to bed, Pat would sit down at the sewing table – cleared of the Janome now – and work on her assignments, sometimes until two in the morning.

A year into college, books started turning up, books that my brother Daryl had told me to keep an eye out for. There was *The Women's Room* and *The Feminine Mystique*, and when I mentioned that one to Daryl, he said, 'Well, let that put the fear of God into you, Med, because I know a bloke whose missus brought that book home and read it and threw it down and said, "Things are going to change around here!" and next thing, the poor husband was having to push the carpet sweeper around.' He said, 'You want to make sure she doesn't turn into a Women's Libber.'

I'd seen stories in *The Mirror* about Women's Libbers. I wasn't entirely sure what it meant. It seemed to be something that was mostly happening in the cities. But then one day Pat brought out a list of things she did around the house – the washing, folding, sweeping – and showed me how if she got paid for doing each thing, she'd be earning more than me.

I said, 'But those aren't paid jobs, Pat.' Obviously, I missed the point.

There was one other thing about Pat's college that was good. It changed for the better in the way things were done in the bedroom. Now, I don't want you to think I'm one of those rogue blokes who never left his missus alone whether she wanted it or not. I was never like that with Pat. I did have my expectations – wasn't that why people got married? – but pretty soon I understood that my sex drive, and Pat's, they were out of whack. To be honest,

Your Honour, I'd been surprised how little sex there was in wedlock. I'd been led to believe it would be on tap once I got married. That's what young men think. Older men know better.

The truth is, Pat didn't really like it. I was okay with that. Some women don't. But sometimes I'd say, 'Pat, would it really be that much of a big deal for you just to do it sometimes?' What I meant was, I don't need bells and whistles, just some relief. But Pat looked at me like I was scum of the earth when I said that. It turned me off, quick smart.

That changed when Pat went to college, though. I don't know whether it was the women's books or the other ladies at the college that changed her mind, or that the kids were older and not likely to come barging in, but for a while there, it seemed she was into it, and even wanting to try new things. I don't want to overstate it. It's not like we started swinging from the chandeliers, but there was a bit more.

Then one day, Pat actually spoke to me about sex, or at least, about contraception. She said, 'I don't want to have another baby, Med. I want you to get the snip.'

My first reaction was, 'You can forget that, Pat.'

She said, 'Alright' and then it was back in the doghouse for a few more weeks.

I went crawling back. I said, 'Why do I have to get the snip? That's an operation. I don't want anyone coming near my old fella with a pair of scissors.' I know what you're thinking – typical bloke.

Pat said, 'I've been on the pill nearly 10 years. People say you shouldn't go on it for that long.'

I asked her about getting her tubes tied. I'd heard that some women did that, got knots tied in their tubes. Pat said, 'Why does it always have to be me, Med? You are the one that wants it all the time, you should get the snip.'

I talked it over with Daryl. He shocked me, said he'd already had it done. His wife had made him too. He said it was no different.

'You still shoot,' he said. 'But you shoot blanks.'

Daryl's wife gave Pat the doctor's number. There were eight men on the ward having the same thing done. We all came up sore. I joked with them, 'Better be worth it!'

'I was too tender to try out the doctor's handiwork for the first couple of days, but then I said, 'Well, Pat, should we give it a whirl?' I didn't tell her that the Doc had said we'd have to wait six weeks. Six weeks! I thought, come on, if there's a knot in it, there's a knot in it, so we had a go.

Ten weeks later, Pat came home from college, and instead of making for the kitchen to put on the tea, she took the keys to the Falcon off the hook, got in the car and drove straight into a fence post.

I ran out onto the porch. I could see Pat behind the wheel – forehead on the wheel – the windscreen shattered, and barbed wire coming in through the glass.

I ran over to the car and pulled the driver's door open. I said, 'Have you lost your mind, Pat?'

She said, 'I'm pregnant.'

I helped her out of the car, back up to the house. I put

her on the lounge. She was like a doll. I had to put her knees together. I had to get a tissue to wipe her face.

For a long time, she didn't move. I told her I thought she might have been. She'd been sick and she'd been tired, and she figured she had a virus, and I'd told her to go to the GP, thinking maybe she's fallen in. He'd pressed on her belly and said, 'Mrs Atley, you're pregnant' and she said, 'This can't happen. He's had the snip' and the GP said, 'Did you wait? You have to wait six weeks. It doesn't take straightaway. Med would have had live ones in the system.'

She said, 'Did you know that, Med?'

I said, 'Pat, I was groggy at the hospital. I didn't take it all in.'

She said, 'You knew that, didn't you, Med?'

I didn't have the kind of marriage that allowed for lies, Your Honour. My life isn't the type that allows for lies. I told her, yeah, I knew. But I thought it would be alright.'

It was the only time she ever hit me, Your Honour. Or almost hit me. I grabbed her wrist just in time. I didn't hit her back. I'm not that kind of man.

When I saw she'd calmed down a bit, I got on the blower and called up the old man and told him the news. He had cancer by then. It wasn't like now, where you fight it and fight it. We knew he was on his way to the grave. He loved the grandkids. I knew the idea of another one would cheer him up. He said 'Your swimmers must be strong bastards.' He knew I'd had the snip, and he was proud of me for getting around it. He and Mum had pushed out eight, remember?

To them, two kids wasn't a family. Four was getting close, but two?

After I'd chatted a bit, I went back to Pat on the lounge.

She said, 'Pregnant, at my age.'

I didn't think she had to worry. Mum had been over 40 when the last of us came along. These days, 40 is when they get started! But it wasn't that she was really worried about.

She said, 'I've done this, Med. I've done the nappies and the bottles and the broken sleep and the potty.'

I said, 'Don't worry. I'll get the change table out of the shed and we'll pick up a bassinet at the op shop. We don't have to spend a fortune. And the kids will love it. Why don't we tell them now?'

I was thinking, just give her time. She'll come around. It's been a bit over 10 years since she had one in the oven. She'll get used to the idea.

Well, that obviously didn't happen. The pregnancy wasn't easy for Pat. The smell of anything – me and my smokes, especially, or maybe just the whiff of me – made her sick. I'd leave the house in the morning to the sound of Pat with her head down the toilet and I'd come home and find her the same way, or else she'd be at the sewing table working on a college assignment, kids not fed, no tea on the table, and she'd say, 'Don't ask me to get up, Med. I'm going to finish this course before the baby comes if it's the last thing I do.'

And then, well, Donna-Faye came. And she was nothing at all like the other two, not like Kat or Blue. She wasn't carrot-topped, for one thing. She had brown hair and was round.

Straightaway, I thought, ah, this is my girl! With her

big belly, she looked just like an Atley. I know you're not supposed to love one more than the others, but it wasn't long before people were saying she was Daddy's girl. I'd carry her around in the crook of my arm. Maybe it was experience. I wasn't as nervous as I'd been with the first two. I knew they didn't break if you dropped them. The crying and the fussing didn't faze me. I knew it didn't last.

I suppose I should tell you, it was me who gave her the nickname, the one she's been saddled with her whole life. I was the one that called her Fat. I can't say precisely how it happened, only that we had Pat, and Karen, who became Kat, and then Donna-Faye, shortened to Faye, was Fat. Like, Pat, Kat and Fat. And she *was* fat. Chubby-fat. Her legs had rolls. Her arms, too. The first time she sat, flat on her bottom, her belly swelled out like Buddha.

Around the same time, there was a show on TV called *A Country Practice*. It had a wombat called Fatso. I'd say, 'Come on, little Fatso' and Fat would crawl across the floor, or else I'd say, 'Into the car, Fatso' making a big show of what a hefty unit she was. So, Fat just stuck. It was never a mean thing. It was about how we loved her.

Back to Pat, though, pretty much the second Fat arrived, she sank into the baby blues. Did I have sympathy for her? I did, but I also thought, come on. The baby's here, and the baby years don't last long. You've got to pull yourself together.

What she did instead was pull up stumps. I mean that literally. No warning, nothing. She got up one morning and said, 'No, to hell with this.'

I remember it like it was yesterday: twenty months after Donna-Faye was born; Kat was 12, and Paul was 11 and Pat got out of bed as normal, calm as you please, and said, 'Med, to hell with this.'

At first, I had no inkling what she was on about.

I said, 'With what, Pat?'

She said, 'With this. With you. With Fat. With Kat, with Blue, with my life out here, the washing, the drying, the folding, the putting away. To hell with it.'

She wasn't mad or anything. She was calm. I said, 'Come on, Pat. We've got it good. The washing machine. My mother never had a washing machine. The linoleum' because I'd put down linoleum by then, over the cement sheets. It was easier to clean, and it looked good.

She said, 'God damn the linoleum.'

I shook my head and went to work, thinking, 'Baby blues.'

I must have been worried though, because around noon, I said to the boss, 'Mind if I use the phone?' And he said alright, so I called home and the phone rang out.

I knocked off a little early and, as I got close to the house, I could sense something was different. I went through the flyscreen and there was no Pat, and no Blue, and no Karen, and no Fat. I might have panicked but then Blue and Karen drifted in, saying, 'Where's Mum?' I said, 'College' and Blue, he said, 'College?' because it had been a while since Pat had gone off to college, and I suppose I thought Blue had forgotten about it.

A short time later in came Mrs Cochrane from the

property one block over, with Fat in her arms. She looked at me and said, 'Everything alright, Med?'

I said, 'I don't rightly know' and I took Fat from her, and put her down to bed, and put dinner together and then I sat up in the armchair, waiting for Pat to come up the drive, but come morning, there was still no Pat – and there never was Pat, never again, not after that.

Now, I know I'm taking a bit for granted, but if you're anything like me, Your Honour, the fact that Pat did that – the fact that she walked out on me, on Blue, on Kat, on a baby 20 months old – well, that floored me. I mean, a woman doesn't do that, does she? A mother doesn't walk out on her kids, and especially not a baby, 20 months old. It's not natural. It kind of defies the laws of nature, doesn't it?

I know that's what my own mother thought. She told everyone, 'It's not normal. To my mind, there's something wrong with a woman who would do what Pat's done.'

I said, 'Pat hadn't been happy about the baby' and Mum, who'd had eight kids, had said, 'What's happy got to do with it? People have responsibilities.'

I have to admit, I agreed with that. I didn't think Pat had the right to go. I thought, I never once came home drunk and beat her or the kids. I didn't gamble my pay. I handed over the whole pay packet. I lived on what Pat gave me.

I thought, 'There's got to be some law that prevents Pat – that prevents anybody's missus – from picking up and leaving, no reason given.'

I'd think, Remember our vows, Pat? For better or worse, richer or poorer, death do us part? Remember saying that?

My old man was dying – his cancer would shrink, then grow again – but the upside of dying is you lose interest in minding your own business, and you start telling it like it is.

He asked me, straight out, 'Was everything alright in the bedroom department?'

I said, 'I'm not sure I know' but even now, I reckon it would be wrong to conclude that the marriage broke up over sex, because if marriages broke up over sex, the divorce rate would be a damn sight higher than it is.

I was hurting like hell, obviously, and I was embarrassed, too, to be the bloke who got walked out on. Edna had told me, 'The whole town wants to know what happened.'

I said, 'Well, you can tell them I'm buggered if I know.'

There was a bit of confusion in the beginning about how I'd manage. Mum said she'd come up and take care of Fat but I thought, I'm probably a bit old to go relying on Mum. Besides which, Trish had cancer by then, and Dad did, too.

I said, 'No, it's okay.' Maybe I was thinking Pat will come back, and she'll go ape when she sees that Mum's taken over, so I set it up with Mrs Cochrane that she'd take on Fat during the day. She was happy to do it, wouldn't even take any money. I told work I couldn't be doing night shifts or weekends. A week went by, then a month. After three months, I suppose even I could see that Pat wasn't coming back.

One year into it, papers for a divorce turned up in the letterbox. Just like that, papers for the divorce. No note, no by your leave, nothing. I tore them up. I thought, No, Pat, I'm not giving you a divorce. You can go to hell. I got married for life, and so did you.

But then more papers came and these ones said I *was* divorced. I didn't accept it at first. I thought surely a man has got to agree? But, actually, a man doesn't have to agree. The courts these days, they just wave the divorces through, and they call them 'no-fault' and that's how it goes down in history – this marriage has ended, and it's nobody's fault. So mine was over, and if you want more of an explanation as to what happened, I suppose you'll have to ask Pat, because she's the one who pulled the plug.

# Chapter 3

THERE ARE PROBABLY SOME PEOPLE WHO think Fat is the way she is because her mum walked out when she was little. I don't believe it, and part of the reason I don't believe it is that Fat didn't actually seem that bothered when Pat walked.

Obviously, she wasn't yet two years old, and the first few days after Pat had gone, she cried a lot, and she said, 'Mum? Mum? Mum?' and Edna and Mrs Cochrane had to rock her and rock her.

The fact is though, Pat hadn't had much time for Fat. She wasn't ever the sit-and-read-to-them-, or the rock-and-cuddle-them type.

I thought, well, at least with Mrs Cochrane somebody's giving her the time of day. Years later, after Fat did what she did, social workers told me, oh, when a mum leaves, or

41

there's a divorce, it cuts deep, and it can take years for the wound to come to the surface.

Maybe that's true. At the time though, my big worry wasn't Fat. Part of my worry was actually me, and how hard I was taking it. I even went to the GP in Forster to ask him, 'Doc, is it possible to die from pain?' He was pretty shocked at that, but honestly, that's how I felt, like the pain in my chest might squeeze the life out of me. The GP was good. He said, 'You're not going to die, Med.'

I said, 'It feels like I'm dying. It's bloody agony.'

He said, 'It might feel like it. You might even be hoping that something will kill you. But it's not going to happen.'

He said, 'What you've got to know is a marriage break-down, it's like a death. That's what they say in the medical books. The stress level, it's like when somebody dies.'

He said, 'I can give you some pills' but I didn't want pills. Nobody I knew would have taken a pill, not in those days, and not for that. What I wanted was for Pat to come to her senses, but seeing as I didn't know where she'd gone, and seeing as she had no people – no family, nobody to call – there was no way to even try to talk her around. For a while there I was pretty sure I was seeing her everywhere. I'd see a lady in the supermarket, dark hair, about the right length, and my heart would leap up and I'd think, 'Pat!' and it never was Pat.

That went away after a while. The pain did, too. If I had to describe how that happened, I'd say it burnt through me. That's what it felt like, like I was burning inside and it had to burn itself out, and then, believe it or not, there came a point where it didn't hurt every time I thought of it, and I even began to feel some gratitude towards Pat. Not for leaving. I mean, I'll never forgive her for leaving. I still don't get what I did to deserve it. But I was grateful she didn't take the kids. So many blokes I knew, when the marriage went south, the wife took the kids, and the blokes, they weren't just divorced, they were ruined.

I still had the house. I still had my job at the Shire. I still had the kids. No bloke I knew ended up with the kids. Most blokes I knew, when the wife wanted out, they lost the lot. So there was that to be grateful about.

There were people who thought I should get married again, and in a hurry, because I wouldn't be able to cope with the kids. But there was nobody else I wanted to marry. Not then. Not now. I said I'd rather cope on my own.

I went to my manager at the Shire and I said, 'Mate, I need you to organise for me a five-day week, nine to five, no weekends, permanent.' I said, 'I know you've got things that need work, but I've got a little one at home, and her mother can't care for her' and he didn't ask any questions, he just said, 'Med, that's no worries.'

Next up, I went around to Mrs Cochrane and made an arrangement where she'd take Fat in during the day, and I'd pick her up from there, and that was okay with Mrs Cochrane. She'd been doing it since Pat left. Why not carry on?

With Fat organised, I went up to Forster to talk to the teachers there about what had happened. Kat's teacher, she told me straight, 'Kat will be fine.' Well, I knew that.

43

Kat was star of the school and if I had to say anything about how she was acting in that first week after Pat took off, I'd say she was having the time of her life. She was the centre of attention. She was the girl with Big News, and lapping it up.

The teacher, she said to me, 'She's so bright' and I said, 'Yeah, I know that' and the teacher, she said, 'There's two ways you can handle this: you can keep her here and we'll do our best, or you can send her up to Sydney to board.' A lot of country girls, in those days, they still did that – went to Sydney to board. I said, 'Oh, no, I can't afford that' but the teacher said, 'Oh, Kat will get a scholarship' and I said, 'We don't want something to which we're not entitled' because, until then, I thought scholarships were for people who couldn't afford the school. The teacher set me straight. She said, no, there were schools that wanted kids like Kat – smart kids – to lift the grades of the whole school, make them all look good.

She told me, 'The school can say they've got a straight A student in the HSC, and everybody else gets charged more fees' and I thought, Do you really want to be part of that, Med? and also, I didn't want people to think, Oh, he's sending her out to board. Maybe he's not coping but the teacher said, 'It's probably not fair to hold her back' so I raised it with Kat, and she didn't surprise me when she said, 'Yes, Dad, please, Dad, I want to go, Dad!' It was actually Kat that rang the school and got the forms sent out, and she was the one who figured out what day she had to go into town to sit the test, and she got Edna to drive her in and wait for her, and Edna told me she was full of beans all the way home, talking about how great it would be if she could go. And just like the teacher said, she did pass, and she passed easily, and the next thing, a creamy envelope landed in the letterbox, this time with a brochure of the school with the indoor pool and the place for lacrosse and the list of things that Kat could do – French, Latin and water polo, and so on.

It took a whole afternoon just to fill out all the paperwork and another day to pick up everything she needed – summer uniforms, winter uniforms, striped tie, straw hat – and then, just like that, she was gone. Boarding in Sydney, and happy as a lark about it.

Did I have doubts about the life she was living at that school? Yes and no. I mean, I'd raised Kat to understand that some people, by luck mostly, have more than others, and some have less, and neither of those things tells you anything about the person. Edna thought oh, maybe the school will set her up, give her expensive tastes, or make her jealous of what others had, but Kat was stronger than that, and anyway, when the reports came in – bound reports, mind you, not scraps of paper like at the State school – they said Kat was top of this, or head of that, or captain of the swim team, and so I figured she was coping fine.

Things were a bit different with Blue. He wasn't bright like Kat. He wasn't stupid, just not exceptional and, in any case, what he lacked in brains, he made up for in his heart. Honestly, I've never seen a kid with such a heart. He'd make friends with anyone, and if he saw a kid being picked on, he'd be first to step up and try to put a stop to it. He was also the kind of kid who brought home stray dogs with rib bones showing through, and he'd feed them up and take them to Pet Day, proud as punch of his dusty mutts and he couldn't understand why Pat wouldn't have them in the house.

When his mum took off, his marks started to go down pretty much straightaway, and by 15, well, he was ready to quit and I was fine with that. I mean, you'd be a loser if you quit school at 15 these days, but back then, it wasn't so unusual. Lots of boys left at 15; the girls did, too, and Daryl and me, we were able to get Blue onto the apprenticeship program at Forster Shire, and he stuck at that until he was 18 and fully qualified as a fitter and turner, and then he also got a driver's licence, and then he told me, 'Old man, I've got it in my mind to hit the road.'

I was a bit taken aback. Blue hadn't been driving all that long and he'd only just started making the adult wage, but I thought, okay, that's normal enough for a kid to want to get around and see things. I said, 'Where do you plan on going, Blue?' and he said, 'I have in mind Lightning Ridge' and I thought, 'Right. You've still got those dreams of striking it rich, have you?' He'd had those dreams for a while. At 12 or maybe 13, he'd come home with a note from school saying the class was going to Sovereign Hill in Ballarat and could he go? I cobbled the money together and off he went.

He came back wide-eyed. He'd panned for gold, he told me. He'd found some flecks. Maybe I should have told him that they put gold dust in those troughs to make more of the experience, that it was fool's gold, not real gold, but he had lights in his eyes, and I thought, ah, let him believe it, and that was the only time I remember that Blue ever got an A for anything, when he did a school project on the gold rush.

He drew maps of the mines, he cut out pictures, he taped his gold dust down on the poster paper with sticky-tape, and he gave it all to a teacher, who was pretty impressed. Blue said, 'I wish I'd been there to strike it rich' and the teacher told him, 'There's still places where a man can stake a claim, Blue, not just for gold but for opals.'

Well, Blue came home that day, brandishing his A, saying, 'I'm going to go back one day and stake my claim.' And I'd said, 'You can't stake a claim in Ballarat anymore, Blue. But you can stake a claim at Lightning Ridge. Go there for black opals, they'll make you rich.'

Blue went straight back to school the next day, into the library, and confirmed to me that I was right, it *was* black opals, and some were as big as a man's hand, and that was the type he intended to find. Meantime, could we get a gold detector and have a look around our own property for whatever gems might lurk there?

I told him to forget it, there was nothing but rocks where we were, and he said, 'You never know' and I was taken with his interest, and so we got ourselves an old metal detector from the *Trading Post*. I asked the bloke who sold it to me, 'You ever find anything?' He said, 'Three pennies, and 42 tin cans.' I said, 'Well, let's see if we have better luck.' And weekends, I'd go with Blue into the hills, with him wearing the earmuff, headphone things that came with the device, and we'd beep-beep and swing the pole, and bugger me, we did find three pennies and 43 tin cans, so one better than the other bloke.

Over time, I lost interest in the fossicking but Blue never did. Right up until he was eighteen, he'd often be out near the dam, beeping and digging, and so I suppose I shouldn't have been too surprised when he announced that it was time to try his luck at Lightning Ridge.

'We should go, all of us', he said, but I put that idea to bed. By this time I'd been on the property outside Forster for almost 20 years and had no desire to pull up stumps. Tell me, Your Honour, do you reckon that might have been because some part of me still thought Pat might come back? Christ, I hope not. Then, too, there was Fat, who had only that year started at the local public school, and Kat, who at least needed a place to come home to if she ever felt inclined.

Blue made the point that Kat never wanted to come home, and he saw no reason why Fat couldn't come with us to the Ridge, saying there must be schools there, but I said, 'Fat's got the same right as you, to stick to one school.'

Blue said, 'Well, if you'd prefer I hung around . . .?'

I said, 'What in the hell you want to hang around here for when there's a fortune in them thar hills?' and he laughed with me, and said, 'Maybe I better stay to keep you company, old man' and I said, 'I'm not much in the way of company, Blue. Just ask your mother.'

Well, it had been some time since Blue had spoken to his mother. A package came one Christmas, when he was about 14, and letters came from time to time, too. I never asked what they said, and Blue never told me, and I don't recall that he ever even wrote back. Maybe that was loyalty to me, I don't know. In any case, he tried once more to get me on board about Lightning Ridge, saying, 'It'll be better with two of us to go over the claim' but I said, 'Blue, I'm just not the moving kind.'

For about a week after that, I heard no more about Lightning Ridge, and I started to think, Med, I hope you didn't kill off that idea, so one night, I got the maps out and said, 'Hey, what about we mark the route?' I said, 'I reckon you take the Golden Highway as far as Dubbo. From there, it's dual carriageway. You don't want to be doing it at night. You can pull over at Dubbo, sleep in the car, and then keep going.'

Blue, he said, 'I dunno, old man, it was just something I was thinking about' and I said, 'It's something you were thinking about precisely because it's on your mind.'

I folded the maps up that night, but I was careful not to put them back where they were kept, with Pat's Bible in the hall cupboard. I kept them out on the kitchen table so they'd be there, looking at him, whenever he came in for tea, beckoning him to have another look, but a week or so later when the maps were still there, and not touched, I took a Camel from the pack and opened a beer, and tapped the cap against the kitchen tabletop, which was my way of saying, 'Take a seat, Blue. We're gonna talk about this.'

I said, 'You given any thought to how you gonna get there, Blue?'

He was still wavering. He said, 'I haven't even made up

my mind to do it, old man' but I said, 'You're mind's made up. You just need a shove out the door.'

Blue said, 'It's not that simple' and I said, 'In what way are you not simple?'

He grinned. He said, 'I got no wheels.'

I said, 'There's the Jeep.' I'd taught him to drive in the Jeep. It was old when I got it and was now older still, and Blue, he said, 'Old man, that shitbox won't make it to the end of the street. It's got weeds comin' up through the floor' and I said, 'It's served us well for 20 years' but Blue, he was right.

I said, 'I reckon we can get enough together to get a ute from Forster Motors' and that was the right thing to say, because having his own wheels was something that no kid would say no to.

We drove into Forster and I told Blue to sit tight, I'd do the deal, and I did it the way deals were then done. I took Camels from my top pocket and the dealer took his Marlboros from the top drawer and we stood and smoked and talked and smoked a bit more and ground the cigarettes and walked out to look at a Holden ute, and looked it over and opened the bonnet and driver's door and turned on the engine and closed it up again and went back inside and came back out and shook hands.

I got back in the car with Blue and said, 'Alright, that one's yours.' It had a hundred thousand on the clock. It needed brake pads but the bloke had reckoned we could get them down the wreckers, so we drove around to the wreckers and I went inside and spoke to the bloke there, an old bloke in a tin shed, radio on, and came out with a tool and walked with Blue down the back of the lot and found an identical Holden and prised the pads off, and gave them to Blue to hold and went back into the office and put my hand in my back pocket and pulled out a wallet and handed over some dollar bills.

We fitted the pads at Forster Motors, lying right there on the ground, and took the ute home the same day and parked it near the house. Fat, who would have been nine or ten, she came out and sat in the driver's seat and tooted the horn.

I said, 'Quit that, Fat.' She did it again, and I said, 'Fat, I said quit that' and she did it again and bolted.

Following day, I put a rag over the oil cap and removed it and took out the dip stick and wiped it on the rag and saw the thing was nearly empty. I poured the oil and put the dip stick back and took it out again, and this time, it gleamed. I screwed the cap back and wiped my hands on my jeans, and I was thinking, this might be the last time I clean something up for this boy who'd become a man.

I said, 'I reckon it'll get you there.'

There was no real conversation about when Blue might actually hit the road but then the day came, and we both knew it. He packed up a few things – a shirt, a pair of boots, plus the ones he was wearing – and I went into the kitchen and took some bread from the bread box, cut some ham sandwiches, put an apple and a banana together, put the whole lot back into the bread bag and plonked it on the kitchen table with the maps.

I said, 'You got smokes, Blue?'

He said, 'Yeah, I got smokes.'

I said, 'You got something to listen to on the road? There won't be radio all the way.'

He said, 'Yeah.'

I said, 'That Cold Chisel bullshit?'

He said, 'Chisel, Angels, you name it.'

I said, 'I don't expect you to phone up every week but once in a while you drop me a line and especially when you strike a vein.'

Blue said, 'Old man, if you're thinkin' I'm gonna be makin' this family's fortune you may well be disappointed.'

I said, 'Well, you never know.'

We had a different dog in those days – not Dog, who's with me now as I write this, but some other, equally ugly mutt – and it had a feeling, like dogs do, that something was afoot, and it was hanging around the two of us.

I said, 'You reckon you want to take that dog?'

Blue said, 'That mutt? No.'

I said, 'Right then, she's yours.'

We walked out to the ute together, and I opened the passenger door and helped the dog up. She had a grin on her face like something grand might happen. Blue, on the other hand, was chewing his lip.

Fat came out and stood on the porch and said, 'You gonna bring me an opal, Blue?' and Blue said, 'Biggest one you ever saw, Fat. You're gonna hang it round your neck and it's gonna give you neck ache and people are gonna be wondering why you're always looking down at your shoes.'

Fat said, 'Yeah right, retard' and went back in, the flyscreen banging behind her.

I knew that he meant it. First decent stone, he'd send down to Fat.

I said, 'You better get on your way' and Blue said, 'Right' and I said, 'Do me a favour and stay in touch with your mother' but he didn't respond, just ground his cigarette into the dirt.

I said, 'Don't give me cheek about it, Blue. Just write to her.'

He said, 'Righto' and got in the car and started the engine and turned on the radio and rolled down the window and said, 'Right then.'

And I said, 'Okay' and Blue pulled out, and there was a bit of dust and that was it, he was gone and so yeah, that was Kat off, and Blue was off, and it was me and Fat, and I've got to tell you, I missed the other two, but it was great with Fat. People might think, oh, an old man and a young girl, that's got to be boring for her, but we weren't bored, or maybe they think, that's got to be hard for him, but to be honest with you, the stuff that Pat used to make such a commotion about – getting the kids out of nappies, onto the potty, getting them to give up the dummy – it was nothing really to complain about.

Now, I know you must be thinking, well, this is all very well, but when did things start to go wrong because obviously, things have gone wrong for Fat, and when I look back I can see things, signs I didn't see then. Fat wasn't great at school. She struggled with the basics – letters and numbers. There'd be days when she couldn't get her words out properly. She'd go to say octopus and it would come out hopperpus, or she'd go to say loveheart and it would come out huvlart, but I mean, that's not really the kind of thing that would stop you in your tracks, is it? The teachers were worried, I do admit that, but I thought, be careful, you might just be comparing her to Kat, who was so bright, and maybe Fat just isn't that bright. But I must have been a bit worried, because I remember cutting open the Cornflake's packet and lying it flat and writing the times tables on it, and getting Fat to sing them with me. One way or another, we got her into high school and then, of course, the first parent-teacher night, they told me, 'Donna-Faye's really not coping with the schoolwork' and I thought, right, here we go again. But it wasn't just that. Fat didn't know how to make friends either. I really didn't get that. At home with me, it was hard to get her to stop talking but the teachers said, no, she doesn't play with the other children. She was getting fatter, too. I know that's not unusual now, to be 12 or 13 and fat, but in those days, there was only one fat, strange kid in every school, and Fat was it. Anyway, we muddled on, and then one Saturday night, when Fat was about 14, there was a knock at the door, and I went to open it, and there was a Chinese boy standing there.

My first thought was, is this a delivery? I mean, on some level, I must have known it couldn't have been a delivery. There was a Chinese place in Forster – the Golden Palace with the red velvet chairs, but they didn't deliver, not in those days. So this boy wasn't from the Chinese but my brain was clearly not ready to accept that he might be Fat's boyfriend, and I just went with the idea that he was delivering food.

I hollered back behind me, 'Fat, did you order Chinese?' but she was ahead of me. She was already at the door. She pushed past me and went outside with this boy, and sat out on the kerb with him, fidgeting. She came back in, and I said, 'What's all that about, Fat? Who is that Chinese boy?'

She said, 'He's not Chinese. He's New One.' That's what I thought she said, 'He's New One.' I said, 'He's the new what?' Maybe she meant, 'A new Australian?' but she said, 'That's his *name*, Dad, New One' and I see now, it was probably Nyugen, because isn't that what they're all called? The ones at the Shire are. But at the time, none of it was making any sense at all, and then Fat said, 'He's not Chinese. He's Vietnamese.'

I said, 'He looks to me like the bloke that takes the orders at the Golden Palace.'

She said, 'He's not Chinese!' and the way she said it, all defensive, it dawned on me – she was interested in this boy. She said, 'You don't get it. His family came out on a boat. You don't know what they went through.' I thought, I know well enough what my brother went through. Now, don't get me wrong, Your Honour. I'm not opposed to people coming here from places where there's strife. It happened when I was at school, the Balts turned up, and the Italians and they were wogs for a while, and then they came good. The Gooks – that's what we called them, before we knew any better – they were a challenge for some when they first starting arriving but I went along to one of those meetings they had in the Forster Town Hall, around 1978, back when Malcolm

Fraser was Prime Minister, and Fraser himself had come out and explained that these Gooks were our Gooks, they'd been fighting on our side and now had to get out or else they'd be killed, and so we were obliged to take them. I got that, and I didn't mind that. I just didn't expect to find one standing at the front door, speaking like an Australian.

I said, 'Fat, don't tell me this bloke is your boyfriend?' and that started an argument, our first real argument, with Fat saying, 'You don't understand!' and me saying, 'I understand perfectly well' and Fat saying, 'You're racist' and me saying, 'Fat, I don't care if he's black, white or brindle. You're not old enough for boys' and Fat saying, 'It's not 1950 anymore, Dad' and me saying, 'I wasn't even born until 1950, Fat' and Fat saying, 'Things have changed' and me saying, 'They haven't changed that much' and so on, until Fat went to her room and wouldn't come out.

Now, I thought I'd won the argument but, of course, those arguments – the ones you have about who your daughter can go out with – they are not winnable. New One didn't come back to the house but I know that Fat kept up with him, and here's how I know: One afternoon, not too long after he'd first turned up at the house, Fat came home with three ducks. They must have come from him because who else would have given her ducks? I said, 'Come off it, Fat, we can't keep ducks, we've got the cat' but Fat said, 'They'll be good for eggs' and I said, 'What they'd be good for is fattening up and taking down to the Chinese Palace and getting your friend to sweet and sour them' and Fat, she said, 'He's not Chinese!' and I said, 'Well, whatever he is, you can take your ducks straight back where you got them from' but she wouldn't have it, and she got so emotional that I gave in.

I said I'd build a pen with wood and wire, but Fat said, 'No, they've got to stay under lamps until they get their real feathers' and I tried to explain, 'It's not normal lamps you need, it's heat lamps' but she wouldn't listen. She put the ducklings in a box near her bedside lamp – she had one of those beds with the wooden bedhead and light built into it. The next day, two of the ducklings were stiff as boards, and Fat was crying and I couldn't stand to see her crying, so I went up to Forster hardware and got a heat lamp. And to my surprise the duck lost its down and got feathers and started leaping out of the shoebox and shitting on the floor and Fat thought that was marvellous. I said, 'It's time we put the duck outside, Fat, and I put a cage together, with wood and chicken wire, and the duck went into there, and what happened? I woke up and Fat was making this strange, gulping noise, and I got out of bed and went into the kitchen, and there was Fat, with red eyes, wet face, pointing towards the duck cage. I went out and there in the cage, there were two feet. That's all that was left, two orange feet, and one beak.

I thought, 'Jesus Bloody H. Christ.' A cat had gone in over the top and torn the duck to pieces. I thought Fat was going to choke she was crying so hard. I admit I didn't know how to handle it. I said, 'That idiot, New One, tell him no more ducks around here' and that made her cry even harder.

Anyway, pretty soon after that, the romance with him, the

puppy love or whatever it was, burnt out and, for a while, there were no blokes around, and I thought good. And then Fat started playing netball for the school team. She hadn't wanted to do it – sports weren't exactly Fat's thing – but the other girls wanted her. They had a bad team at Forster. They never won a game. Fat was big. Not many kids her age would get past her on the netball court. She'd always be wider than the girl with the ball. It hadn't happened to her all that often, that people were interested in her, so she took up netball, and it went pretty well for a while, and then one Saturday afternoon, the year that Fat turned 15, she went to netball, and came home on the bus, all agitated, and I said, 'What's so exciting?' and she said, 'We won!' and they never won, so I said, 'Hey, that's great, and why don't we go into Forster, and get some chicken packs to celebrate' and she thought that was a great idea.

Normally, we would have gone into Ollie's Trolleys on Main Street, but Fat wanted the buns with gravy and Ollie's Trolleys didn't have the buns with gravy, so we went to Red Spot on Harrison Street, instead. We drove home and I was putting the chicken and the peas and the buns and the gravy on the plates and the phone rang and it was for Fat, and it was never for Fat, and I thought, well, they really are excited about this netball thing.

She spoke on the phone for a bit, and then came into the kitchen and said, 'Dad, I'm going out for a while' and I said, 'What about the chicken, Fat?' and she said, 'Oh, but there's some friends from netball getting together and I want to go.'

I was taken aback a bit. Like I say, Fat hadn't fitted in at school and there weren't all that many times where she had somewhere to go.

I said, 'But how will you get home?' and she said, 'It's alright, Dad. My mate's mum will bring me back.'

I said, 'What mate is this?' and she said then what might have been her first ever lie to me. She said, 'Lana' and I knew Lana. Lana was the daughter of a family in town. I said, 'Well, okay' because, I mean, it was a Saturday night and it was daylight saving, still light outside. I said, 'Okay, but not too late' and secretly, I was pleased. My Fat, making a friend.

So Fat went out the front door and I went into the kitchen to put foil over her chicken plate and put it in the oven, and watched while Fat got on the bus – the bus stop wasn't a hundred metres from the front door – and watched the bus drive off. I had my chicken in front of the TV and watched a bit of *Hey Hey* and then some other rubbish came on and I thought, Time for me to hit the fart sack. Fat still wasn't home but that was fine. I didn't want to sit up with the rolling pin. I didn't want to ruin her night out.

Next morning, I got up, I opened the door to her bedroom, and first thing I noticed was that Fat's bed hadn't been slept in. I thought, no, that's not right. I went and checked the other rooms – Blue's old room, the sewing room – but no Fat. I went and poked my head around some of the sheds on the property and even wandered down to the dam to see if Fat might be there, but she wasn't near the dam. Like most families, we used to keep the Rolodex near the phone, and I flipped through it, looking for L for Lana, but there was no

Lana, and I was buggered if I could remember Lana's last name.

I sat on it for a bit, thinking of what to do, and come 9 am, I phoned the cops at Forster, and spoke to the duty officer. He didn't seem that worried. He said, 'How old is she now, Med?' and I said, 'Fifteen' and he said, 'And let me guess, 15 going on 23?' and I thought that was a bit cheeky, but I laughed along, and the cop said, 'Well, Med, she's probably just run off.'

I had my doubts about that but the duty officer said, 'Mark my words, Med, she'll be back by teatime.' I said, 'You reckon you could do a bit of a search?' and the duty officer said, 'I'm on my own here, this being Sunday. Why don't you go look around the places where she might go, and if nothing's turned up by teatime, you give me a ring back.'

'Well, I knew the Shire better than the cops did, anyway. My work was with the Shire, basic maintenance, all around the council parks and gardens, the toilet blocks, the skate bowl, the golf course. I put down the phone and made some rounds. Time to time, I'd come across a neighbour and roll down the window and say, 'You seen Fat?' and they'd say, 'No, mate' and I'd say, 'Keep a bit of a lookout, will you?' and they'd nod and say, 'Sure thing.'

Lunchtime came around, and I went home. I poked my head in Fat's room again and I went through the sheds on our property and still no Fat. I made myself a sandwich, and I ate it slowly, because in my head, I was thinking, act normal, and everything will be normal, but I kept looking out the window, and there was no bloody sign of her.

I went back to the house and kind of busied myself, and then dusk came on, and I got the plastic torch, and I walked right up to where the highway starts, to what used to be the main road into Sydney, and I shone the beam up and down, and even in the ditches. No Fat. At 9 pm, I rang Forster police again and said, 'It's Med Atley here, I called this morning about my daughter, Donna-Faye' and the duty officer said, 'Yeah, I've got a note of that, Med. She still not back?' I said no, and he offered to send a man around, and I said, 'What I really need is a hand with the search' and he said, 'I've only got the one man. Let's leave it another hour, and see how things go.' I said, 'Right, then' and the duty officer said, 'You've got to remember she's a teenager now, Med. They grow up. We don't like to think they do, but they do.' I wasn't inclined to believe him but what could I do? I couldn't force him to come searching with me and, as it turned out, I didn't have to, because at 10 o'clock, Fat walked in the door like she'd never been gone. No explanation, no apology, no hurry, just through the door.

I said, 'Where the hell have you been, Fat?' She'd got the shock of her life, being that I jumped out at her like that. I said, 'Where have you been?' and she said, 'Nowhere!' and I said, 'Don't give me nowhere!' and I went for her, to shake her, but she was too fast, she got past me, and took off down the hall to the bedroom.

I was right behind her, saying, 'Fat! Get back here, Fat' but she was already in the room and she'd locked the door. I cursed Edna that day. It was Edna who had told me I should put a lock on the door, because Fat needed a lock because Fat was a 'developing girl' and girls needed their privacy.

I was saying, 'Open up!' and she was shouting back, 'Go away!' and then, 'You're not the boss of me!' and I was saying, 'Too bloody right I'm the boss of you' and 'You open this door' but she wouldn't and after half an hour standing there, feeling like an idiot, talking to the closed door, I had to give up and go to bed. I lay there fuming, but also confused, because really, what was it all about?

She was out of the house the next day before I got a chance to collar her, and when I phoned the school, they said she was there, and all was normal, and when I got home from work, she was back in her room with the door locked.

I ask you, Your Honour, what does a man do in that situation? I didn't have any experience with girls running off. Kat had never done it. I wasn't about to kick the door in. I wasn't about to belt her. I thought the best thing to do was to put that missing 24 hours behind us but a few weeks later she did it again – she slipped out, and didn't come back and I had to call the police again and they made all the right noises but did nothing and I just waited until Fat came home of her own account. This time, I grounded her. I said, 'Fat, that's it. No netball, no going out with friends' and I moved my TV chair to where I had a good view of the front door, so she couldn't slip out without me seeing her go . . . and so she went out the window. Like I've said, we had an old house. It had sash windows, and some were practically painted shut, Fat's included, and you could hear when someone was using the heel of their hand to get one of them up, and I heard it, and I got up, and went to her door and tried to open it but she'd locked it from the inside. I ran around to the front of the house, but I wasn't quick enough. She was gone.

I called the cops a third time. I said, 'I've just seen her make a break for it. We've got time to catch her' but this time, the duty officer, he surprised me, he said, 'You're not going to like this, Med, but I know where she's going.'

I said, 'How do you know where she's going?' and he said, 'I heard she's seeing the Haines boy.'

I said, 'You are kidding me' or maybe, 'You better be kidding me.' The cop, he said, 'That's what I heard, Med' and well, I couldn't believe it. He offered to go up to the Haines property and bring Fat home, but I said, 'I think I can do that myself' and he said, 'Well, okay, but take it easy, Med.'

I got straight in the car. I drove out to the Haines place, out on Haines Road. It wouldn't have taken me more than 15 minutes to get there. There were no lights on. I knocked on the front door. Nothing. I waited a while and said, 'Goddamn it' and drove home, and there was Fat. Obviously, she'd heard me shouting after her, and she knew she'd been caught going out the window and she'd done a lap, and come home again, and was now trying to pretend she'd never been gone.

Well, I said, 'I know where you were headed' and she said, 'You don't' and I said, 'You've been with that Haines boy' and she said, 'It's not your business'. I said, 'How is it not my business?' and she said, 'You don't even know him.' She was wrong about that, Your Honour. Know him personally, no, but I knew plenty about the Haines boy. I'd

63

been living in the Shire for 40-odd years so there weren't too many kids around the place I didn't know, not unless they were new to town, and the Haines boy, he wasn't new to me.

Paul Haines was the youngest of four boys living out on Haines Road, so called because there had been a Haines out there for as long as anybody could remember. The first Haines I knew was old Mr Haines – that would be Paul's grandfather – who had the brickworks, although the place looked more like a junkyard, with the main house and the two sheds and the Nissen hut that came on the back of an army truck one day and the hay bales and the caravan.

When Grandpa Haines died, he left the place to his son, John Haines, who married a woman who spoke to nobody and kept up the Christmas lights all year round. They had four boys, three of them with J-names – Jack and John and Jethro – and then, 10 years after that, another child arrived, this one called Paul, and he was about the same age as my own Blue Paul, or maybe the same age as Kat, and there was a tragedy in the late 70s, when the main house that these boys lived in caught fire, and both the parents were killed, and people said it was the Christmas lights, but who knows? Anyway, the burnt shell stood for years before it fell down, and from what I could gather, the boys – they were grown up, obviously, except for Paul – they just moved into the other buildings that were on-site, including sheds. There were wrecks of cars and bits of motorbikes and bald tyres on the lawn, and people thought maybe the parents had left some money, because none of the J-boys had means of support, none had jobs, and no matter what time of the day or night you drove by, one of them would be out on the porch, poking at a fire in an old keg, or else under a car.

I don't know why the authorities allowed those boys to raise Paul but he was at school with my two for a while. He was the odd kid, the one that every school's got, with no manners and no lunch, and he prowled the playground, chasing girls, trying to look up their skirts and one time, he took Blue's marbles and when Pat went up to complain about it, he outright lied, even when confronted with the evidence. The teachers, they told Pat, 'He's uncontrollable' and it's true, there was barely a day when he didn't end up in a chair outside the principal's office. By age 10, he was skipping classes on a fairly regular basis. I'd see him down at Forster creek with a stick in hand, poking at carcasses of rabbits. More than once I heard the story that he was killing animals, that he took kittens from cats on his property and threw them off the railway bridge in a hessian bag, or else put them in Tupperware and sealed the lid and watched them get frantic and lie down and die.

From memory, he dropped out of school at age 11 but the J-brothers must have kept him on the roll or else why wouldn't the truant police have come? The mums were happy about him not being in the school but then he started roaming the neighbourhood, knocking down letterboxes and belting cars that were parked by the kerb. Then one day, when he was about 12, he went up to the railway bridge with a boulder in both hands, and set it onto the tracks, and hid in the grass and waited for the night service to come through from Newcastle to see if he could derail the engine.

The train didn't come off the tracks but the driver had to make an effort to stop and the sound of the wheels on the steel was heard half a kilometre away. Then the cows that had been on board had to be offloaded onto the road and half the town came out to see it. Not one of us failed to notice the Haines boy there.

Now, it's my view that police should have given Paul Haines a walloping that night, because sometimes, that's all that's needed, somebody to show him that there's rules, and they're for everyone, and if not, there will be consequences, but nobody did wallop him and so he was allowed, in a sense, to carry on his merry way. And he did carry on, until one day, he nearly killed someone.

The year was 1984, and the Haines boy would have been about 13, which means Donna-Faye would have been about two or three, so their paths hadn't yet crossed. There was a kid in town whose name was Conan, who himself had problems, by which I mean he was a simple kid. It was a stinking hot day, and like every hot day, the kids from Forster and surrounds were up at the creek, trying to beat the heat. Now, the point of being at the creek for kids in those days was to jump off Big Rock into the water. It was totally banned, and had been ever since a kid had gone in off Big Rock, and come up with a submerged branch through his jaw, but in those days when things were banned, it just meant you weren't really supposed to do them even when you did, and on really hot days, on 40-plus days, you just couldn't stop kids from going down there, and no matter how many times I'd drive down, as Shire maintenance manager, and tell them to skedaddle, they'd wait for my back to be turned, and they'd be back, jumping in again. And so on hot days, I made it my business to go down there and get in the water and make sure nobody had tried to sink a car or something over winter, so when the kids jumped, they wouldn't kill themselves.

So I'd been down that morning, and I'd seen Conan at the creek, his pants hiked up to his armpits. Bigger boys were scrambling up Big Rock and bombing down but Conan wouldn't have had the guts to do that. He was a little kid, and although not every light in the house was on, he knew enough not to try to copy them, so he'd get up to the top of Big Rock, still in his shoes, and he'd say, 'I'm a gonna jump down!' and the older boys would say, 'Don't do it, Conan!' and he never would do it, because Conan couldn't swim. I saw Paul Haines there, and as far as I could tell he was the only one really egging Conan on, saying, 'Go on, Conan! Jump, Conan!' but Conan wouldn't jump. He'd get to the top of a rock, he'd stand there for a while, looking like a goose, and then he'd climb down, and sit on the water's edge, grinning and putting his shoes in the water. I should have said to Haines, 'Lay off him, you lout' but I didn't, and that's stayed with me because maybe if I'd done that, what happened next would not have happened. Anyway, it was understood in those days that come six o'clock or thereabouts, with daylight fading and tummies rumbling, boys would get on their bikes and dink each other home in time for tea, and so I suppose it was around six o'clock, maybe seven o'clock, when Conan's grandma – he lived with his grandma – noticed he was missing. According to what I heard, the grandma had asked some girls in the neighbourhood to go out looking for Conan, and they were walking along, saying, 'Conan, Conan' and they came across the Haines boy, running his stick along the palings of a fence, and they asked him, 'Have you seen Conan?' and he said, 'Yeah, he's in the creek' and they said, 'How do you know?' and he said, 'Because I pushed him in' and the girls ran home and got Conan's grandpa and he bolted over to the creek and Conan was exactly where the Haines boy had said he'd be, in the water. He was face up, thank God, but the grandfather had to drag him up onto the bank and push water out of his chest, and hold his head while he vomited on the grass, and then carry him home. They laid him down on the floor between two single beds in his bedroom, and waited while the ambulance came. The paramedics said, 'He's bloody lucky' and it's true, he could have drowned and it was a close enough call for Conan's grandmother to say to police, 'I want something done' and what she wanted done was for police to go around to the Haines place and have a word to him, and to his brothers. And the police, they did that.

They went around to the Haines place and the older brothers were there and the police said we need to speak to you about Paul and the brothers said he wasn't there, and the police explained what had happened, and the brothers said 'It weren't Paul. Paul was home today' and then carried on fixing their cars, or doing whatever they'd been doing.

Now, my feeling is, if the brothers hadn't said that, if

the brothers had said, okay, we'll give him a clip over the ears, the police might have let the thing go, but when the brothers wouldn't even get off their butts and answer the charge that Paul had very nearly killed a kid, well, the grandmother said, 'Alright then, I want charges laid.' The cops explained to her that it wouldn't be that easy, the Haines boy was only 12 or 13 years old, and you couldn't charge a boy that age with attempted murder, not on the basis of a kid being pushed into a creek. But the grandmother, she was a feisty one, and she pushed and she pushed, and she said, 'That Haines boy is a delinquent, and he ought to be in a home for delinquents.'

Maybe the cops agreed, because they did try. They referred the matter to the bigwigs in the prosecutor's office in Sydney to see whether there was enough evidence to charge the Haines boy with anything and the big wigs did agree to have a hearing, and it was held in Sydney, and the cops made sure the Haines boy turned up, by driving out to his property every day to pick him up and deposit him in a swivel chair in the centre of the room, while the story played out around him. I went along. I had to go along. I'd cleared the creek for jumping that day. I'd seen Conan on the rock, and I'd seen Haines, too. There was a chance they'd want to speak to me. What I saw, it amazed me. Paul Haines was chewing gum, and blowing bubbles, and then peeling exploded gum off his chin, and feeding it back into his mouth. Halfway through proceedings, they gave him a glass of Quik milk and he gulped that down and then spent half an hour trying to suck the glass up to his face, so it would stick there without him using his hands. That's how seriously he was taking things.

Other kids who'd been at Big Rock that day were gathered up and put in a room next door to the courtroom and they got a microphone, so we could hear what they were saying, and one of those kids told the magistrate that he met up with Conan on the street outside his grandmother's house that morning and they had made their way to Big Rock, and there were kids jumping off the rocks, and Conan didn't want to jump, and he said the Haines boy had picked Conan up 'like this' and then thrown him down 'like this' and Conan went 'splash, into the water'.

The prosecutor wanted to know whether Conan was kicking or struggling and the witness, who was about seven, he said, 'Yep, he went like this, and he went like that' and he waved his arms and legs around, like he was dancing in his chair.

Now that was pretty damning stuff, but if you think the Haines boy was worried, you'd be wrong. He just sat there dangling a shoelace over his nose, trying to catch the ends of it in his mouth, like none of it had anything to do with him.

Next up was one of the girls that Conan's grandmother had sent out to look for Conan, the one who said she had seen the Haines boy in the street and said, 'Do you know where Conan is?' and Haines had said, 'In the creek' and she'd said, 'How do you know?' and he'd said, 'I put him in there' and she ran to get the grandpa, who had found him face up.

The grandpa told the magistrate that Conan was 'lying back like this' – he put his own head back, eyes rolled towards the ceiling – but his body was straight, and his first thought was, 'We've lost him' but he dragged the boy out and thumped his chest and pumped on his stomach and water came out and the blokes from the ambulance had told him, 'You got lucky.'

Legally speaking, Haines didn't have to take the stand on account of his age, but his lawyer said he had nothing to hide, and anyway, he seemed to want to get up there and say his piece. He'd given up the story that he'd been at home all day, and hadn't been at Big Rock. He said, 'Nah, I wasn't home. I was at Big Rock' and he said he'd been pretending to be King Kong, hollering and banging his chest, and Conan had wanted to do the same – get on the rock and jump off – and the rock was slippery and Conan went over the edge and into the water.

The magistrate said, 'Did you go in after him?' and Haines said, 'I had to get home for my tea.'

The magistrate said, 'Did you see him come to the surface?' and Haines said, 'He come up on his own' and with that, the hearing kind of ended. I mean, it just ended. There was no real result. Haines never faced a charge. There were a lot of people who didn't understand that but the cops told me, 'Med, we can't put Conan on the stand, because he won't go on the stand' – he went pretty much mute whenever Haines was around – and the other witnesses, being so young, couldn't be relied upon, and so we all filed out, and that was that, except for one thing – Haines started to change. I don't mean physically. He was already half a head taller than me, which made him close to six foot, and maybe more – but he started gaining in confidence, too, like he understood that he'd dodged a bullet, and now he figured he was invincible.

I'd see him in town, what my mother called 'louching' along – slouching along, I suppose she meant, but louching covered it better, since that's like a louse – walking down the street, drinking from a Coke can, always in the same clothes: black vinyl tracksuit pants with press-studs down the legs, and a mullet haircut and a packet of Winnie Blues, and if the parents had left the boys any money, it must have been gone because the cops told me he stole his first bike at 14, and followed that up with stealing other stuff, like he stole the whole bubblegum ball machine from the milk bar and took it down to the school and tried to sell the balls to the other kids for five cents, instead of two cents, and at 15, he got caught down at Forster creek with a girl whose dress was torn and whose knees were knocking. The cops who interrupted them wanted to know what the hell was going on but the girl fled on foot, over a hill, through a valley and was gone.

At 16, he got an old wreck and took it up the highway and floored it, shooting through two sets of red rights and leaving an old lady ghost-white on the footpath, her clothes pinned to her skin. The cops gave chase but had to give it up lest somebody get killed, and that set up a new game for Haines, tricking up old cars to see if he could burn off the cops. He got banned from driving, and apparently that made him think, well, what can they do to me now? I don't have a licence to lose.

Now, had I known, back when I was hearing all these

stories, that Haines would one day be sniffing around Fat, I might have taken the law into my own hands but, like I say, I didn't see it coming. I just never would have imagined one of my girls would have been interested in a dickhead like Paul Haines – who, by the way, was 25 to her 15, which surely made the whole thing illegal. Looking back now, I ought to have done more about it, but what is a man supposed to do? The more you say, 'You can't do something' to teenagers, the more determined they become to do it.

There was something else, too. I didn't want Fat mad at me. I didn't want to yell at her, or to ground her too much. I didn't want her telling me she hated me, not even when I knew she didn't mean it. She might have been 15 years old, and womanly in all ways that matter, but she was still my little girl, the one who'd had to grow up without her mum, who hadn't been able to make any friends, who got teased for being big and, who, like most teenage girls, probably wanted nothing so much as a bit of attention from a boy, and this one – this idiot, Haines – was the only one who was paying her any.

People might say, well, your girl hanging around with a loser like that, it's just more evidence that she's long been off the rails, that she had no discipline, that she was bad news. That's fine. People can say that, but it's not the way I feel about Fat, not then, and not even now. I know what she's done. I'm not in denial. I can see how people say, oh, she's evil, or she's insane. I hear them say that, and part of me can even see where they are coming from, but it's not the way I see it.

When I look at Fat, I see a little girl, going from nappies

to big girl pants, and being so proud of that. I see her putting on her new school shoes and getting into bed with them, and sleeping through the night with those heavy things on her feet.

I see her standing in the kitchen, pushing Vegemite and butter worms through the holes in her Vita-Weats. I see a little girl who used to pretend at being her own pony, who'd tie a rope around her waist and the other end to the Hills Hoist, and go galloping around.

I see her out on the gravel drive, and I see me holding the seat of her pushbike, and I see her heading towards the front gate, with her training wheels off, and I hear her shouting, 'You can let go now, Daddy!'

*You can let go now, Daddy.*

Well, I did let go. I'm not letting go again.

# Chapter 4

I DON'T WANT TO LEAVE ANYONE with the impression that I did nothing at all about Haines, once that romance had started. I did drive around there, intending to tell that mongrel to keep his hands off my daughter. I parked out front and I walked up to the door. I knocked and I knocked again, and I was about to turn my back, thinking 'He's not home' when the door opened, and there he was, standing there, chewing gum.

It was the first time I'd seen him up close since he was a boy. He had one tooth in his head. His face was pockmarked, from boils. Every knuckle on his hands was scabbed and scarred over. He had tattoos on the wrists and neck, and he'd come to the door in bare feet. He had footy shorts on, and a mullet haircut. He was everything that would make you think, 'Mate, you're a clown. Get a haircut. Get a real job.'

I said, 'You Paul Haines?'

He said, 'Yeah.'

I said, 'Med Atley's my name.'

He said, 'Yeah.' He knew who I was.

I said, 'You know my daughter, Donna-Faye, she's 15 years old?'

He said, 'Yeah.'

I said, 'You don't think you'd be better off with a girl your own age?'

He looked at me, still chewing gum. A dog had come out. It was one of those big black and tan bastards, a Rottweiler with a muscle chest and a studded collar. Haines was patting its meaty head. He shrugged and leered and said, 'Yeah, well, I like your daughter.'

Should I have taken a swing? Maybe I should have taken a swing. Instead, like an idiot, I said, 'I want you to know, I'm watching you.'

There was a bit of silence and then Haines said, 'Alright. You're watching me' and then just stood there looking at me until I had no choice but to turn around and head back to the car.

When the phone went that night – by this stage, it was going off every night – Fat took the call and then came into the kitchen and squared up to me in the lounge room and said, 'Did you go to Paul's house?' and 'Are you trying to ruin my life?' and 'You can't stop me from seeing him.'

I said, 'Fat, you're 15, he's way too old for you.' She said, 'What do you know, Dad? WE ARE IN LOVE!' and I thought, oh, heaven help me, in love? With Paul Haines?

I said, 'Come on, Fat.'

She went into her room. A few days later I phoned up Edna and I said, 'What do you reckon?' and Edna said, 'Well, at least put her on the pill' and that got me riled. I said, 'I'm supposed to approve of this?' and Edna said, 'Don't go square on me, Med. She's 15, she's seeing somebody. What do you want to happen?' and I said, 'You want me to say to my own daughter let's go and get you on the pill and then you go out and do as you please with a man who's 25 years old?' and Edna said, 'Med, she can go and do all that on her own' and I guess that was right. Fat was seeing the Haines boy, and there was nothing short of bolting her to the bed that I could say or do that would make a damn bit of difference, and it wasn't long before he had got so cocky about it that he'd drive up to the front door, just drive up, all mag wheels and bits of plastic stuck to his bonnet, and lean on the horn, and Fat would fly out the front door and get in the front seat, and they'd go through the gate, and I'd sit like a lemon in the TV chair in front of *Hey, Hey*, trying not to think of what they might be doing, and this went on and on, until the second that Fat turned 16, which was when Haines knew for sure he wouldn't be getting done for carnal knowledge. He came in his ute, and picked up the white dressing table with the wing mirrors I'd bought Fat for her thirteenth birthday, and put her collection of stuffed toys in garbage bags and slung those in the back while she took clothes that were still on hangers and tied them together and lay them on the tray, and then, with Haines sitting behind the steering wheel, smoking a cigarette, Fat gave me a hug and a kiss and got in the passenger seat, all excited, and waved and waved through the windscreen, while he revved up, spun the wheels and took off.

Now, I know that some parents, when their kids take off with blokes they don't like, they cut them off. They say, I won't have that bloke in my house, and all hell breaks loose, and it takes forever for things to mend. I didn't do that. I didn't cut Fat off. I didn't like the fact that she was 16 and living with Haines – in fact, it gave me a real bad taste in my mouth – but Fat and me, we still spoke to each other on the phone and from time to time I would still go out there, to Haines Road, to see how she was travelling. It was never much fun, not if he was there. They'd taken up residence in one of the old sheds. I wish I could tell you whether the other brothers, the J-boys, were still there, but I don't remember if all of them were, or if some had gone, or if they were living in other sheds and caravans around the place, or what. Fat would answer the door and let me in and Haines would have his feet on the table and the TV would be on, and I'd say, 'Paul' and he'd say, 'Med' which annoyed me, because it was like I'd given him permission to call me Med, and I'd never done that, but I'd say, 'Much going on?' and he'd say, 'Goddamn Roosters got beaten again' and I'd say, 'And how are things on the employment front?' and he'd say, 'Me back's been out' and Fat would say, 'Lay off him, Dad' and Haines would get up, and put his feet into moccasins, and go into the kitchen for a beer, and bring back just the one, and he'd sit back down and sip away and wipe foam from his mouth and, never mind if it was 40 degrees in the shade, he'd never offer me one. More than once, I said to Edna, 'I have never met such a rude bastard in my life' or else I'd say, 'He's a sad and sorry excuse for a man' and I know Edna thought I was just arking up because Fat had grown up and gone with a bloke, and she thought I'd have arked up whatever bloke she'd have gone with but I wasn't riled because Fat had got a fella. I was riled because she'd picked such a loser. But Edna said, 'You're going to have to get used to it, Med. You either get used to it or you'll lose her for good' and so I forced myself to get used to it. I'd go around when Haines wasn't home – hard to predict when he'd be out because he pretty much did nothing – and I'd pay her a visit and help her out a bit, by putting out garbage, or nailing a paling back on the fence, or whatever else that useless bastard never got around to doing. And when she turned 18 in the year 2000, I actually turned over some of Pat's things to her, things Pat had left behind, like a jewellery box with a few bits and pieces in it, and Fat seemed pleased to have those things. She'd started working by then, selling Avon. She'd dropped out of school pretty much on moving in with Haines. He told her flatly he didn't want her going to school. Too many boys there. She was his wife now, he told her. I was half-tempted to say, 'If you're his wife why hasn't he done the right thing and put a ring on your finger?' but to be honest, the fashion for living in with a bloke, it appealed to me, at least when it meant that my girl wasn't getting hitched to Paul Haines.

Anyway, Fat did talk sometimes about going back to

school but the reality was, they needed what money she could bring in and she did get into this Avon thing. She showed me her kit, which was basically lipsticks, perfumes, soap-on-a-rope, that sort of thing, and I did hear from one of the ladies at the Shire that she was a good sales girl. She didn't mind stopping in for a cup of tea with the older ladies, who maybe wouldn't have a visitor that day. She was kind like that, and she was reliable. She didn't keep the money they gave her. Didn't steal it, I mean. She delivered the things they'd ordered, and made sure they got the right change, and, well, it was hard not to be proud of her, given that counting money and writing things down, it was never that easy for Fat.

So anyway that went on for a while and then she finished with Avon and started with what she called Nutrimetics, which was like Avon, but all natural, and not tested on animals, which was what people wanted, because there had been a few stories about make-up being poured into a rabbit's eyes, or something like that, and suddenly, animal-cruelty free, that was the way things had to be. But the trouble for Fat was, Nutrimetics wasn't sold door-to-door, like Avon, it was sold at parties. Fat would have to go and show the ladies how the products worked, and with Haines, that was never going to last. He didn't want Fat going to parties, not even to see old ladies, so it was never going to fly, not by his rule book, which riled me even more, because it wasn't like he was working and bringing in money so who was he to set the rules? But when I complained to Fat about that, she just looked at me and said, 'Oh, Dad, it's not worth arguing with him about it' which I took to mean he'd make her life a misery if she tried to defy him.

So Nutrimetics was over and then Fat told me she'd decided on a pony show. A pony show! I said, 'What do you even know about ponies, Fat?' because as far as I knew, she'd had a pony picture on her wall for five minutes when she was about ten and that was the extent of her interest in ponies, but she said, 'Oh, Paul is keen' by which she meant he'd managed to find, or more likely to steal, a horse float of some kind, and with Fat's money from Nutrimetics, he'd bought two ponies, neither of them more than nine hands high, and his idea was to have Fat take them around to school fetes and do pony rides up and down a track with little kids on the back. I said, 'But who is going to load up the ponies? And who is going to drive the float?' and I didn't have to wait long for the answer because the answer was, most of the time, I was going to have to do it, because Haines couldn't get off his sorry arse on a Saturday morning, not if he'd been on the sauce the night before, which inevitably he had been. Not that I minded. I mean, I loved spending time with Fat and liked seeing little kids getting a kick out of riding those ponies. We soon settled into something of a routine – me going round to Haines Road at 5 am to help Fat get everything ready, then driving down to wherever the fete happened to be, and spending the day together, Fat and me. If anybody had asked, I would have said that was quite a good time, maybe the best time in my life, but of course it went sour, and that was

Haines' fault, which everything always was. Basically, Fat called me up one afternoon, and said, 'Dad, will you come to court?'

I said, 'To *court*?' because never in the history of the Atley family, not as far as I knew, had any one of us ended up in court. We weren't that kind of family.

Fat said, 'Paul got provoked and there's an assault charge he's got to face.'

Paul got provoked? I could believe that, but I could also believe – and was more inclined to believe – that he'd just as likely be the one who did the provoking.

I said, 'What did he do, Fat? Tell the truth' and that set off an argument with Fat saying, 'You've always been against him' and, 'You've never liked him' and, 'Forget it then, Dad. We'll go without you' and then she hung up, so I had to phone back. She was a bit sulky but she obviously wanted me around because when I said, 'Alright, Fat, you tell me when, and I'll come along' she said, 'He's pleaded guilty. He's not going to contest it' and she gave me the time and the date of the sentencing.

The day came and I put on my suit – I've only ever had the one tan suit, which I realise doesn't go with the beard, but I put it on – and I went to the courthouse in Forster and, well, I'm not even going to try to summarise what went on in court that day, Your Honour. I'm not even going to try to explain it. What I'm going to do instead is paperclip the whole judgement here for you to read, because my feeling is, unless you read the judgement for yourself, you can't really understand what it was like for me to be there in that courtroom, and to have it dawn on me exactly what kind of bloke my daughter had got herself involved with.

## Jurisdiction, Forster Local Court

**Presiding, Senior Magistrate Barry Brain**
**Date of hearing, December 10, 2003**
**Matter of, Paul Jack Haines**
**Judgement.**

Paul Jack Haines. Will you please stand?

Mr Haines, you stand before me today having pleaded guilty to a breach of the Crimes Act (NSW).

It is my task today to pass sentence upon you.

For the benefit of this court, I note that you were born in the Forster Hospital in 1971 and you are now 32 years old.

You have a long history of criminal offending. At 16 years of age, you pleaded guilty to theft. You were put on probation. You breached probation. You have criminal convictions in the juvenile courts for theft of a motor car, driving without a valid licence, speeding, dangerous driving and evading police.

In 1999, when you were 28, you returned to this court to plead guilty to one count of assault occasioning actual bodily harm, and one count of damage to property.

Those offences related to a fight in a pinball parlour. You knocked the victim to the ground. You used a cricket bat to smash the window of the pinball parlour.

You pleaded guilty to those offences and you were released on a good behaviour bond. The probationary period was set at 18 months.

In 2001, you pleaded guilty to a second set of offences. One of those offences was interference with a motor vehicle. The other was aggravated robbery.

You were sentenced to three years imprisonment for these offences. That sentence was suspended. You gave an undertaking that you would attend courses at Alcoholics Anonymous. You were again released into the community on a bond, requiring you to be of good behaviour.

You stand before me now charged with a new set of offences.

You have pleaded guilty to several offences relating to the control of a motor vehicle.

You have been convicted of driving without a licence; driving an unregistered motor vehicle; driving under the influence of alcohol; failure to observe a stop sign; failure to report an accident; leaving the scene of an accident.

They are serious offences, but they are not the most serious offence. The most serious offence is a charge of aggravated assault, occasioning actual bodily harm.

On February 13, 2003, you attempted to break into a Holden Civic sedan owned by Mr Adam McCain of Forster.

You have testified that you wanted to steal a CD player from the car. You intended to sell the CD player.

Mr McCain disturbed you in the process of breaking into the vehicle with a screwdriver. You lashed out at Mr McCain with the screwdriver. You struck the victim in the throat.

When Mr McCain reached for his throat, you pushed him to the ground and kicked him about the upper body and head. Mr McCain was left unconscious. You took Mr McCain's wallet from his pocket. You were apprehended not 500 metres from the scene of the crime.

The prosecution has directed my attention to Mr McCain's victim impact statement. Mr McCain has taken pain-relief medication on a daily basis since the assault. Mr McCain still requires medication to sleep.

Mr McCain has said in his statement that he fears going out at night. He no longer parks his car in car parks that are not well-lit.

In the normal circumstance, this court would order you downstairs, Mr Haines, to serve the three year prison sentence for this second set of offences, committed when you were on a good behaviour bond for the first set of offences.

This court has, however, provided you with a Legal Aid lawyer. That lawyer is your counsel. Your counsel has asked this court to consider suspension of your sentence.

Your counsel notes that you have pleaded guilty, in the process saving this court time and money.

Your counsel points to your co-operation, and your remorse.

I turn now to your personal circumstances.

At the time of this offending, you were addicted to alcohol, cannabis and prescription drugs. You had taken Valium, used cannabis, and consumed a substantial quantity of port wine.

Your counsel has submitted that your use of alcohol and drugs stems from the events of your childhood. Your parents died when you were young, and you were subsequently accused of the near-drowning of a young boy. You were cleared of blame but your counsel has submitted that rumours about your involvement have dogged you throughout your life.

You first began using cannabis at age 12, and were using it daily at the time of your most recent offending. You have taken prescription medication since the age of 18 and your doctor-shopping, to which you admit, suggests to me that you are also addicted to Valium.

Following your arrest for your most recent offending, you were in custody for seven days.

The experience of being incarcerated came as a shock to you. You have described that experience to me as being 'like a wake-up call.'

Your counsel asks this court to consider a noncustodial sentence. The prosecution opposes that course. The prosecution argues for a custodial sentence. The prosecution points to the seriousness of your offending, and to the repetitive nature of your offending.

The prosecution notes that the maximum sentence for aggravated assault is 20 years in prison.

The prosecution directs my attention to the injuries sustained by your victim.

The prosecution submits that your lack of compliance with previous good behaviour bonds does not augur well for your future compliance.

I say to you now, Mr Haines, the prosecution is determined to have you incarcerated. I myself am of that mind.

Three times, you have appeared before this court. On two occasions, you have been given the benefit of a good behaviour bond. Twice, you squandered those opportunities to change your ways.

Your counsel submits compelling reasons to suspend the jail sentence that I intend to impose upon you.

Those reasons are this: your guilty plea; your show of remorse; your new insight into the impact of your offending; your willingness to abide by a drug testing regime; your stable employment; your stable relationship; the 'wake-up call' you received, upon being imprisoned for seven days.

Then, too, there is the matter of your impending fatherhood. Your long-time partner, Donna-Faye Atley, is expecting a child, Mr Haines. Without your support, your business, and her business conducting pony rides at local fetes is likely to close. Beyond that, there is the possibility that the responsibilities of parenthood will help mature you, Mr Haines.

It is with these reasons in mind that I intend, Mr Haines, to sentence you to three years imprisonment, for those offences to which you have pleaded guilty.

I intend also to suspend your sentence, and to order you to enter into a bond in the sum of $1500.

It occurs to me, Mr Haines, that in suspending your sentence, I risk making a fool of myself. This court has been lenient to you in the past. You have made a mockery of its leniency. But this court is giving you another chance, a final chance, to rehabilitate yourself, and the reason I'm doing that, Mr Haines, is that you are soon to become a father. That will be a transformative experience. There will soon be a young person – a tiny baby – entirely dependent upon you, Mr Haines.

At the risk of your continued mockery of this court, and its processes, I will suspend your sentence, but I say to you now, Mr Haines, if you do not take the chance, the final chance, that I am now giving you, you will be imprisoned. Come before this court again, Mr Haines, there will be no leniency.

Mr Haines, you may sit down.

# Chapter 5

So, there you have it, Your Honour. That's how I found out that I was going to be a grandpa. Sitting in court, listening to the father of my daughter's child getting sentenced for assault.

How did I react? First up, I felt rage. I thought, how could I be so thick as to not know that Haines was up to his old ways, thieving and thumping people? I thought of myself going around there, trying to make nice, saying, 'Hey, Paul, how about those Roosters?' I felt – excuse my French – like a prize dickhead.

On the other hand . . . Fat was pregnant! That was what the magistrate had said. There was going to be a baby. I'd been sitting next to Fat on one of the benches at the back of the courtroom and when he'd said it, I'd looked down at her belly and I'm buggered if she looked pregnant – she didn't –

but then Fat had always been a bit on the heavy side, or else maybe she wasn't yet far enough along, so you couldn't tell. But that's definitely what the magistrate had said, Fat was having a baby.

Now, I don't know if you have grandkids, Your Honour, and if you don't, it's going to be hard for me to explain how a man feels when one of his kids – his daughters, especially – announces that she's got one in the oven. First up, you think, hang on, I'm old enough to be a grandpa? I don't feel old enough to be a grandpa! Then you start puffing up, like a big old balloon. I mean, I was obviously rapt about it, and maybe it felt especially good because there had been times, up until then, that I'd wondered whether any of my kids would ever get around to giving me a grandchild. I mean, this was 2003. Blue was 30, and Kat, she was 31, and neither of them looked even close to having kids. Kat had gone from her boarding school to university and from there she'd got a place at a law firm in the city, and they'd been so impressed with her, they'd offered to send her to London, to work in their London office, and she'd jumped at that opportunity, like she jumped at every opportunity. She'd met a fellow there, David, and before I knew what was happening, he'd slipped a rock on her finger that was the size of an iceblock and they were engaged. Early in 2001 they'd moved to New York and they'd planned to get married there and Kat had told us that she'd fly all of us – Blue and Fat and me – to New York for this big wedding they were going to have, at Windows on the World, on top of the World Trade Center, and at first, I'd said, no, no, because it was David's money, wasn't it, and I wasn't sure I could accept so much, not to cover me and my adult kids, and then, too, you've probably guessed, I'm not the travelling overseas type. I'm more the type that thinks this is the best country in the world and nothing I've seen on TV has convinced me otherwise. Then again, how many times would Kat get married? Maybe only once, and so I'd just about made up my mind to go when those attacks happened at the World Trade Center and it seemed for a while like the world had changed. Kat said David's parents, who had been real jetsetters, suddenly didn't want to fly, not from London to New York, and besides that, Kat didn't feel like a big party, not when the Windows on the World had been blown to pieces. So they ended up having the wedding in the registry office, and sending pictures back to us. I did try to get Kat to come home for a while. I said, 'Kat, why not raise any kids you'll have somewhere safe?' I mean, who wants to live in a place where somebody's trying to kill everybody? But Kat said, no, no, she was more determined than ever to stay, and David said, 'We can't let the terrorists win, Med' and so they stayed on, and I thought, well, that might mean that they're not having kids, because who would raise kids in New York, with all the crime and so on? And when I talked to Kat, I did get the feeling that she wasn't inclined that way because it was always how she wanted to achieve this and she wanted to achieve that, and nothing at all about wanting to settle down and raise a family.

As for Blue, well, I'd encouraged him to think pretty hard before settling on a girl to marry, reminding him that his mother and me, we'd tied the knot too young and look how that had worked out, and he seemed pretty happy with that advice and as far as I knew, there was nobody serious on the scene and how could there be? Out there on the Ridge, where he was living, blokes outnumbered women something like eight to one. Plus, you have to take into account how Blue was living. He'd staked his claim and tunnelled down and from time to time, a black opal would come to the surface, but for the most part, he had a tarp, and a drop toilet and no plumbing, so when it was time to have a shower – and believe me, that time didn't seem to come around all that often for folk on the Ridge – he'd rig a bucket up on a rope and let water come down over him, and while the simplicity of it had its charm for a bloke like Blue, I couldn't see a woman enjoying herself out on that drafty loo.

As for Fat, well, as I say, this was 2003 so Fat was coming up to 21, which was older than Pat and me had been when we'd had Kat, but still, who would have thought, of the three kids, Fat would be the first to fall in? But that is what seemed to be happening. I mean, I'd sat in the Forster Local Court and heard it from the Magistrate. Med Atley, ready or not, you are going to be a grandpa, and so I walked out of court that day on that cloud that people talk about, just light with a kind of disbelief, and Fat was beside me, and we pushed through the heavy doors and went out onto the footpath, and I was about to say, 'Well, you've put the wind in my sails' when Fat said, 'Have you got your chequebook, Dad?'

I said, 'Chequebook?' and Fat said, 'For the bond. We need you to put up the bond, or else they won't let Paul come out.' I thought, 'So that's why it was so urgent for me to be here' and, had I not heard the news about the baby, I might have thought, 'I'm buggered if I'm going to pay money to keep this bloke out of prison' but Fat took me by the arm and led me back through the heavy doors to the counter where there was a lady sitting behind glass, and Fat said, 'We're here for Paul Haines. The sentence was suspended. We've got to pay a bond' and she pushed me forward. I found myself going through my pockets. I had no cheque-book on me. Fat went pale. She said, 'Dad, you've got to get it or they'll take him down.'

I said, 'Let me go get it.' The lady said, 'We close at four.' I said, 'I'll be back by three-thirty.' I drove back up to my place, all the while thinking, Grandpa, Grandpa, Grandpa, and imagining myself at the local club, showing a picture of my grandkid around. I took the chequebook from the drawer in the sideboard and drove back to the courthouse. Fat was still waiting by the counter. I made out the cheque. I signed it. Fat passed it under the glass. The lady stamped it, and stapled it to some paperwork. She said, 'Mr Haines should be out shortly' and she wandered off, to do whatever filing she had to do, and while she was gone, Fat hugged me and I hugged her gently, so as not to squash the baby, and then I held her at arm's length. I looked down at her belly. I said, 'Fat, why didn't you tell me?'

She said, 'Tell you what?' and I said, 'That you've got one in the oven!' and her face, it just fell. You know how a person's face just falls, like they've just realised that what they've been thinking about, and what's been making them

93

feel happy, isn't the same thing you've been thinking about and isn't the same thing that's making you feel happy?

Fat said, 'Come on, Dad, look, here's Paul' and Haines came towards us, rubbing his wrist where the cuffs had been. He said, 'Hey, Pop' and grinned at me, with that one tooth of his and Fat said, 'Paul!' like that, sharp and short, and she marched off down the street, away from the court-house, towards where we'd parked. I followed, with Haines, after stopping to light himself a smoke, coming up behind me. And it was only when we got near the car that Fat turned and said, 'There is no baby, Dad.'

I said, 'What?'

She said, 'There's no baby. We just made that up because Paul can't go to jail.'

Well, it was like a punch in the gut. No baby? The judge had said there was a baby. The very reason that Haines was walking out of this court, right now, it was because there was going to be a baby. I said, 'What the hell are you talking about?'

Fat, she said, 'There's no baby!' and she got in the passenger seat, and Haines, he was grinning, and grinding his cigarette, and making like he was going to get in the car, too.

I said, 'You hang on a minute, Haines. You got off prison with that baby story. You come right back into that courthouse with me, and you tell the judge that was a load of bullshit, and you take what punishment is coming to you' but it wasn't like either of them was listening. Fat was already in the car and she wouldn't look at me, she just kept staring out the windscreen, and Haines was blowing the last of the smoke out of his toothless gob and getting in the driver's seat and pulling the seatbelt around him and starting up the motor. I knocked on Fat's window. I said, 'Fat, what you've done, that is a crime. It's perjury' but what would Haines have cared about that? He just pulled out of the car park, and left me standing there, outside the courthouse, like a bloody fool.

It was a month before I heard from Fat again. She phoned me up. The conversation we had, it was the grunting kind, with Fat saying, 'How's the Shire? How's the dog? ' – and me saying as little as possible, until it became too excruciating for her to go on, but the next week, she called again, and look, the truth is, when it comes to that girl, I'm just a softie. I was then, I am now, even with all that's happened. I let her win me over. She said, 'Come on, Dad, we had to do it' and, 'I couldn't have Paul in jail' until I finally said, 'Fat, you doublecrossed me. You lied in a court of law. That's not the way you were raised. You need to have a good look at what that bloke has done to you.'

She wouldn't have that, of course. I mean, she was blind to his malice. It was all, 'Oh, you don't understand him, Dad' and, 'People have always picked on him' and, 'He's not like you think' and in the end, I just said, 'Fat, you pull a stunt like that again, it will be you they put in prison, you know that, don't you?' but she didn't seem to get that, either, she just said, 'Come *on*, Dad. Paul's good. Just forget about it and come over to the house.'

I said, 'I've got no desire to see that man. You want to

say hi, you come here, and you don't bring him, because I won't be held responsible for what I'd do to him if he dared to show his face around here' and Fat said, 'Well, have it your way' and hung up on me again but then my birthday came around, and she brought over a gift – socks, I think, it was always socks – and although I wasn't home when she came by, I did go around to her place, the day after my birthday I believe it was, and I thought Haines must know he's on his last chance with me, because he tried to engage me in a conversation. He said, 'I put up a new shed' and I'd seen that on the way up the drive. He said, 'I'll show you round.' We actually walked out of his house together, and through a back paddock to where he'd put this new shed up. I said, 'Pretty impressive' and it actually was and it was cleaner than the building they were living in, which was always a bit smoke-filled and slumping, whereas this place had guttering and downpipes and electricity, and it was bloody enormous, too, and like a fool, I said to Haines, 'And what are you going to do with it?' because to me, it didn't look like the right kind of thing for ponies, and Haines, he said, 'Oh, I'll figure something out' and we walked back to the house again, and Fat passed both of us a beer and that actually wasn't such a bad afternoon. Only later, when I mentioned the shed to one of their neighbours, a bloke I knew from the Shire, he said, 'You're not serious, Med? Mate, that shed he's built, it glows all night. He's growing dope.'

I was astounded. I thought, Do not tell me that Haines has walked me around his dope growing enterprise, and done so with pride and made a complete goose of me in the process? But that was the kind of bloke he was, just brazen. Like with the new car. Not too long after the shed went up, out of nowhere, Haines started driving a new Holden ute, a special vehicle, tricked up to the nines, in a lairy purple with a Bundy bear on the rear window, expensive as anything and, as far as anybody knew, he didn't have a job.

I said, 'Fat, is Haines dealing?'

She said, 'Dealing what?'

I said, 'Well, at five bucks a ride I find it hard to believe he can afford an HSV from the pony shows? Do you take me for an idiot, Fat? What's going on in that back shed?'

Fat said, 'You always think the worst' and that was fair enough. When it came to Haines, I always did think the worst and so far, I have not been wrong, and it was for that reason that I kept trying, at least in those days, to get my girl to see sense, that she had hooked up with a loser but there was still time to get out, and she could come home and go back to school and start fresh but who was I kidding? Fat had been out on Haines Road since she was 16 years old. Her world revolved around that bastard. She was completely isolated from her cousins, and even from Auntie Edna, who wouldn't go out to the Haines property, not after the first time she'd gone there and found Haines with footy socks on, his knees wrapped around a milk crate, using brass scales to weigh the dope.

She said, 'I'm sorry, Med. He gives me the heebie-jeebies.'

I said, 'You didn't say that when I first mentioned to you that she was going around with him.'

She said, 'I thought it was just a passing thing' and it was good to hear that she was on my side, but still, a little too late. Anyway, Edna said, 'Well, things could be worse. She might actually have been pregnant' and I said, 'Touch wood' and I tapped the table, but that obviously doesn't bloody work, because the minute those words were out of Edna's mouth, the minute we'd discussed the possibility that Haines might actually father a grandchild of mine, rather than just pretend to do it as a 'Get Out of Jail Free' card, Fat turned up with news. I'd just made a cuppa and I made another for her and we were sitting at the kitchen table and she said, 'So, you're going to be a grandfather' and at first I thought, don't tell me she's trying to make a joke of what happened because I wasn't ready to see the funny side. But then I saw she wasn't joking and I said, 'Says who?'

She said, 'Trust me.'

I said, 'You been talking to Kat?' I mean, that's what made the most sense. Up until that point, Kat hadn't seemed to have a ticking clock, but maybe it had kicked in? But Fat said, 'Nope' and she was smiling this strange smile, and I said, 'What then?' and she said, 'It's me.'

Well, I was wary as hell. I said, 'Course you are. And the court case is when?'

She said, 'Come on, Dad, will you let that go? It's true this time.'

I pushed back from the kitchen table and walked around to her side and looked her over and there was something of a bump there under her shirt. She smoothed the fabric down, to show it off a little more, and she said, 'Come on, give it a pat.'

I didn't give it a pat. I was that scared it might be bullshit. But Fat said, 'Come on, Dad. Let bygones be bygones. There's a baby in here'.

I said, 'Well then, when are you due?'

She said, 'Christmas Day.'

I said, 'Christ!' and she said, 'We're not calling him that!' and then she said, 'Can you at least be happy for me?' and I said, 'Well, I don't know, Fat' and she looked upset, so I said, 'Well, are you eating right?' and she said, 'Day and night' and I said, 'Morning sickness?' and she said, 'All day sickness' and I said, 'And what does the father say about this?' because it had got to the point where I could not say that bloke's name, but Fat said, 'Well, he wasn't keen. He's never been that keen. But now it's on, he's come around.'

I said, 'Well' and then I said, 'You got a preference, boy or girl?' and she said, 'We already know' and I said, 'Well, go on, then' and she said, 'Are you sure you want to know?' and I said, 'I'm going to find out eventually, aren't I?' and she said, 'I thought you might like a surprise' and I said, 'So go on, surprise me' and she said, 'Okay' and I said, 'No, I mean, surprise me now' and she said, 'You sure?' and I said, 'I'm sure!' and she said, 'Okay, it's a boy' and I said, 'A boy?' and she said, 'Yep' and I said, 'And what will you call this boy and for Christ's sake don't tell me Med, because I've had problems with that name all my life' and she said, 'No, it will be Seth' and I said, 'Seth? What the hell kind of name is that?' and she said, 'Paul thought of it' and I thought, well, that would be right.

So we had that cup of tea, and I gave Fat a bit of a hug when she went out the door, and I could feel the baby there, firm between us, and I was chuffed. I admit that. I was chuffed. I told Edna. I told everyone. I was going to be a grandpa. This time it was for real and not five minutes later, or that's how it seemed to me, Fat had swelled up like a beer keg, and then it was December, and Fat was at Forster Hospital giving birth to Seth, and oh God, it's so hard to talk about this. It's so bloody hard. I couldn't get to the hospital fast enough and then I found myself in the shop near the kiosk, buying balloons and a stuffed toy, the biggest one you've ever seen, and I was trying to get down the hall with it, and the thing was so bloody big I couldn't see around it, and a nurse had to come and take me by the elbow and direct me into Fat's room, and there she was, sitting up in bed, not under the covers, just bare legs, with swollen ankles on the sheets, her stomach still looking like there might be a baby inside it, except that right there, in the room, in the cot next to Fat, there was Seth.

Fat said, 'So what do you think?' and what did I think? He was ugly as buggery, obviously – he had skin flaking off him and his face was wrinkled like a walnut and at the same time he was absolutely, 100 per cent, the most handsome little guy I'd seen in my life.

Fat said, 'You want to hold him?'

Absolutely, I wanted to hold him but like most males, I didn't think I was all that good with babies. They are so bloody small! So fragile. I said, 'I'm all thumbs' but Fat said, 'Oh, go on' so I lifted him out, keeping his little apple head in my paw, and for a second, he didn't do anything, just stayed lying there, in that grip of mine, and then the cry came – he had this perfect little pink mouth, like a cat's mouth – and quick as lightning, I had him over to his mum, just handed him like a parcel, and she popped a boob out, and he fixed on, and I tried to make like I was looking anywhere else, and then she was finished, and handing him back to me, and she said, 'God, I'm tired' and I said, 'You sleep' and soon as I said it, her eyes clapped shut, just folded shut, and she was gone, like she was exhausted, and I had this little guy in my hands, his head in the palm of my hand, and I didn't dare move a muscle and I swear, I sat like that until I was all cramped up, until a nurse came by and said, 'Here, let me' and took the baby and lay him down, and that's when Fat woke up, too.

She said, 'You still here?' She was dreamy. I said, 'Where have I got to go?' and we sat a bit more, me not saying much because I was thinking that my voice might wake the baby, but Fat, she seemed to get that nothing would wake him, not after that feed, and she started chatting away, saying, 'They make him stay in with me, you know' and I said, 'Oh, right' and then she said, 'Were you there when Mum had me?' and I said, 'You bet I was' and then she said, 'I wonder if Mum knows?' and I thought, Gee, so that's what's on her mind. Her own Mum, and that made sense.

I said, 'I reckon she does, Fat.' And Fat said, 'Maybe I'll get in touch, tell her she's a grandma' and as a joke, I said, 'You do that, Fat. And you make sure you say hi from me!' and that was it, Your Honour. That was it. It was 23 December 2005. My baby girl was 23, and still missing her mum, and her son, my grandson, wasn't yet one day old, and how could I have known that I'd be able to count on the fingers of both hands the number of times I'd see him again?

On Boxing Day Fat took Seth home, and set him up in the nursery I'd painted – the only clean room in that ramshackle house – and I shook hands with Haines and said congratulations and then I returned to work, and although there were times when I'd swing by after work, with a rattle or some other thing I'd picked up in town, Haines would often say, 'They're asleep, Med' or else, 'Rough night. Can you come back?' and so I suppose I'd seen Seth only five, maybe six times, before I got that call, at 10 minutes past 11 one Saturday morning in March 2006 and it was Fat saying, 'Dad, you've got to come quick, Seth's in the hospital.'

# Chapter 6

THEY HAVE THESE RUBBER DOORS AT Forster General, rubber doors that separate the people waiting from the ones that have gone through to emergency. By the time I got out there – it cannot have taken more than 15 minutes from the time I got Fat's call for me to get out there – Seth had already gone through, and it was only Fat and Haines in the waiting room. Fat's face was all screwed up. Her eyebrows kept coming together. She was chewing on the inside of her lip. I said, 'Where is he?' and 'What happened?' and Fat said, 'We don't know' and I said, 'You don't know where he is?' and Haines said, 'They've taken him somewhere' and Fat said, 'He was limp, Dad. I went to wake him this morning, and he was limp. He was chucking up. I didn't know what to do.'

I said, 'You've done the right thing. You've brought him to

the right place.' I went over to reception, where the nurse who does the admissions sits, and I said, 'I'm Med Atley. I'm the little boy's grandfather. His mother, that's my daughter. Can you tell me what's going on?' but the nurse, she looked over my shoulder towards Fat, and she said, 'Well, the baby's gone into emergency' and then Fat came over and put a hand on my shoulder and led me away, saying, 'We've asked all those questions, Dad.' I said, 'Well, it's ridiculous to have you out here. A baby needs his mother and what did the doctor say?' and Fat said, 'We didn't see a doctor' and Haines said, 'They sent out a nurse' and I thought, 'That would be right. Public hospitals, can't they even afford a doctor to see a baby anymore?' and I said, 'I'll get a doctor' and I started going towards the reception again but Fat said, 'Sit down, Dad, you're making a scene' and so we sat down, the three of us, and it was torture, listening to the clock tick and watching people around us going through the old magazines, and watching other kids going through old toys in the milk crate, and watching a bloke come in on crutches and put his leg up on a chair and get a weight off, and finally hearing a woman come out from behind the rubber door with a clip-board in her hands, saying, 'Atley-Haines?'

I thought, Atley-Haines? Who is that? It didn't immediately register but Fat jumped straight up and the woman with the clipboard said, 'You're Seth's mother?' and Fat nodded, and the woman said, 'Would you come with me?' and Fat and Haines, they both started following, and I said, 'I'm coming, too' and the woman looked at Fat, and Fat nodded, so all three of us went through the rubber doors, and into a small room, with a table and plastic chairs. I said, 'What's this?' and 'Where's Seth?' and the woman said, 'Seth's in emergency' and I said, 'Well, let's go straight there. Let's do the paperwork later' but the woman said, 'Seth's been stabilised. We need to talk to his mother' and she walked back out the way she'd come.

I pulled out a plastic chair – they had those ones with brown steel legs, like from Fat's primary school – and I motioned for Fat to sit down, and Haines took a chair, too, and I couldn't help thinking how stupid he looked, so bloody enormous, so tattooed, with that big forehead, those big hands, in that little chair.

We didn't have to wait long for the people who wanted to see Fat. They were two women – one young, maybe 20, or 22, and the other one older, like in her 50s – and straightaway, I thought, they aren't doctors. Don't ask me how I knew. It was something about the way they looked, too scruffy, and not with the right look of caring that you get with doctors.

They introduced themselves. I don't remember their names. I do remember they said they weren't from Forster. They were from the John Hunter, the big hospital nearer Newcastle, and like I thought, they weren't doctors. They were social workers. It wasn't the first time I'd met one. We'd put on a few at the Shire, starting in the early 1980s. They were people who were supposed to dream up ideas for what local kids could do, or else be in charge of some graffiti project that made the town look worse. I couldn't see the point of them.

The older one, she spoke first. She said, 'Donna-Faye,

we'd like to talk to you about Seth, about what happened to Seth.' I thought, Well, this is ridiculous. We haven't even seen the doctor. What were we supposed to talk about? I said, 'Where is Seth?' and 'When can we actually see Seth?' and that's when the younger one piped up, and said, 'Seth's going to be transferred to John Hunter' and that made my blood run cold, because like everyone in Forster, I knew, if the local hospital couldn't handle something, it was down to John Hunter, so if Seth was going to John Hunter, something was serious, and something was up.

I said, 'When can we see the doctor?' but I might as well have been talking to myself, in terms of the answers I got. The younger woman, she was pulling sheets of paper out of a manila folder and passing them across the table to Fat, and saying they were the transfer papers, and could she sign them, so the hospital could get the ambulance on its way? Fat was signing and crying and signing and crying, and then when everything was signed, the younger lady pulled the paperwork together and shoved it back in the envelope and left the room and then came back and sat down, and that's when the older one got down to what was really going on, which was basically that they were about to accuse my daughter of bashing her own son.

They didn't come out and say that. Not straightaway. What they tried to do instead was to trick Fat into admitting that was what she'd done, or else get her or Haines to dob the other one in. That was the name of the game, I can see that now.

The older one, she said, 'Ms Atley, how old is Seth?' and I thought, come on, they know how old he is! They've just come up with a phone book's worth of documents on him. But Fat said, 'He was born December 23' and the two women, they nodded, and they said, 'So, about 14 weeks, then?' and Fat nodded, and said, 'He just got a three-month booster' and they nodded and smiled, and the older one said, 'And why did you bring Seth into the hospital today, Ms Atley?' and Fat told her what she'd told me. 'He was dozy, and he was chucking up, and we didn't know what was wrong with him.'

The older social worker said, 'And was that last night he was vomiting, or was that this morning, or when?' and Fat said, 'Well, I worked the night shift last night' and that seemed to surprise the two women, because they looked at each other, one of those looks that gives everything away, and then the older one said, 'You're working the night shift? You've got a 14-week-old baby!' and Fat said yes, she was doing three nights a week to Woolies, stacking the shelves. Haines didn't say anything, didn't even look ashamed of himself, which surely he must have been, because what kind of man, what kind of father, sends a young mother out to the night shift with a baby not three months old? But from Fat's point of view, what choice did she have? Haines might have had money for his V8 ute but nine times in 10, when I went around there, it was beer in the fridge and no milk, and I don't think that would have changed just because there was suddenly a baby on the scene.

But anyway, the older lady said, 'What time did you

get home last night?' and Fat said, 'I finished up around midnight' and the older lady said, 'And was Seth asleep?' and Fat said, 'Paul tried to put him down, but he wouldn't go down, and in the end, he'd had to put him in the cot, but he was still crying a lot.'

The older lady said, 'Oh, you poor thing! It must have been exhausting for you, to come in after a long shift, and have to settle the baby' and Fat said, 'Paul said he was crying all night.'

The younger lady said, 'Does Seth cry often?' but before Fat could answer, Haines jumped in and said, 'He never bloody stops' and the older lady, she lit up at that, she put on this fake smile, and she said, 'Oh, that can be so difficult, can't it? That can be so hard when the baby won't settle' and she smiled at Fat, and she smiled at Haines, and I thought, Hang on, what is going on here? Where is this heading? but the younger one had jumped in, and she was saying, 'So frustrating! Some babies, they just won't settle!' and Haines, being the dickhead, couldn't stop himself from agreeing with her, saying, 'Yeah, this one's a real bastard.'

Fat said, 'I tried to give him the bottle. Paul had been trying to give him the bottle but he'd been chucking it up everywhere' and again, the older social worker jumped in and said, 'And that must have been so frustrating! Did you find that frustrating?' And again, there was this brightness in her voice, like she understood, like she was concerned, like she got that Haines and Fat were struggling with this baby and everybody knew how hard that could be, and there was no shame in saying they weren't coping. Encouraged by her,

Haines said, 'The doctor said he's got the colic' and Fat said, 'Not colic. He said reflux' and Haines said, 'Colic' and Fat went mute.

The older woman said, 'Well, colic or reflux, that must make it more difficult to settle him' and then she said, 'So, did Seth settle at all last night? Did anyone get any sleep?' and Fat said, no, it just got to the point where she just gave up and put the baby in the cot and let him cry it out and drop off, and then it was morning, and she'd gone in to check on him, and he was all floppy.

The older woman, she was making clucking noises through all of this, sympathetic noises, nodding her head. She said, 'Mmm, floppy, and anything else? He was vomiting, you said?' and Fat said, 'He'd chucked up all over the cot. There was chuck all over him' and she'd peeled back his nappy and it was yellow poo, exploded out of his nappy, all over his back, and Haines said, 'And it stunk like anything' and the older woman, she was tut-tutting and nodding, and saying, 'That's got to be frustrating! Now you've got all that cleaning up to do!' and Fat was saying, 'I get more tired than anything' and the younger social worker was saying, 'I'm sure you do! You must!' and then, 'And what about you, Dad?' not meaning me, but meaning Haines. 'You must find it frustrating, wanting to help and not really knowing what to do to help?' and Haines, he snorted and said, 'Doesn't matter what I do. That kid pays no respect to me.'

There was a bit of silence then, just half a second of silence, maybe only enough for me to pick up that the mood was changing, and then the younger social worker said,

'You know, sometimes, parents, they try everything with a newborn baby, and it's so, so hard. It seems like nothing you can do will solve the baby's problems. The baby just cries and cries and cries.' And I thought, What is she getting at? But of course, I knew. I knew what was coming. They were about to point the finger. I was ready for it but I'm not that sure Fat was ready for it.

The older social worker, she said, 'Sometimes, when you're handling a baby, you can lose your grip and drop the baby when a baby is fussing or crying or screaming. You didn't drop the baby, did you?'

Fat shook her head, no. The older woman, she then said, 'And he didn't fall, did he? He didn't roll off the table or anything, while you were trying to change him, did he? He didn't fall?'

Fat shook her head again, no.

There was a bit more silence, and then the younger woman, the one who was apparently in charge of all the forms, she reached down and opened her briefcase, and she took out a sheet of paper, and I noticed her tone had completely changed, and she said, 'Ms Atley, Mr Haines, I need to inform you that we will be heading to court this afternoon, and we'll be applying for a care and protection order. Do you understand what that means?'

And Fat, poor Fat, she just said, 'What?'

The young woman said, 'Ms Atley, your son, Seth Atley-Haines, has suffered a serious injury, and we believe the injury was a non-accidental injury. You haven't been able to provide us with an explanation for that injury. That being the case, we do not intend to return Seth to your care. I'm required to inform you that today we will be applying for an order to take your son into the State's care, pending a full investigation.'

Now, up until this point, I had managed to stay pretty calm, but now I moved away from the wall where I'd been leaning, and I said, 'You what?' and 'This is ridiculous' and Haines, too, he suddenly got mobile, getting out of his chair, saying, 'You're doing what?'

The older woman, she said, 'Please sit down, Mr Haines' and Haines said, 'I won't bloody sit down' and the older woman said, 'Lower your voice' and Haines said, 'I'll raise my voice. I'll bring this roof down' and for a moment there, I thought things might explode, except the younger woman, she pressed some kind of button, some button that must have been under the table, and the door opened, and a security guy came in – not a real bouncer, but dressed like a bouncer, with a torch in his belt and a walkie-talkie on his chest, to make him look menacing – and he ordered Haines out of there, and me, too, and Fat as well.

Haines walked straight back through the rubber doors, through the waiting room, out into the car park, where he lit a smoke. I stood in the waiting room, waiting for Fat, but she didn't come out, not straightaway. I strode around, head full of steam, marching up and down, with out-patients in their plastic chairs and their arms in their slings and their heads in bandages, no doubt thinking, What's with this guy? and then the nurse on reception beckoned me over and said, 'This is a hospital, sir. You're going to have to calm down' so I went

111

outside and stood in the car park and lit my own smoke, and that's where Fat found us – me and Haines – at opposite ends of the same forecourt at Forster General, our backs to each other, steam coming out of our ears.

I was thinking, I'm gonna kill him, I'm gonna kill him, I'm gonna kill him if he's touched that boy, because of course I knew, even on that first day, that if anything had happened to Seth, it wouldn't have been Fat that had anything to do with it. I mean, no way, not even knowing what I now know, there was no way. It would have to have been that violent bastard she'd ended up living with, and so when Fat came out, we both moved towards her in an equal hurry, and she kind of stuck each hand out, as if to clear a path for herself, and said, 'I want to go home' and so of course that gave Haines permission to put his arm around her, and start guiding her towards their car. I said, 'Wait, Fat, what's going on?' and she half-turned, and put a hand in her pocket, and a sheaf of papers came out – yellow, pink, green papers, like duplicates of something she'd signed – and she shoved them at me, and she got back under Haines' arm and kept going towards their car, leaving me standing there like a stunned mullet, looking after them as their car went out through the exit barrier, and down the road, in the direction of the Haines property, and only when they were gone did I get a chance to look down at the papers Fat had shoved in my hand, and I pretty near vomited, right there in the hospital forecourt, because what they were, those papers, they were basically an application to take Seth into State care, and down the bottom was Fat's signature, which could only mean she'd somehow been made to sign them.

Well, I was that angry. I mean, Fat was no longer a child, but I had my doubts that she would have known what signing those papers meant. No way would she have understood the jargon, and she was in shock. She was a mother whose baby was on the way to John Hunter. I thought, this is an outrage. I went back into the hospital. I held up the papers. I said, 'I want to see the social worker that gave this to my daughter.' The girl on reception, she was trembling a bit, like I was making her feel anxious, or maybe she had seen this kind of thing before and knew it didn't end well. That made me feel guilty. She had nothing to do with it. I hadn't meant to frighten her. I'd just wanted to figure out what was going on, so I softened my tone and I asked her again, 'Can I see the ladies who gave these forms to my daughter?' but the girl on reception said, 'I don't think they're here. I think they've left' and I thought, 'Is she bullshitting me?' but then, no, I suppose it was possible that they were already on their way back to Newcastle, to get their child-abduction – really, that's what I thought it was – underway, in the courts.

I said, 'Well, then, can I see my grandson?'

The girl said, 'Could you just wait here a minute please?' and I waited and a bloke came out. I don't know who he was, but he was a kind bloke. He was in some kind of scrubs. He said, 'Mr Atley?' and I said, 'Yep' and he said, 'Your grandson is Seth Atley-Haines?' and I said, 'Yes' and he said, 'Seth has been stabilised. We're about to get him

113

on his way to John Hunter. It's going to take an hour to get him there.'

I said, 'Well, let me see him before he goes' and the bloke said, 'I can't do that, Mr Atley, and it's not even really because of all that paperwork. Seth's a very sick boy.'

Well, that was the first time, Your Honour, that I'd heard that. Seth was sick. Really sick. I mean, I'd heard he'd had a temperature. I'd heard he'd been vomiting. I'd heard he wouldn't take the bottle. He had to go to John Hunter but the women with the paperwork, they'd been all about, 'What happened?' and not how sick Seth was.

As softly as I could manage it, I said, 'Mate, I'm his grandfather. His mother, she's my daughter. She wouldn't have had anything to do with this. If I hang about, don't make a nuisance of myself, sit quietly, why don't you let me look in on him, just pop my head through the door before he goes?'

As I say, the bloke was kind. He said, 'Look, Mr Atley, let me make a deal with you. Why don't you head home, and phone up later, and I'll make sure I leave a note with the girl on reception, and she'll be able to tell you what's happened once he's been transferred.' Well, I didn't want to accept that. I didn't want to leave. I thought I'll hang around the back and wait for the ambulance to come out and rush up and look in the window, but no matter how I looked, I couldn't see where the ambulance would come out, so eventually, I did go home, and at six o'clock, I did call the hospital but it was a different nurse on the reception, and she didn't know anything about this deal I'd made with the bloke in scrubs.

I said, 'Let me speak to the bloke I spoke to before, the one who said I should phone up' and she said, 'Do you know his name? I don't really know who you mean' and I said, 'He didn't give me his name' and I tried to describe him, and she said, 'We have 30 staff in the building' and basically I got nowhere, so I put down the phone, and got out the Newcastle *Yellow Pages*, and looked up the John Hunter, and called them there, and basically got a brick wall. So I got in the car, with the aim of driving down the Pacific Highway, down to the John Hunter, if that's what it took to see my grandson, who shouldn't have been allowed to be on his own, not sick like he was, but on the way, of course, I had to pass the Haines place and the lights were on so I pulled up the gravel drive, and it had started to pour with rain, and there were puddles and patches all over the drive, and my car got splashed and I had to hopscotch through the puddles and I knocked on the door. When nobody answered, I thumped on it and said, 'Open up, Haines' and the door opened, and it was Haines.

I said, 'What have you heard?'

He said, 'We've heard nothing, except they've moved him down to John Hunter.'

I said, 'Where's Fat?'

He said, 'She's asleep.'

I said, 'Don't give me, she's asleep. How could she be asleep?' and Haines said, 'I gave her one of my Valium' and I was appalled at that. I mean, drugs? That was Haines' answer to everything. Drugs.

I said, 'What the hell went on here this morning?' and

Haines said, 'Don't you start on me' and I said, 'Start on you about what?' and Haines said, 'Well, what do you think went on, Med? What we said went on, went on. Seth got sick. We took him to hospital and now they're blaming us.'

I was still standing in the rain. There was none of this, 'Come on in, don't stand there in the rain.' I had water pouring off me. Lightning cracked, and I had to shout. I said, 'You think this is about you? This isn't about you. Or is it about you?'

Haines shouted back, into the wet, into the dark, 'You listen to me, Med. That's my son there in the hospital, not yours, and if all you're going to offer is banging on my door and hanging it on me, you can piss off. I mean that, Med. Piss off, and don't come back. I've put up with you because you're a lonely bastard whose wife did a runner, but let me tell you, I've had it with you. You come here hanging Seth on me, you're dead to us.'

Well my head it felt like it might explode. My heart, it was coming up, out of my chest. I said, 'You goddamn –' and I made for him, and he put a hand up against my chest and said, 'Alright, Med, you want to take this outside? Let's take this outside' and he stepped out from behind the security door, like to have a punch-up with me, right there in the rain on the gravel drive, but then through the screen door, I could see Fat – my Fat, now with milk down her shirt, in purple tracksuit bottoms and a pair of moccasins, red-eyed from crying – and she was coming towards us, saying, 'Will you two just cut it out? Can't you just *stop*', and tears were pouring down her face, and she was saying,

116

'Can't you think of Seth for once', and she reached out, grabbed for Haines, and he stepped back into the house. The door closed and I was left outside, standing in the dark and the rain.

# Chapter 7

I DON'T LIKE TO CALL ON people for help. Men don't, do they? From the youngest age, my old man told me, see if you can do it yourself. Only if you can't, get someone to lend a hand. What he was talking about, though, was things like servicing the car or fixing a tap. With Seth, I didn't even know what was going on, really. I was out of my depth, and I was buggered if I could think how to handle it, and so I called Kat. I called her in New York. It was something I hardly ever did, so I knew she'd know it was important.

I reached her in her office. It was a weekend, but in those days, she was always in the office; Saturdays, Sundays, night-time, that's where you'd find her. Her husband, David, was the same. When it came to working, they couldn't get enough. They told me everyone was the same. The

Americans were at war. They'd had a recession. Everybody was working hard just to hang on.

I was confused by the way she answered the phone. She said, 'Ka'aren Atley.' Say what you like, but when your little girl has been known all her life as Kat Atley, she doesn't just become Ka'aren Atley – 'Ka'aren' like Car-ren, Your Honour. The whole way that Kat spoke, it changed when she went to that school, and it changed again when she moved overseas. Australians are like that, aren't they? Chameleons. They adapt.

Anyway, I first thought, oh, I dialled the wrong number here, but when I said, 'Is Kat there?' she said, 'Oh, Dad, it's me!' and then she said, 'What's wrong?' because obviously, I didn't call all that often, and it was mostly when I had news.

I told her I phoned up to talk about Fat. I said I felt pretty confused. I didn't know who else to try. I'd already tried Blue, but the only way to get him was to ring the local pub in Lightning Ridge, and that hadn't worked out, not on a Saturday night. The barman couldn't hear me or couldn't work out what I wanted, and Blue never came on the line so I'd phoned Edna, and told her what had happened – Seth was in John Hunter, and they wouldn't let me see him – and she couldn't understand, either. She kept saying, 'But that doesn't make sense, Med. Why is he in the hospital? What happened to him?' and I kept having to say, 'That's it, they won't tell us' and she'd say, 'But that doesn't make sense, Med' and after a while it was clear that Edna wasn't going to be of much help, although she did put the idea into my head to call Kat, when she said, 'If they keep this up, Med, what you're going to need is a lawyer' because wasn't Kat a lawyer? That's what she'd done at university. Law. She'd know what to do.

I explained the situation. I said, 'You know, Kat, how Fat had the baby . . .' and Kat did know that. She'd sent one of those 'I heart NY' baby suit things and she'd been on at Fat to send a picture on the email but we hadn't managed to work out how to do it. I said, 'Well, Fat came in from the night shift at Woolies and Seth was grizzling and the next day he was chucking up, and she took him into hospital, and now they're saying it's somehow Fat's fault . . .' and Kat, she was as stunned as me. She kept saying, 'Fat? They think Fat hurt her own baby?' and I had to explain how Fat hadn't been home, that Haines had been home, and Kat said, 'But that still makes no sense, Dad. If the police think Haines did something to the baby, what's that got to do with Fat?' and I had to say, 'I don't know, I don't get it' and Kat said, 'It sounds like Fat needs a lawyer' and I said, 'Aren't you a lawyer?' and she said, 'Oh, Dad, I'm not that kind of lawyer. I do patents. I do business agreements.' She didn't say the obvious, which was that she was in New York and even if she'd flown out that very afternoon, it would take her two days to get to Forster. She said, 'Well, have they told you when Seth's coming out?' I mean, that's where we were at, Your Honour. We were still saying things like, *'Have they told you when he's coming out?'* I mean, really, that shows how much we knew about how serious this thing was, which was sweet bugger all.

Anyway, Kat, she said, 'Look, Dad, I've got to get moving

but give me an hour, and I'll have a Google around, and I'll see if I can find somebody to have a look at the paperwork for you' and I could hear in her voice that she had to get off, and I said, 'Well, okay' and Kat, she said, 'It'll be fine, Dad. I have a good feeling about it' and so I rang off and sat stewing, and not really knowing who else to call, or what else to do.

Now, the following day, being Sunday, I couldn't do much. I did one drive by John Hunter – hour there, hour back – but stopped myself from going in, in case I somehow made things worse, but my heart was just racing and pounding, thinking of Seth in there and not knowing what was wrong with him, and what they were doing to him, or anything, really. Then, on the Monday, I took the papers into my work, and showed them to the bloke who worked on legal matters for the Shire, a bloke called Barry. I said to him, 'Barry, mate, I need a favour. Can you look these over for me?' and he looked them over, and he looked a bit shocked, and then embarrassed, and he said, 'Med, this is a care application. That's your daughter, Donna-Faye? The State's made an application to take her baby into care.'

I said, 'Yeah, I get that.'

He said, 'What's gone on, Med?'

I said, 'I don't rightly know. Fat – Donna-Faye – she phoned up Saturday morning and said Seth was in the hospital, chucking up and whatnot, and I went to hospital, and they wouldn't let me see him, wouldn't let any of us see him, said the baby had to go to John Hunter, and two women came in and said somebody must have hurt him, and gave Fat these papers and sent her home without the baby.

Barry, he said, 'Well, you need to find out what has happened here, mate, because this application, it's to take your Seth into State care. It's the first step to making him a State ward.'

I said, 'No grandchild of mine is going to be a State ward.'

He said, 'Well, that's what's underway.'

I said, 'What can I do about it, Barry?' and like Kat, Barry said, 'You need to get a lawyer', but he wasn't the kind of lawyer I needed. He said, 'Med, mate, this kind of thing, it's not my bag. You need somebody who knows their way around the Children's Court.'

I said, 'Anybody you can recommend?' and Barry thought for a minute, and said, 'Look, there's a practice in town. I can make a call for you' and he went though the Rolodex, and found the number and phoned up, and I heard him explaining the situation, saying, 'Yeah, welfare already involved' and, 'Yeah, the grandfather works here, he's a good bloke, and he's pulling out his hair' and then looking embarrassed because aside from the beard, I don't actually have much. He said, 'Okay if I send him over?' and then he nodded and put down the phone, picked up a pen and wrote down the address.

He said, 'She can't make any promises, but she's willing to have a look.'

I said, 'It's a lady lawyer?'

He said, 'Yeah, but she's good.'

I took the address from him. I said, 'This is just between us, right?' and Barry, he said, 'Med, we haven't spoken.'

I took the afternoon off and sat down with the lawyer and went over the situation again, and she had much the same to tell me. Seth was on his way to being a ward of the State.

I said, 'Can they just do that? I mean, they haven't even told us what's wrong with him.'

She said, 'They do it every day' and in case you don't know, actually that's true. Probably I don't need to tell you this, Your Honour, but the number of kids that are wards of the State in this country, well, you wouldn't believe it. I'm talking 30,000. That's no exaggeration. That's more than when Pat was in the home, way back when. The only difference is, they don't have kids in homes anymore. The homes are gone. They've got them fostered out instead, and from what the lady lawyer said, that's what they had in mind for Seth, to take him from my daughter and give him away to somebody else.

I said, 'So, what do I do to put the brakes on this?' and she said, 'Well, you've got a battle on your hands' and I said, 'But how can that be? How can they just take a baby?' and she said, 'Well, look at it from their point of view. Seth's got a serious injury and nobody can say how he got it. What would you do if you worked for welfare?'

I said, 'I wouldn't say straightaway oh, let's take the baby away. That doesn't sound right to me.'

The lawyer, she looked at the paperwork again and said, 'Well, if they think one of the parents shook the baby, or dropped the baby or hurt the baby somehow, I don't see what choice they've got.'

I said, 'But you've got it all wrong. Fat wouldn't hurt Seth. Fat's absolutely over the moon with Seth. It's agony not having him with her.'

She said, 'But Fat doesn't live alone, does she?' and then she said, 'This bloke your daughter lives with, what's he like?' Well, what could I say? That he was an absolute no-hoper? A drunk and a drug addict with an aversion to a hard day's work? But that Fat seemed to think that the sun shone out of his arse?

I said, 'Well, let's put it this way. He wouldn't be my choice.'

She said, 'Might he have done something to the baby?'

I said, 'Well, look, he's not good for much, but to be honest with you, I can't believe anyone would do anything to a little baby.' I mean, deliberately hurt a little baby? That was seriously the way I was thinking. How could anyone have hurt Seth? He was only just learning how to hold up his head. He still had that strange way of sleeping, where his hands would move like they were conducting an orchestra. Hurt him? You've got to be kidding. It was all I could do not to bawl when I saw him.

The lawyer said, 'Well, people can surprise you, Med.'

I said, 'I can tell you the chance that Fat's done anything, it's got to be nil, and they're keeping that baby away from his mother. He's got to need his mother.'

The lawyer sighed, and she said, 'Well, whatever the rights and wrongs of it, that's what they've got planned and at all costs, I'd try to avoid this baby going into State care, Med, because my experience is, when a child goes into State care, it's difficult to get them out.'

I said, 'Well, my grandson is not becoming a ward. That's just not an option', and I explained how I'd raised Fat after my wife took off, and I'd take Seth and raise him myself before I'd let the State have him.

She said, 'Oh, Med, if only it were that simple.'

I said, 'Will you take the case?' and she said, 'Well, Barry says you're a good bloke' and she smiled at me, and for some reason, that made me feel a bit more confident about where we were at. I thought, if this lawyer – and Barry had said she was a good lawyer – was prepared to take the case, maybe we had a chance.

See how much I didn't know? I didn't know that lawyers, they take cases. That's their job. They take cases because they get paid.

Anyway, I left her office and I drove home. I phoned up Fat, and the phone rang out, so I phoned again and phoned again. I figured they had to be home. Where else would they be? It was Haines who finally picked up. I stopped him before he could say, 'Med, piss off.' I got in first. I said, 'Look, Paul, forget about the other night, I've got a lawyer for you.'

Haines hesitated. He hesitated, and then he said, 'We don't need a lawyer, Med.'

I said, 'Do you have a better idea?'

He said, 'We've got justice on our side.'

I said, 'It won't hurt for you to speak to her. I will pay. She's a nice lady. We'll just make sure we all understand what's going on and what we have to do.'

For once in his life, Haines didn't argue. I made an appointment for the three of us – Fat, Haines and me – to see her again, and by the time that appointment came around, we'd had another letter from the court, this one telling us what was going on in the minds of the bureaucrats. It said that Seth was a victim of the Shaken Baby Syndrome. Now, I should say here, I'd never heard of Shaken Baby Syndrome, not before I read that letter. I didn't know what it was. It's pretty rare. It's also pretty new. Sixty years ago, they didn't have it. Or else they had it, but they called it something else.

It was the lawyer who told us what it was. She said it was when the parents took the baby by the shoulders, and gave it a good rattle to make it shut up.

She said some people – new parents, mostly – they get so frustrated with a crying baby, they shake it, and they don't know it's a deadly thing to do. They don't understand they are rattling the baby's brain around, doing real damage.

I thought, well, that explains what those two women at Forster General were on about, with all their questions about how frustrating it is to have a baby in the house.

I looked at Fat. If she heard what the lawyer was saying, her face didn't show it. Her expression even then, it was often blank.

The lawyer said, 'The Department isn't saying which one of the parents they hold responsible, only that they believe that somebody shook the baby, and since neither of you admit to it, they don't want to run the risk of it happening again.'

Haines said, 'Yeah, well that's bullshit.'

Fat said, 'I just want my baby back.'

Our lawyer looked at Fat, and she flashed that smile that

she'd given me. She said, 'Well, of course, Donna-Faye. That's absolutely why we are here, to get your baby back.'

She reached into her top drawer. She brought out a contract. It was all about what we would pay to get Seth back. It was a pretty penny. But, she said, that was 'the easy part'. There were other contracts, too. If we won, we'd sue, and if we won money, she'd get 48 per cent.

'But that all comes later,' she said. 'For now, let's concentrate on bringing Seth home.'

# Chapter 8

IT WASN'T LONG BEFORE THE FIRST day of the hearing about Seth came around. I'd had to park the car a mile away from the Children's Court, the one in Parramatta. I had to run down the street in my suit – again with the tan suit, although just the pants this time, and a white cotton shirt, which I was hoping wasn't too yellow under the arms – so I wouldn't miss the start.

I shouldn't have bothered. I wouldn't have missed the start. I shouldn't have bothered with the suit either. I mean, nobody else bothered to get dressed up, not even if they were fighting for their own kid.

One example – there was a woman sitting on the steps out front when I arrived, with her feet basically in the gutter and her head between her knees. I know I'm not supposed to notice these things, but her boobs were falling out. She

129

had a Jim Beam singlet on, and no bra, and her boobs were falling out. Like Haines, she had tattoos all over her hands. Hers were swallows.

I thought, is she drunk? I mean, it was 9 am but her head was lolling around, and she was moaning. She wasn't drunk though. She was grief-stricken, and nobody was helping her. I wasn't sure what do to. I looked around, and it was clear that nobody else was going to intercede, so I went over and bent down and said, 'Ma'am? Can I help you, Ma'am?'

She looked up at me. She looked like a racoon. Her eye make-up, it was smudged down her face. She said, 'They took my bloody baby!'

I was pretty shocked. I said, 'Who took your baby?' She said, 'They did. The effing system (except she didn't say effing, she said the real thing). The courts. The cops. The effing system.'

I was thinking about what to say to her, what to do, really, when another woman started coming down the stairs. She was dressed properly. She had on a skirt, with a jacket. She was a big lady, but she looked neat. She had a briefcase.

The woman with the swallows on her hands, she looked up, and she saw this woman and she started spitting – I mean, literally spitting on the ground. She said, 'There she is, the baby-snatcher. There she is, the dog. There she is, the mole. That's what welfare looks like in the State of NSW. That's the dog, the mole.'

She said, 'I've got nothin' to lose now, bitch' and, 'Better watch your back, bitch' and, 'I'll be getting Byron back and you can suck my old man's dick, mole.'

The woman with the briefcase didn't look up. She walked down the stairs without turning back and went up the street and when she was gone, the tattooed woman turned to me and said, 'Have you got a cigarette?'

I gave her one. What else could I do? I gave her one.

I looked at my watch. I was late. I headed up the stairs into the building. There was security at the front door, like at airports. I put my wallet and my keys on the conveyor belt, and got waved through by those wands. I went up an escalator. It wasn't like a normal court. There were no blokes walking around in horsehair wigs. There was no fancy wood panelling.

There were TVs mounted on the walls, flashing the names of the cases, like airport arrivals. I could see 'Atley-Haines' so I knew where to go. We were in court six. I felt a bit anxious. I thought, 'I'll just go the loo.' I don't know if you've seen it but the toilets at the Children's Court in Parramatta are covered in graffiti. Covered, like a mural. The cleaners must have given up. Most of it is permanent marker. I read some of it. One person had written, 'You find yourself in this place, you might as well kiss your kids goodbye.' Another said, 'Welfare workers steal your kids and give them to Koori carers to cover their own arse.'

I thought, 'How has this happened? Us Atleys, we're good people. How did we end up in a place like this, dealing with this kind of mess?'

I did my business. I made my way out of there. I found court six. I was just in time to see Haines meandering over, in

131

his Adidas pants and his moccasins. He was talking loudly.

He said, 'Can you believe it, Med? Got held up by security. Bastards took my Swiss army knife.'

I thought, he's kidding. He was not kidding. He was exactly the kind of moron that would take a Swiss army knife into the Children's Court.

He said, 'I better get it back.'

Fat was trailing behind him. Her face was swollen from crying. She was saying, 'It's alright, Paul.'

I thought, He's upset about the *knife?*

She said, 'The security guard told us to remind them on the way out.'

It was all I could do not to say, and hey, maybe we can get Seth on the way out too? I said, 'Are you alright, Fat?' I put my arm around her. She was bigger than me around the middle. Like I've said before, she just carries weight. She shrugged. She said, 'I'm okay.'

Haines said, 'I'm bloody not. I've had that knife five years.'

Our lawyer wasn't outside court six. Neil Cowan was there, though. I know what you are thinking. Who the bloody hell is Neil Cowan? I might as well tell you, since I'm the one who was responsible for getting him there. Neil Cowan is a quack.

I found him on the internet. I wish I hadn't, but I did. It was Kat that gave me the idea. A couple of years after she moved overseas, when she was back on some short break, she put a computer in what was Blue's room, and she organised some kind of connection with Telstra. She showed me how you pulled the cord out of the back of the phone and stuck it in the back of the computer and you could get the internet.

She was raving about how great it would be, sending emails and photos and whatnot. To be honest with you, I stayed away from the thing for years. I'd unplug the phone to use it, and forget what to do next, and then forget to plug the phone back in and Edna would come around and say the line's been busy for two days. So it was more of a nuisance than anything. But then when all this started, so many people said to me, oh, you should look on the internet. There's so much information on the internet. So I made an effort and I got a connection and I put in 'Shaken Baby Syndrome' and this bloke, Neil Cowan, he'd popped up. He had a whole page on it.

From what I read, it seemed like he was an expert. He said Shaken Baby Syndrome was a myth. Not just a myth. A fraud. He said it wasn't real, and welfare departments, like the Department of Community Services, made it up so they could steal babies from poor homes, to keep social workers employed.

Looking back now, I can see that Neil Cowan was deranged in some way. He was obsessed with governments and conspiracies and cover-ups and fraud. But I couldn't see that back then. What I saw then was that he'd put realms of material about Shaken Baby Syndrome on the internet, and he had a phone number in Sydney, and I was so desperate for help, I would have grabbed at anything. I remember phoning him from my place – pulling the plug out of the computer, putting it back in the phone – thinking, he's a doctor, he probably won't be easy to reach, but maybe I'll be able to leave a message with his receptionist and maybe he'll call back.

Well, there was no receptionist. Neil Cowan himself picked up the phone. He said, 'Neil Cowan' and, surprised, I said, 'Are you the doctor on the Shaken Baby website?' and it was like he came alive.

He said, 'Yes, yes, that's me' and I said, 'Well, I'm Med Atley' and I explained what we were up against, and straightaway, he started saying oh yes, classic, classic, that is so classic, like classic was his favourite word in the world.

He said, 'Oh, this is a classic case' and then he said, 'Where are you?' and I said, 'Forster' and he said, 'Allow me to come up there. I'm compelled to hear more about this.' I thought, uh oh, how much is this going to cost? I said, 'What are your fees?' but Cowan said no, no, no, don't misunderstand me, I don't want money, I want to help you, this is a classic case, a classic example, you really don't understand what a classic example of the Shaken Baby myth this is, and he invited himself up to Forster, to our lawyer's office, and to my credit, I think, the moment he walked in, I did think, uh oh, because there was something not quite right about him. I wish I could explain it better than that, but something just wasn't right, in terms of the way he presented himself when he was supposedly a doctor, a professional, an expert. His pants were a bit too short and too tight, like they were from an old suit that didn't fit right, or else one that belonged to somebody else, maybe a smaller brother, and he had pens in the top pocket of his shirt, all lined up, and my experience is, nobody who actually works does that with pens, because those things, they leak, and that's something you find out on the first week in the job, and you don't do again.

He sat down and he took a pen from his line of pens, and he said, 'Ned, I've decided to make your case the test case, the one that will go all the way to the High Court' and our lawyer, she nearly spat out her tea. She said, 'The High Court? We haven't even been to the Children's Court.'

But Neil Cowan, he wouldn't be swayed. He said, no, no, this is the classic case, this is the one I've been looking for, the one we need to smash this conspiracy wide open, and then he launched into what I figured was his usual spiel, the one his mates (if he has any) must threaten to bash him for, if he raises it again, about how Shaken Baby Syndrome is bogus and how he'd been looking for a case for a while that would help him prove it, and this one was classic, just classic, and what he intended to do was show that Seth's injuries weren't caused by shaking and how what he'd prove instead was that these brain injuries were caused by vaccinations.

He said, 'Had Seth had his shots?'

Well, of course Seth had his shots. He'd had his three-month shots not five days before he went to hospital, and when Cowan heard that, he practically jumped out of his chair, saying, 'See, see, and they'll tell you there is no connection between the shots and the brain injury! It's classic, just classic! There is so much evidence that these shots cause brain damage, but the drug companies, they don't want to admit it, because every baby in the western world is getting shots and that's a lucrative business. So what's happening is parents are turning up at hospital with babies that had been jabbed with all kinds of poison, and the hospitals are saying,

"Did you shake this baby?" because they were in cahoots with the drug companies.' Having said that, Neil Cowan slapped his hand down on the lawyer's desk, and made us all jump.

Haines said, 'Well why can't we just go in there and say we didn't do anything? They've got no proof we did.'

Did you get that, Your Honour? *They've got no proof we did*.

But Neil Cowan, he wouldn't be swayed. He said, no, no, no, he'd been studying this for a long time. Vaccinations were poison and the drug companies knew it and governments knew it and Seth's case, it was just classic, classic, and he said, 'This will give me the ammunition I need to blow this conspiracy apart' and then he pulled out a letter and showed me the letterhead, which said 'Office of the Prime Minister and Cabinet' and he said, 'I've been in touch with people at the highest level, and they have acknowledged my work in this area!'

I had a quick look through the letter. I didn't want to be rude but to me, it looked like one of the letters we used to send people from the Shire, when they wanted us to come and cut their lawns and we couldn't come and cut their lawns, because it's not our business to cut private lawns. It was basically a letter that said, 'Thanks for the incredibly boring material you've sent us about this, we've filed it away, and now please, piss off.'

I handed the letter back to Neil Cowan, and I was actually on the verge of saying, look, maybe this isn't the best idea, maybe you shouldn't testify for us after all, but there was just no stopping him when his mouth started to run, and it was Haines who finally said, 'Yeah, okay, we get it' and I felt a bit embarrassed, but Cowan, he didn't seem put out at all, like he was used to people telling him to shut up.

I did venture one question: Why would the welfare department want to steal babies from their mothers? Cowan, he acted like he had that all worked out. He said, 'Imagine, Ned, if there was no Shaken Baby Syndrome! What would happen to all the social workers? What would happen to the occupational therapists, the speech therapists, the cognitive therapists, the lawyers and the judges? They wouldn't have jobs!'

Now, I know what you're thinking, Your Honour. Neil Cowan was a quack and I should have known it, and maybe I did, but I hope you can also understand how desperate we were, when we went looking for people to help us. Seth was still at John Hunter. We hadn't seen him since that day they'd taken him behind the rubber curtains at Forster General, and my Fat was falling apart, being away from her baby. She'd started walking around in circles, crying and holding one of his bears, like it was a baby. I could hardly stand it. I would have grabbed hold of anyone who told me they could help her.

The other thing was, our lawyer said some of what Neil Cowan was saying was actually true. Not the bit about how drug companies were poisoning the nation's babies and the government was turning a blind eye, obviously, but she said, 'It is true that it's very difficult to prove that a baby has been shaken.'

I thought, But how can that be? Because, I suppose, like a lot of people, I thought a shaken baby must look like a rag doll, all limp and loose and floppy and that it would be obvious to anyone that it had been shaken, but our lawyer, she said, 'Actually, no. A shaken baby looks like any other baby. They don't have bruises. They don't have broken bones. The damage is all on the inside. You've got to do a scan and even when you do, it's hard to say Shaken Baby because all the scans can tell you is that the baby is injured, and not how it got injured.' I thought that was interesting, but still, even after she'd said that, our lawyer said, 'Look, I'm still not sure Neil Cowan is the right person to have on our side' and then Haines butted in and said, 'But why not? He makes sense to me. And at least he *is* on our side' which made me think, Haines, you're not so stupid after all, are you? You know I'm not on your side and so it was Haines who gave Neil Cowan the go-ahead to come up to the court on the day of the hearing and so there he was, standing outside court six, in the same white shirt and too small suit pants, with the same row of pens, trembling with excitement, ready to testify for us.

# Chapter 9

WE'D BEEN IN THE WAITING AREA about 10 minutes when a voice came over the intercom, saying, 'Haines, Atley. Parties for Haines, Atley' which meant it was time to go in and get started, and while I realise that you already know the outcome, Your Honour, I think it's important that you see how things looked from where we were sitting.

I'm not going to pretend I can remember every word. What I am going to do instead is give you the guts of it.

We went into the court – me and Fat, Haines, and Neil Cowan – and we took up the seats in the middle row. The Department's people – a doctor who had treated Seth; the older woman that had talked to Fat in the waiting room, and so on – took their seats in the same middle row, but on the other side of the room.

The lawyers sat up front, facing the magistrate, and when

the magistrate came in, their team stood up so we all stood up, and they bowed their heads a bit, so we bowed our heads a bit, and the magistrate sat down, and everyone else sat down, and then nothing happened for a while, and I noticed there was a woman tapping on a strange machine, like a little typewriter, but half the size, and I remember thinking, well, at least there will be a record of this, and then the Department's lawyer stood up and gave her name, and said, 'I'm here for the Department' and our lawyer got up and gave her name, and said, 'I'm here for the parents' and another lawyer got up and said, 'I'm here for the John Hunter hospital.'

I wanted to get up and say, 'I'm here, too' but our lawyer, she'd already said, 'Don't do that. Just sit quietly at the back with Donna-Faye' and she'd given instructions to Donna-Faye on how to sit and what to wear and Haines, too, was supposed to be neat and clean, but he hadn't paid any attention. But anyway, there were people bobbing up and down for a while, giving their names and whatnot, and the woman with the little machine was tap-tap-tapping, and then the magistrate looked up and said, 'And are the parents here?' and our lawyer, she said, 'Yes, Your Honour' and the magistrate said, 'Okay then, let's go.' Now, our lawyer had already told us that their side would get to go first and it might seem like the magistrate was only getting their side of the story and not to panic, because we'd get our turn.

Now the first person to go into the witness box was Teddy Blewett, who is the paediatric registrar at John Hunter, which, in plain English, means he is the top doctor for sick kids. I didn't know him, not then. I know him now. We're great mates now. But I'm going to write this like it happened then, before we met.

Teddy had notes with him. Thinking back now, it was impressive how professional he was, how sympathetic and calm. He asked the magistrate if he could read from his notes, and the magistrate said, 'Please do' and he basically read the thing. He said, 'Seth Atley-Haines, born 23 December 2005, presented at Forster General with his mother, Donna-Faye Atley and his father, Paul Haines, shortly after 11 am on 27 March 2006. Seth's mother told staff that her baby was sick and needed a doctor.'

He said a trainee doctor was assigned to the case, and she stripped Seth out of his jumpsuit and his nappy, which was stained with diarrhoea. She put a thermometer under Seth's armpit, and recorded his temperature at 41, which was high. She asked Ms Atley why she'd brought Seth into the hospital, and Ms Atley said Seth had been 'chucking up' (meaning, vomiting); that he had been 'whinging' and 'crying', had 'runny, yellow poo' and a 'runny nose'. She thought he was 'hot' and he seemed 'more floppy' than usual and he was refusing his bottle and was obviously extremely unwell.

The hospital's lawyer interrupted at that point. He said, 'And those symptoms, are they typical of anything in particular?' and Teddy, he said, 'Those symptoms – they could be anything.'

The lawyer said, 'By anything, you mean . . .?'

Teddy said, 'Oh, accidental poisoning, infection, anything.'

141

The lawyer said, 'Okay, so what happened next?' and Teddy said, 'The team at Forster General didn't have the equipment necessary to conduct the kind of tests that were needed to find the cause of Seth's distress, so he was transferred to us at John Hunter, where I myself conducted a series of tests.'

Their lawyer said, 'What kind of tests?' and Teddy said, 'First a blood and a urine analysis. It all came up clean' and the lawyer said, 'And so the next step was?' and Teddy said, 'I organised an MRI to see if there was any swelling or bleeding on the brain. I'd already noticed that the fontanelle – the soft spot on Seth's head – was bulging, and Seth's head was larger than it should have been, too.'

The lawyer said, 'Do you have the results of those tests?' and Teddy said yes, he had the slides with him, and with the court's permission, he'd show them, and the magistrate nodded, because that was obviously fairly standard, to get the results of the tests out, and a lightbox was switched on, and Teddy put the scans, like X-rays, on the light board, and he said, 'This is an MRI scan of Seth Atley-Haines' brain on the day he was admitted to John Hunter' and I have to say, that was upsetting, to see our boy's skull, or his brain to be more accurate, up there on a lightbox. Teddy used a rod to poke at it and say, 'In a normal scan, there would be a one- or two-centimetre gap between the brain and skull, and in Seth's scan, see here, there is no gap. The brain has swelled right up to the edge of the skull, and the gap's filled with blood, and so we had to operate, to drain that blood.'

'I was feeling so upset, looking at that, Your Honour, and

I was grateful when the slide came down, but then another one went up, and it was worse. It was like a giant eye – Seth's eye, but blown up on the screen, to be the size of a head – and it had long veins, like rivers running through it – and Teddy, he said, 'This is a retinal scan, taken on the day Seth was admitted. These dark spots' – he pointed to them – 'they are retinal haemorrhages or, if you prefer, spots of blood, behind the eye.'

Their lawyer said, 'And what do these scans tell us?' and Teddy said, 'Well, I believe Seth Atley-Haines was shaken, and vigorously, some time in the 24 hours before he was taken to the hospital in Forster.' Now, I have to tell you, Your Honour, it was a shock to hear somebody say it. We'd been expecting it, we'd seen it in the legal documents, but it was still a shock to hear somebody say that somebody had shaken that little boy. Fat, she kept her head down, but I knew that she was crying. Haines, he snorted, 'That is such bullshit' and our lawyer, she turned around and gave him a look.

The lawyer, he said, 'And did you speak to Seth's parents about that?' and the doctor shook his head no, and said, 'We have a team of people at John Hunter – we call them the Child Protection Unit – that swings into action when we have a suspected case of child abuse' and the lawyer said, 'And did that unit swing into action?' and Teddy said, 'It did' and the lawyer said, 'And do you know the conclusion to which it came?' and Teddy said, 'The Child Protection Unit is also of the opinion that Seth was shaken' and the lawyer said, 'And, just so we are clear, a diagnosis of Shaken Baby Syndrome, it's something that you come to fairly easily, or only reluctantly?' and Teddy said, 'Not *reluctantly*, but carefully. It's not something you want to get wrong' and the lawyer said, 'And in this case, you are of the view that Seth Atley-Haines was shaken sometime in the 24 hours before he was admitted to hospital?' and Teddy said, 'I really have no doubt about it.'

Haines let out another snort. I heard him say, 'This is crap' and again, our lawyer looked sharply at him. Their lawyer said, 'You know, don't you, that Seth's parents say they didn't shake him? That they'll argue in court, if not today then tomorrow, that something else must have caused the injury? In your opinion, Dr Blewett, could these injuries have been caused by a baby falling from a bed, or being dropped, or perhaps by a vaccination?' But Teddy, he said, 'No, no, vaccination, absolutely not, that is junk science, and it's not a fall, no' and the lawyer said, 'How can you be sure?' and Teddy said, 'Well, I hope I can make the court understand this, because it's important. When a person shakes a baby, the brain moves around inside the skull, and it's the rotation of the brain that does the damage.' He said, 'There are little veins that run between the brain and the skull. In a shaken baby, the veins are torn away from the skull, as the brain swirls around. We call it a shearing injury, or else a rotational injury, and we only see it when a baby has been shaken, not when a baby has fallen, and not when a baby has jerked forward in a car seat, and not when a baby has been bounced on somebody's knee.'

The lawyer, he said, 'And that's the kind of injury that Seth Atley-Haines has, a shearing injury, a rotational injury?' and

Teddy said, 'Yes, he does' and the lawyer said, 'And he remains in hospital to this day?' and Teddy said, 'He does' and the lawyer said, 'And why is that?' and Teddy said, 'Well, it's still unclear whether Seth will survive' and that hit me like a hammer, that statement. The magistrate, who'd been scribbling away, she seemed to have got a shock, too. She said, 'You mean, Seth's condition is still critical?' and Teddy said, 'He remains on life support. Yes' and the magistrate said, 'Why hasn't life support been removed?' and Teddy said, 'Because of these proceedings. We don't know who has legal responsibility for Seth – is it the State, or is it the parents?'

The magistrate said, 'So you're waiting for my decision, so you can ask either the State, or Seth's parents, to remove life support?' and Teddy said, 'That's right' and the magistrate sighed, and shook her head, and made a scribble on her pad, and Fat, who was sitting beside me, put her forehead on her knees and started making loud choking noises and I had to lean over her back to muffle her and also to hide my own crying, because it was around then that I realised what was actually at stake in that court. We'd gone there thinking, oh, we're going to bring Seth home. We hadn't really understood that even if we won, so much of Seth was lost.

# Chapter 10

I GUESS YOU KNOW BETTER THAN me what it's like to be in court, Your Honour. One side gets up and puts their case and it seems like you're gone for all money, and then your side gets up, and suddenly, there's hope. That's what happened in the court case, with Seth. Their side went through the arguments, the injury, and how it must have happened, and how it couldn't have been an accident, and how the parents must be to blame, then our lawyer got up, and it seemed like the tide was turning.

The first question our lawyer put to Teddy was this one: 'Do you know for certain that Seth was shaken?' and of course, Teddy had to say, 'Well, no, I don't know for *certain*, but I *believe* he was shaken' and that gave our lawyer a chance to say, 'But you don't know for certain, do you?' and he had to say, 'No, I don't, it's my opinion' and our lawyer said, 'But you do know that Seth's parents say that they absolutely did not shake their baby, don't you? You know that they say the opposite, that they took their sick baby to hospital for treatment – that is something that good, caring parents would do – and they have had to fight the accusation ever since that they did something to harm their child?'

Teddy said he couldn't really comment on that, but if our lawyer was asking whether he believed the baby was shaken then the answer was yes, he did.

Our lawyer said, 'Yes, but you don't know for *certain*, do you? Come to that, you don't know for certain what happens when any parent shakes a baby, do you?'

Teddy looked perplexed. He said, 'It causes brain damage.' He said, 'The baby usually dies, and if the baby doesn't die, the brain is so badly damaged that there is no quality of life.'

Our lawyer said, 'But how do you know that? I mean, has anybody – and by anybody, I mean a medical professional or a social scientist – ever taken a group of babies, and shaken some, and not shaken others, to see what happens when you shake a baby?'

Teddy said, 'Of course not.'

Our lawyer said, 'Well then, how do you know what happens to the brain when you shake a baby?' and Teddy said, 'I've looked at scans of babies whose parents have admitted to shaking their babies' and our lawyer said, 'And those scans, they are from babies the same age as Seth, are they? The same size? The same weight? They were shaken in the same way? The same number of times? With the same force? By a person with the same strength? Suffering the same level of frustration?' and of course Teddy said, 'Well, I can't be sure about that' and our lawyer said, 'No, you can't, can you. But can you tell this court whether parents ever admit to shaking their babies?' and Teddy said, 'Sometimes' and our lawyer said, 'How often?' and Teddy said, 'I couldn't put a precise figure on it' and our lawyer said, 'Well then, take a guess. How many parents have admitted it to you?' and Teddy said, 'From memory, two' and our lawyer said, 'Two?' and Teddy said, 'Two that I can remember. It might be more than that.'

Our lawyer said, 'So you've seen scans from two babies whose parents admitted to shaking, and comparing those scans with Seth's scans, you've now decided that he must have been shaken, too?' and Teddy said, no, he was able to compare Seth's scans with the scans of other shaken babies from other hospitals, and our lawyer said, 'But what kind of babies are they? The same age, the same weight as Seth? And do we know that they were shaken, or do we assume that they were shaken, because their scans look like the scans of other babies that were also assumed to have been shaken? This doesn't sound like a very precise science.'

Teddy said, 'I know what you are getting at but it's actually more complicated than that. I might see one or two case of measles every year, but I know when I see it' and that's when our lawyer really pounced. She said, 'But shaken baby is not like measles, is it? There's a test for measles. There's a test for mumps. But there is no test for Shaken Baby Syndrome.'

She paused. She waited. She said, 'Am I wrong? You can't test for it, can you?' and Teddy, he had to say, 'Well, I've looked at the scans, and as I've said, that type of injury – the sheared veins – that doesn't happen when you drop a baby, or when a baby jerks forward in a car seat, or when you're out jogging with a baby in a backpack, or when a baby rolls off the bed.'

He said, 'I've seen babies that have rolled off beds, or fallen onto the floor, and the injuries are not the same. When I see that kind of injury –' and here, he pointed up at Seth's scan on the lightbox, and he said, 'When I see that kind of injury, I know it's a shaking injury.'

Our lawyer said, 'Excuse me, Dr Blewett, but you do not *know* it's a shaking injury. You *assume* it's a shaking injury.'

She said, 'It's an assumption you are making, and given that both parents say that no such thing happened, it's quite a leap.'

She said, 'For the benefit of this court, let's be clear, it is your opinion that Seth was shaken. It is your *medical* opinion and it is your *professional* opinion but still an opinion, and an opinion is not a medical fact' and with that, she sat down.

What was my reaction to that? Well, as I've said, Teddy Blewett has lately become a friend of mine. I respect him. In some ways, I probably even love him. I can look back and think, well, it must have been hard on him, what we put him through. But at the time? At the time, I suppose I had that adrenalin running through me, the kind that people get when they go into court. It's like a battle, you see, you against them, and when you have a bit of a victory, you think, 'Take that!' and, 'We're gonna win this thing!' and you lose sight of the fact that it's not supposed to be about winning. It's supposed to be about truth.

# Chapter 11

AFTER TEDDY LEFT THE STAND, THE magistrate got up from her seat, and that was a sign for all of us to get up while she left the room, and then to sit back down, then get up again and go outside to stretch our legs. Haines made a rollie. I needed a cigarette myself but first wanted to talk to our lawyer. I said, 'How are we doing?' and she said, 'Look, they haven't been able to prove anything' and Haines, picking strands of tobacco from the tip of his tongue, said, 'There's nothing to prove.'

Our lawyer said, 'Tomorrow will be better for us, because it will be all our witnesses.'

At it turned out, it wasn't all our witnesses. The social worker that had questioned Fat on that first day had to say her piece, which was basically that Fat and Haines couldn't explain how Seth got injured, and that people like

Fat and Haines, people who haven't got experience with babies, and who might not be all that smart might shake a baby, not knowing it's the wrong thing to do, just to make them be quiet, and not even realising the damage they've done.

The magistrate asked her a few questions about shaken babies, how old they are when they come in and so forth, and she said the 'peak age' was between eight and fourteen weeks, and so Seth was obviously in that group, and the magistrate wanted to know why that was the peak age, and the woman said oh, well, babies cry a lot, and by eight weeks, the parents, they've gotten over the thrill of having a new baby, and they are sleep-deprived and asking themselves, is this ever going to stop? And then, of course, after 14 weeks, the baby might still be crying but they get too big to shake like that, so the shaken babies drop off after 14 weeks, too.

This woman, she also said Seth had gone into hospital on a Saturday morning, and lots of babies get shaken on Friday nights and the magistrate wanted to know what was significant about Friday nights, and she said, well, people are drinking and the football is on, and when I heard that, I pretty near said out loud, 'Oh, come on, who would shake a baby because the football was on?' But this woman, she said it happens all the time, especially when men – and here, she looked at Haines – have to look after the baby while the mother is out of the house. She said a man in that situation – and by now I knew she meant Haines – will see the baby as a bit of a nuisance, something that's stopping him from doing what he wants to do, which is have a beer and watch the footy, and he thinks if he gives the baby a bottle, or gives it a dummy, the baby should stop crying. But sometimes, babies don't stop crying, and the man will think, 'What kind of baby is this? It's a shit of a baby' and if the crying goes on and on – which it might, if the man doesn't pick up the baby and rock and soothe the baby – then they might take the baby and shake the baby by the shoulders, saying, 'Why won't you bloody well shut up?' and they don't realise, when the baby does go quiet, it's because basically they've rattled the baby's brain.

The strange thing was, when the magistrate asked this woman whether she thought Seth should go into State care, she didn't say yes. She was on the Department's side, but she said, 'Well, that depends.'

The magistrate said, 'On what?'

The social worker, she looked at Fat, and she said, 'It is quite rare for a mother to shake her baby. Mothers do some-times hurt their children, but rarely by shaking. Shaking tends to be something that men – boyfriends, de factos – are more likely to do.'

For a second there, she looked like she might say more, but in the end, that was the closest she got – that anyone got – to saying, look, the chances are this wasn't Donna-Faye. Chance are it was Haines. Fat had been at work, at Woolies. Haines was home with Seth, and it was a Friday night, and he was probably pissed, or stoned, or both, and wanting to lie on the couch, and Seth was probably missing his mum or needing his bottle, and Haines would have got fed up with him, and picked him up and rattled him and dropped him back in the cot, and left Fat to find him there, whimpering, and he'd lied about it, when Fat asked him whether anything had happened, and under those circumstances, why should Fat lose her baby?

I have often wondered, Your Honour, what Fat might have said about that, if she'd taken the stand that day. I don't say that she would have pointed the finger at Haines. She was mad about him but also, in all likelihood, she didn't know, not for sure, what he'd done. I'm absolutely certain she would have sworn blue that *she* had nothing to do with it, and maybe the magistrate would have heard her saying that, really saying it, and come down on Fat's side. But Fat didn't take the stand and Haines didn't either. Our lawyer said, no, it's up to them to prove their case. You don't have to prove your innocence. You don't have to say anything.

That being the case, there was only one more witness, and that was Neil Cowan, and he was so excited at this opportunity to get into the witness box to spout his cock-amamie theories that he practically fell over his feet on the way up to the front of the court, which hardly worked in our favour.

The magistrate said, 'If you could tell me your name, and your occupation?' and he said, 'My name is Neil Cowan and I'm a doctor.'

'The magistrate said, "A medical doctor?", which surprised me. I mean, I'd assumed he was a medical doctor. Why else would we have wanted him there, if he wasn't a medical doctor? But he actually said, no, he was a doctor of something else, and when the magistrate wanted to know of what, he went all cagey and said, 'From a university in the United States' and when she wanted to know which one, he said it was 'online' and I think we can all admit it now, he had one of those degrees that you get in the mail.

Then he said, 'My formal qualifications are one thing. The more important thing is my expertise in the ways of the medical establishment and the welfare industry, and the ways in which they operate – in cahoots! – with each other.'

The magistrate probably didn't mean to roll her eyes but she did roll her eyes, and she made some small marking on the paper in front of her. She pushed her glasses back onto her nose, and said, 'Go on, then' and for Cowan, that was obviously the trigger he needed.

He started by saying, 'I do not believe that Seth Atley-Haines was shaken.'

He said, 'Moreover' – he loved that word 'moreover' – he said, 'I do not believe that Shaken Baby Syndrome exists' and then he went on with his spiel about how doctors create bogus syndromes; and how he had written to the Prime Minister and had received a reply; and how there hadn't been a single case of Shaken Baby Syndrome recorded before 1960, and suddenly, there were hundreds of them; and how that 'epidemic' of shaken babies coincided with a massive increase in funding to the welfare industry, and how 'Seth's parents are sitting here today trying to prove they *didn't* do something. How are they supposed to prove that?'

157

The magistrate listened politely. She did not interrupt. Then she said, 'Well, Mr Cowan, do you have any alternative theories for the massive injuries to Seth Atley-Haines' brain?' and of course, that really got Cowan going, because if there was one thing he had, it was theories. He said, 'Well, it could be anything! Plenty of times, in America, with cases like this, they've found out it was a reaction to the vaccination. And if it's not that, maybe Seth is allergic to something? Dust maybe, or cats? Lots of people are allergic to cats.'

Cats! I thought, please tell me he is not going to argue that cats had left Seth fighting for his life in a ward somewhere, far from his mother, and from me?

But Cowan was just getting started. He had miles to go in his campaign against the vaccinations, and so he got stuck into that, saying 'the drug companies' knew their shots caused all kinds of brain damage and they covered it up because they were in the cosy position of getting their drugs into every newborn in the country, and I have to admit, that made me pretty cross. I mean, like most people my age, I grew up when there was polio, and I saw what it did to some people, and maybe the magistrate felt the same, because she asked no questions about the vaccines. Instead, she said, 'Mr Cowan, have you actually examined Seth?'

Cowan, he said, 'No' and she said, 'No' and he said, 'No, of course not' and she said, 'But you seem to have such strong opinions?' and Cowan said, 'It's not my fault I haven't examined him. They won't let me near him. They know how close I am to uncovering this conspiracy, and to exposing the myths and lies.'

The magistrate, she said, 'So, it's not only that you're not a medical doctor, you've never actually met Seth?' and Cowan said, 'There's not a chance in the world that security guards at John Hunter would let me within a bull's roar of Seth, and do you know why? *They* are in on the scam and, like the doctor, they will lose their jobs the minute I expose this scam!'

I guess it was at that point I really understood the monster I'd created with Neil Cowan. Security guards were in on the scam to disable babies and hide the results? It was embarrassing, not that Neil Cowan was the type to get embarrassed. The magistrate handled it pretty well, though. She said, 'Alright, Mr Cowan (she never did call him doctor), thank you for your testimony' and although he tried to resist standing down, she made him step down, and then she said, 'Am I to hear from the parents?' and our lawyer said, 'No, your Honour' and I have to say, it did feel strange to me that we didn't insist on having our say, and that our lawyer didn't want to give Fat the chance to say, 'I didn't do anything. I would never hurt my baby' because surely that would have helped her? But I guess you always think, The lawyer knows best, but then, suddenly, that idiot, Haines, was on his feet and saying, 'I do have something to say actually, and I've writ it down for you' and before our lawyer could stop him, he'd pushed himself past my knees and was going up the aisle, towards the bench, and he was handing the magistrate a piece of paper.

She reached down, and she took it. It was a small square of white paper, folded many times. She pushed her glasses back on her nose and unfolded it, and unfolded it again, until it was normal size, and she started to read it, and she looked at Haines, and read some more, and handed it back to him, saying, 'Well, thank you, Mr Haines. I'm not sure that's appropriate for this forum' and he said, 'Well, that's your opinion' and she said, 'Yes, it is' and got up, and we all got up, and Haines came back down the aisle, and shoved the note at our lawyer and cracked his knuckles and said, 'Let's go see about my Swiss army knife. They better not have knocked it off' and Fat went out after him.

I said to our lawyer, 'How did we do?' She said, 'I guess we'll find out' and I said, 'What did Haines' note say?' and she rolled her eyes and said, 'Here, read for yourself' and I took it from her, and read it, and I was amazed. I mean, it was absolutely out of line. Completely out of line. I've still got the note. I mean, people who say we didn't care about Seth . . . I've still got every scrap of paper related to every court I've found myself in, and just to prove that, I'm going to paperclip that note here for you, so you can read it for yourself, and see exactly what we were dealing with, with that idiot Haines:

*Donna Faye and me is writing to you to tell you that Seth is not youre kid he is our kid and you think you can just take kids of me and Donna Faye because we are shit and you are not you think your shit dont stink but at the end of the day you sit down and shit on the toilet like every body I will get a lawer and I will go to the highest court in the land and I will fight and see the prime minister and every other person I can think of its game on as far as Im concerned game on we did not do nothing to Seth you will not get Seth he is my boy and he will wear the HAINES name with pride.*

# Chapter 12

**Judgement of Senior Magistrate Anne Albright, in the matter of Seth Atley-Haines**

Citation: Re, Seth (2006)
Jurisdiction: Children's Court of NSW.
Parties: Director General of Department of Community Services, Donna-Faye Atley, Paul Jack Haines
Place of hearing: Parramatta
Date of hearing: 3 and 4 May 2006
Magistrate: Senior Magistrate Anne Albright
Legislation: Children and Young Persons (Care and Protection) Act 1998

1. These are care proceedings.
2. These proceedings have been brought to court by the

NSW Department of Community Services, henceforth known as 'the Department'.

3. These proceedings relate to Seth Atley Haines, born 23 December 2005.

4. Seth is the son of Donna-Faye Atley, henceforth known as 'the mother' and Paul Jack Haines, henceforth known as 'the father'.

5. The Department of Community Services seeks an order that Seth be removed from the care of his parents.

6. Seth's parents oppose the order.

**Case details:**

7. On March 27, 2006, Seth, then aged just under 14 weeks, was brought into Forster General by his parents.

8. Seth's mother told hospital staff Seth was 'sick'.

9. After initial examination, Seth was transferred by ambulance to the paediatric intensive care unit at John Hunter Hospital in Newcastle, where a number of tests, including a CT scan and MRI brain imaging were undertaken.

10. Seth was found to have subdural haemorrhages and retinal haemorrhages.

11. Seth's parents have been unable to provide an explanation for Seth's injuries.

12. Other than the parents, no person had care of Seth in the 48 hours prior to his admission to hospital.

**Evidence for the Department:**

13. This court has had the benefit of oral testimony from Dr Theodore Blewett, paediatric registrar, John Hunter Hospital.

14. Dr Blewett is acknowledged as a leading authority in his field and is well known to the Children's Court.

15. Dr Blewett's report says injuries of the type seen in Seth are typically associated with what has come to be known as 'Shaken Baby Syndrome'.

16. Dr Blewett believes it unlikely that Seth's injuries are due to any other cause.

17. Dr Blewett believes injuries to Seth were most likely caused by 'violent shaking'.

18. This court has also been provided with a written affidavit by Dr Paul Tate, consultant paediatrician at the Sydney Children's Hospital.

19. Dr Tate is a leading authority in paediatric neurology and is well known to the Children's Court. He has examined Seth.

20. Dr Tate believes it is unlikely that Seth's injuries were caused by birth trauma.

21. Dr Tate believes it is unlikely that Seth's injuries were caused by vaccinations.

22. Dr Tate believes 'shearing injuries' – where the veins connecting the brain to the skull have ripped away – are 'almost exclusively' caused by forceful acceleration of the head (shaking) which cannot be accidental, and cannot be caused by the child acting alone.

163

23. Dr Tate believes other explanations are 'rare, and can be excluded' in the case of Seth.

24. Dr Tate believes retinal bleeding – bleeding behind the eyes – is a clear marker for Shaken Baby Syndrome.

25. It is therefore Dr Tate's opinion that Seth's injuries were caused by shaking.

**Evidence for the Parents:**

26. Seth's parents have been unable to provide the court with an alternative explanation for Seth's injuries.

27. It is common ground that Seth was in the care of no other adult in the 48 hours prior to his admission to Forster General.

28. Seth was in the exclusive care of his father, Paul Jack Haines, for six hours on 26 March while Seth's mother worked the night shift at Woolies.

29. There were no times when Seth was in the care of his mother, but not his father, in the 24 hours prior to his admission to hospital.

30. A witness called by the parents, Neil Cowan, has told this court that Seth's injuries cannot have been caused by shaking. He submits that Shaken Baby Syndrome is a myth.

31. Mr Cowan has an interest in Shaken Baby Syndrome that might fairly be called a crusade.

32. Mr Cowan is well known for his campaign against mass vaccination programs.

33. Mr Cowan has not examined Seth nor, in fact, met

Seth.

34. Documents presented to the court by Mr Cowan to support his claim that brain injuries may be caused by vaccination amount to documents downloaded from the internet and pamphlets produced by anti-vaccination groups.

35. There is no evidence before this court to support Mr Cowan's claim that Seth's injuries were caused by vaccination.

36. It is my view that Seth suffered a 'non-accidental brain injury'. I make no findings as to who is responsible for that injury.

**Social matters:**

37. Seth's father has a poor history of impulse control.

38. Seth's father has a history of violence and criminal behaviour, including assault.

39. Seth's father has substance abuse problems.

40. Testing conducted by independent, court-appointed analysts prior to this hearing suggest that Seth's mother is of below-average intelligence. She produced low scores for resourcefulness, although high scores for empathy.

41. Testing conducted by independent, court-appointed analysts prior to his hearing suggests that Seth's father is also of below-average intelligence, and produced low scores for resourcefulness, empathy, and impulse control.

42. Seth's parents have known periods of great stress,

including income stress. Seth's mother provides the only known source of income to the household, and returned to work just 10 weeks after giving birth.

**Legal issues:**
The question the court must resolve in this case is NOT whether either parent is responsible for inflicting the injury upon Seth.

That is perhaps, a matter for another court, at another time.

Likewise, it is not the role of this court to decide Seth's fate.

Seth's parents want Seth to come home. They accept that this is not likely to happen in the short-term but they want to secure their legal rights as Seth's parents, which would enable them to have him home should he recover from his injuries.

World-renowned experts in paediatric neurology have told this court that Seth is unlikely to survive his injuries, and is currently being kept alive by artificial means.

However it is not the role of this court to assume that the death of Seth is imminent.

It is the role of the court to decide whether the risk posed to Seth by the parents would be an acceptable one, were he to recover, and be able to leave the hospital.

If the court decides that the risk to Seth is unacceptable, it must grant parental rights to the State.

**Conclusion:**

This court concludes,

a) There is a high likelihood that Seth's injuries are non-accidental.

b) There is no possibility that they were inflicted by people other than one or the other, or else both, of the parents.

c) One or the other, or perhaps both parents know what happened to Seth but have declined to tell the court.

d) Seth's injuries are extremely serious.

e) While he survives, Seth remains vulnerable to further attack by one or the other or perhaps both of his parents.

f) There is therefore an unacceptable risk to Seth, should he be discharged from hospital and returned to the care of his parents.

FOR those reasons, it is the ORDER of the COURT that,

– Parental responsibility for Seth Atley-Haines, born 23 December 2005 be transferred from the parents to the Department of Community Services.

– Contact with his parents henceforth be prevented.

# Chapter 13

MY FIRST THOUGHT AFTER THE VERDICT came down was, no. I'm not going to take this. This is wrong.

I asked our lawyer, 'How do we appeal?'

She didn't really respond, not then, and not in the weeks that followed. I think she'd got bored. Bored, or else she'd figured out that if we couldn't win this part – the easy part – we'd never get to sue. She'd never get her 48 per cent.

She did say, 'Well, you can appeal, but that means you'll have to take it to the Supreme Court. It can take a while to get a time and a date for a hearing in the Supreme Court. It's expensive, and we might lose.'

I took it from that she wasn't interested in going further, which riled me, because I was fired up. I thought, okay, if she's not interested, I can go to the papers with this. I'll go to *A Current Affair*.

I asked the lawyer what she thought of that. She said, 'I always tell my clients, don't go to the media. It's the dynamite charge. It can do more harm than good.'

But that was when we were still her clients. That was when she had a whiff of some settlement. Now if we went to the media, we'd be off her back, and so she said, 'Go for it.'

I thought, well, the media it is. And Haines, he was with me. I think he thought he'd be able to get some money for an exclusive interview. Child abducted by State! Parents accused! Human rights violation!

That kind of thing appealed to Haines. He might have been an idiot but he had an ego like you would not believe. Trouble was, with the lawyer backing away, I found myself in alliance with Haines. Not with Fat – she was falling into a deep kind of fog, but I was in cahoots with Haines. Obviously, I wasn't thinking straight. It's like I said earlier, you get into a court battle with a big government department, and you feel like that bloke in *The Castle*. You want to keep going, for justice. You want a David and Goliath thing. You want a victory.

Haines was putting on a good show, pretending that he felt the same, at least in the early days. He'd rage about the injustice. He'd say, 'If that smart-arse lawyer is not going to help us appeal, I'm going to take it to Parliament!'

He'd say, 'I'll take it to the highest court in the land! I'll take it to the House of Lords!' He actually looked that up online. He found out you can take things to the House of Lords. He quoted Neil Cowan. He would say, 'It's like Neil Cowan said, you can't have the courts taking babies away from their mothers!'

He'd say, 'What proof do they have that we did anything? They have no proof!'

Always, with the *proof*.

Did I think, It's a bit hard to get proof, Haines, if you are one of two witnesses and the other one, Seth, can't talk? I don't know. Maybe I was still giving him the benefit of the doubt. I don't anymore.

Anyway, he'd say, 'I'm going to make up signs, and tell everybody that my son has been taken away, and I'm going to carry those signs on a march down to Parliament House in Canberra!' He'd say he was going to leave a pile of Seth's toys sitting on the High Court steps. He'd say all kinds of stuff and Neil Cowan was all for it. He encouraged Haines to do it. He'd say, 'We'll start a People Power movement!' He'd say, 'People across the country will rise up, and join us and it will be the start of a revolution!'

They had quite a view of themselves, those two.

It was Cowan who got the ball rolling, for the actual march. He said he'd make Seth 'the poster boy' for the Shaken Baby myth. He went through our photographs. There was a nice one of Seth in Fat's arms, taken about a week after Seth was born. Fat was looking down on him with such love. It was the perfect shot. Haines didn't like it, though. He wanted a photograph with him in it, and that's the one he went with for the poster, a picture of Fat, holding Seth, but with Haines standing behind her, towering over her, his arms crossed, his biceps flexed, not really making our case that this was a normal, happy family, not with his tattoos and the handlebar moustache, like Hulk Hogan used to have.

Cowan took the photograph, and scanned it. That meant he could put it on his website, and he did. I'm ashamed to see it there now. Seth Atley, the poster child for the Shaken Baby myth.

I no longer think it's a myth that babies get shaken. I can see that Seth was one of them.

Anyway, Cowan put the photo on the website. It was the first thing you saw when you clicked on the page. He put up all the documents from the court. He put up transcripts, and scans. He said Seth's case would go 'viral'. He said that meant that Seth would be famous. His picture, and the details of his case, would be emailed all around the world.

Right from the start, the worldwide attention, the myths, the conspiracies, that wasn't my bag. I wanted Seth to come home. That was all I wanted. I wanted my daughter to have her baby in her arms. To that end, I signed myself up for whatever Haines had planned. I wish I hadn't but I couldn't think what else to do.

I let Cowan set up a username for me, and a password so I could get into the site, and talk to people on there. We were trying to build what he called an 'online community' but what that was, I didn't rightly understand, not until it was too late. He said people who felt the way we did would be attracted to the site, and would unite online, and together we'd bring down the system that was trying to abduct Seth.

He was right about attracting people. The site went up in June of 2006 – not too long after the court case – and straightaway, people started visiting. We could tell that from the site counter. We could also tell how they were finding us, on the web. They were putting words like 'child abuse' and 'alibi' and 'shaken baby' and 'vaccination risk' into Google and ending up on our site.

Most people stayed a minute or so and moved on. Maybe they were looking for something quite different. But there were quite a few who hung around – the same ones, every day. Most didn't give us their real names. They had 'handles' or nicknames, things like 'Warrior for Justice' and 'Victim of Injustice'. They used our message boards to talk about child welfare and child support. Some of it was pretty nasty. Blokes would email in, saying, 'Child welfare workers are lesbian man-haters who steal kids!' and, 'How come they've all got fat arses?' and . . . well, my Mum used to say to me, Your Honour, you lie down with dogs, you get fleas, but I suppose that lesson was momentarily lost to me. I was lying down with dogs. I was getting fleas.

It was part of my job to edit the site. I was supposed to keep the worst stuff out, but still give people a place to spill their guts. I could tell that a lot of these blokes had been dying to tell their story. There were men who had been through the Family Court and lost their kids for abusing them, and they were pretty sure the system was corrupt, especially the judges. They would have been happy to do anything to bring down the system.

Haines set himself up as the hero of the site. He gave himself a nickname: 'Seth's Proud Dad.' He answered some of the mail himself. It was like he was the celebrity, the bloke leading the revolution. He'd been at it about a month when he decided that he would lead a march. He told everyone, 'Take pictures of your kids and blow them up big! We're going to carry them through the streets. We're going all the way to Canberra!'

He set a date for the march – 4 August. We put the date on the website, and we wrote, 'Join Us On Our March For Justice for Our Children!' One or two of our readers, the ones who day or night, always seemed to be hovering around the site, popped up with instant messages. They said, 'We'll be there!'

I thought, well, if it's going to happen, I better get with it. I bought poster paper from the Forster newsagent. I made up a few big signs: 'Bring Seth Home' and 'Shaken Baby is a Myth!'

Neil Cowan said I should phone *A Current Affair* and *60 Minutes* and tell them about the march. Haines said, 'Go with the one who offers the most money.'

I made the calls. I told a receptionist at Channel Nine that my son-in-law – *my son-in-law*, God help me – Paul Haines had been unjustly accused. He was going to get a photograph of Seth, blown up big, and carry it on his shoulders, raising hell along the road to Canberra to force the politicians to listen, and to return my grandson.

The girl on the phone said a reporter would get back to me. I waited but nobody did call back. Cowan wasn't daunted. He said the TV stations were sometimes wary because in cases of child abuse, they can't show anybody's face. He said, try radio. I phoned 2UE and I phoned the ABC. I didn't get anywhere there. Cowan said, 'Well, it's hard for radio. It's a march.' He said, 'Try *The Daily Telegraph*' but they said it wasn't their thing, either.

Cowan said, 'Well, that's okay. When we are on the streets with our signs, a hundred deep, blocking traffic, they won't be able to ignore us then!'

The day of the march came around. I was up at 5 am. Others had said they'd meet us in Forster, for the first part of the journey. I got myself ready, packed socks and clean jocks. It was going to take a few days to get to Canberra, obviously.

I drove around to the Haines place. I knocked on the door and when Haines didn't answer, I pushed on it, and went inside and there he was, on the sofa – the saggy, baggy, defeated sofa – with a bowl of mull by his elbow and a blackened bong on the floor. Where Fat was, I don't know.

I had the posters in my hands, the big ones we were going to carry on the road to the High Court. I said, 'Are you ready?' but looking at him, I could see that he wasn't ready. Not for the first time, Paul Haines wasn't going anywhere. He was bolted to that couch.

He said, 'Right, Med. Look, I think we've got some operational problems with this campaign.' He reached for his bong and his lighter and he set the water bubbling. He paused, and with smoke still in his throat, he quickly said, 'Like, where are we going to stay en route? I ain't got no money for motels.' And he exhaled.

I said, 'People will put us up! That was the plan, remember? When they see what we're doing, they'll come

175

out of their homes, put us up! We'll do meetings in town halls and people will come and support us? Remember that?' Looking at him, eyes glazed over, I knew what I was saying was ridiculous. Who, of the good folk of Australia, would have that layabout in their home? Who would welcome his smoke-stained fingers around their cutlery, his tufty moccasins under their dinner table?

Not that he cared what I thought. He'd set the amber water bubbling again. His throat was on fire, the tip of his thumb was sore. He was holding back the bong smoke. He said, 'I dunno, Med. It's a bloody long way to Canberra.'

He fell back against the couch. He was looking at me, but not in a focused way. He was stoned.

I looked at him. I thought, 'You loser. You punk. You prick.' But like every time beforehand, I didn't say anything. I left my poster signs on the floor. I walked out of there. I thought, 'What do I do now?' I'd have to go online, put up a note saying the march was delayed, but maybe it was too late? Maybe people were already massing near the Forster courthouse, waiting for us? I thought I better go there to explain. I need not have worried. There was no crowd. There was one bloke with even more tattoos than Haines. He had a dog with him.

I went home. I went online. There weren't many people on the site, either, just the same two blokes who were always there. I told them, 'The march is off.' One of them replied, saying, 'What march? Was that today?'

I sat back on my own couch. I've got to tell you, it felt strange, having been up early, and bristling with energy, and ready to go, and now to be sitting still and quiet, quieter than I could ever remember it being in my house, just the clock ticking and the dog, who once or twice jerked up to get at an itch under his tail.

I thought, well, what are you gunna do now, Med?

I already had the answer. I was gunna do nothing. And why was I gunna do nothing? Because I'd turned myself into a gunna. You know what a gunna is, don't you, Your Honour? A bloke who is gunna do this and gunna do that. I was gunna tell Haines to lay off Conan that day at Big Rock, but I didn't. I was gunna throttle Haines when he took up with Fat, when she wasn't but 15, but I didn't.

I was gunna stand up to Haines when Seth went into hospital, because of course I knew, like everybody knew, that he must have done it, but I didn't.

What I did instead was hook up with him, collaborated with him on that damn website, attracting every kid-basher and lunatic on the internet, and why did I do that? Because I was gunna get Seth back. Oh yeah, that's what I was gunna do.

Except I didn't. Reading what I've written so far, I can see what I actually did do to save my daughter, and my grand-child, and it wasn't very much, was it? And do you know what that makes me think? It makes me think I'm as impotent as they said I'd be, on the day Fat was conceived.

# PART TWO

PART TWO

# Chapter 14

THEY FOUND HER IN THE MIDDLE of Victoria Road in Sydney's Kings Cross, pacing the white line that separates cars on the left from those on the right.

She was dressed in a long, green military jacket, with insignia on the shoulders. She was naked underneath but had gumboots on her feet.

Her hair was on end; her eyes were wild and desperate; she held her arms wide, in a Christ-like pose.

She was wailing, 'Stop. Everybody must stop!' but the cars, they did not have time to stop. They swerved around her, all except a bus. Too big and clumsy to properly swerve, it ran off the road and through the front window of a shop.

Was there sympathy for this woman – this near-naked, hysterical woman, with her bare, puckered belly and long breasts, with her rubber boots that had chafed the back of her calves – whose antics had caused a bus to career into a store front?

There was some – but only some. Had Donna-Faye Atley been streaking through a cul-de-sac in some suburban idyll, then maybe people would have rushed into traffic, brought her to the kerb and closed the military jacket around her, to protect her modesty, but this was Kings Cross.

Kings Cross, never mind the gentrification – the delicious little chocolate shops and the providores, with their pita chips and their free-range chickens – it's still, for many people, Sydney's boulevard of broken dreams, of strip clubs and sex shops; of the dazed, lying in pools of vomit; of taxis being used as mobile brothels; of addicts on the nod; of Aborigines, buckled in the gutter; of prostitutes with bruised thighs and sores on their faces, knocking on car windows ('You want a girl? You want some fun?'); of street kids with new tattoos and facial piercing; of men with teeth like burnt matches; of junkies with arms that hang like meat; of the drunk, the homeless, the angry and alone.

It is humanity, in all its crooked timber – and people there, they do walk into traffic.

That said, the paramedics who picked up Donna-Faye, after the bus crashed and the glass shattered and the situation became serious – they said she wasn't drunk, and she wasn't on drugs.

She was shaking, and she had a look in her eye like she was running from something nobody else could see. Not something that wasn't there, but something that nobody else who was there was able to see.

She was taken by ambulance to St Vincent's Hospital – it's not very far; in a pinch, she might have been carried there on a stretcher. Nursing staff searched for ID but she had none. They asked for her next of kin but the man they called – Paul Jack Haines – on the number she gave them, he said, 'I want nothing to do with this.'

Her next of kin, in that case – the only person who still had a loving interest in Donna-Faye – was her old man, Med.

# Chapter 15

## Med Atley

IT TOOK FOUR HOURS TO GET down the Pacific Highway to
the place in Sydney where they had Fat. I was so tempted
to leadfoot it, but I thought, Don't do it, Med. You're
not much good to her are you, if you're wrapped around
a tree?

If you'd asked me what I knew about mental illness at that
point, I would have said, not much. I'd heard that people
sometimes went crazy, and there were places where they
had to go when it happened, but these people, well, they'd
never crossed paths with me.

Now I was hearing Fat had a breakdown. They meant it
literally, she'd broken down in the street and been taken to
one of those places I'd heard about and were holding her

185

there and it didn't matter that she was 25 years old. I'd have to go in because I was next of kin.

I didn't know what to expect. I had in mind a place like I'd seen on TV, like something out of *One Flew Over the Cuckoo's Nest,* with people with their arms wrapped around themselves and their eyes popped and their beards half grown out, keeping little birds in their pockets.

I thought of my girl, Donna-Faye, lost in the middle of them, twisting a finger in her hair. Would she know who I was, and how would she react? Maybe she'd try to scratch my face. Maybe I'd have to hold her hands by the wrists and try to calm her down.

Well, it wasn't like that. Those big places, the loony bins, they've gone. Fat was in a normal hospital. There were green signs to show you where the exits were. There was a lady behind reception, and a cafe in the foyer and a flower shop. I went up in the elevator to the mental health ward. The lady on their reception told me Fat had her own room. I thought, please don't let her be strapped down, and she wasn't strapped down. She wasn't even in hospital clothes. She was sitting in a chair wearing a tracksuit with elastic around the bottom of the legs. It was a bit too short or else she was too fat for it, and it was hiked up, over her belly. Her ankles and her wrists were sticking out. Somebody had washed her hair. It was pulled back into a ponytail, and it was too tight. Her eyes looked a bit Chinese. So she didn't look completely right – she was not in her clothes, and not wearing her own face – but she didn't look crazy, either.

She was quiet, I give you that. She was quiet, and

twitched a bit. I'd seen that before. She'd twitched a bit in adolescence, and now she was twitching again, and looking down at the floor a lot, and whispering, like we had a big secret. I said, 'Fat, you don't have to whisper.' There were no other people in the room. She looked up at me and nodded, and motioned me closer.

I sat on the edge of her bed. She looked around, like somebody might be there, in a room we could all see. She whispered, 'I'm sorry, Dad.'

I said, 'What on earth have you got to be sorry about?' She said, 'All this fuss' and I said, 'Come on, Fat. You're no fuss. You're alright. You're just a bit lost.'

She said, 'Where have I been?'

I said, 'You're here now.'

She nodded. Half an hour later, she said, 'Where have I been?'

I thought, well, she's confused. But I had faith in the system in those days. I thought, she's in the right place. She's going to get proper help, a bed in a hospital, a psychiatrist to see her through. She'll get medication. She's not going to be sent out to fend for herself.

I tracked down the matron in charge of the ward. She told me there was paperwork to fill out. There always is, isn't there? I've come to the conclusion they give you the paperwork to make you think they're on top of things. What they are on top of is piles of paperwork.

The matron told me Fat would be given what they called a 'caseworker' and this caseworker would come and see me once I'd had my visit with Donna-Faye. I asked her what a caseworker was – they assume that you know, when I had no idea – and she said, 'Ah, well, it's a person employed by the mental health service to manage Fat's case.'

Does that sound good to you? It sounded good to me. Somebody was managing Fat. They knew where she was, and what treatment she needed, and whether she was getting it. That's how it sounds, doesn't it? It isn't how it works. How it works is, you have a caseworker and then you get a new one pretty much every time you walk in the door. You've got to explain everything all over again because usually that person hasn't had time to read the file.

I said to the matron once, 'Why does it have to be this way? Why don't they hand over the file and explain what's gone on, so we don't have to do it every week? Better still, why can't we keep the same person?' She was sympathetic. Everybody is very sympathetic. She shrugged and said something about resources, and people moving on, and the workload, which is what you hear in every government department you go near these days.

They have no money. They have no staff. Everybody is burnt out. Mental health is the worst.

Anyway, after I'd spent a bit of time with Fat, mostly just sitting with her saying, 'You'll be right' and, 'We'll get you on your feet again' I went and met the caseworker. I was up-front. I said, 'I'm Donna-Faye's father. I want the truth. Is she mad? Because something about her doesn't look right.'

The caseworker shook her head. She said, '*Mad* is not really a term we use anymore.'

I wasn't in the mood for that. I said, 'They found her walking stark naked down the street. That sounds mad to me.'

The caseworker said, 'I'm not sure the term is all that helpful.'

She asked me to sit down, and I did. We had a long conversation. She was the first to tell me what had actually gone on, which was that Fat had had an acute psychotic episode. I didn't know what that was. Was it the breakdown they'd talked about on the phone? The nurse who called me said she'd had a breakdown. The caseworker said, 'Yes, okay, for your purposes, breakdown is fine. She's had a break-down.'

I didn't mind that diagnosis. I thought, Okay, you break down, you get up. It might just take some time.

The caseworker wasn't so sure. She said some people – people like Fat – they have these brain snaps in their late teens, early 20s, and people think, oh, they'll be alright. They might have been under a bit of strain – Fat had had her baby taken away remember – but they'll be fine when things start going right for them. It doesn't always happen.

It's hard for people to accept,' the caseworker said. 'Some-times people don't go back to where they were.'

I wanted to know if Fat was going to be locked up. I mean, if she was never going to be normal, would she have to be locked up? The caseworker said, 'No, no, we don't lock people up, not anymore.' She said, 'Fat will stay on the ward for a couple of weeks' and they'd get people out to talk to her, to understand what had happened to her, and when she was stable, she could go, which sounded pretty good.

I said to her, 'And when will she be stable?' but she couldn't say.

I thought, well, I'll go home, come back when they know more, but the caseworker said, no, stay. Let's talk. She asked me about our family – not about Seth, because it seemed like everybody on the ward knew all about Seth – but age-old stuff, like how Fat had come along 10 years after Blue, and how she'd had to grow up without her mum.

The caseworker said, 'Maybe Fat always felt like a mistake?' I said, 'Well, she was a mistake! A happy accident, I used to call her.' The caseworker said, 'That can be hard on a child' and I said, 'No. Pat had a problem with it, but that was Pat's problem. It wasn't my problem.'

She asked me about Haines and why I thought Fat had hooked up with Haines. I said, 'I'm buggered if I know. I tried to put her off the idea.' She said, 'It sometimes happens with young women. An older man – a more powerful man – might make her feel special.'

I said, 'That makes it sound like I'm to blame for her ending up with him.' She said, 'Maybe Fat blames herself for her mum leaving home. Maybe she thinks you blame her, too.' I said, 'Well, I don't.' I also said, 'It's strange to me that people see Fat as the problem. She's not the problem. That idiot Haines, he's the cause of our problems.' The caseworker paid no attention to that. She said, 'Why do you call your daughter Fat?' and I had to say, 'It's not fat-fat. It's Fat. Donna-Faye. Faye. Fat. Rhymes with her mum Pat, her sister, Kat.' She said, 'But she's not a small girl, is she?' and look, I admit, that was the first time I thought, well, maybe it wasn't a good idea to have saddled her with that nickname.

The caseworker nodded and said, 'Well, thank you, Med, and that's it for the first session, and you can go and sit with Donna-Faye if you want' and it wasn't til then that I realised I was even in a session. I went and said bye to Fat, but she was zonked out, so I headed back to Forster. It was after midnight when I got home. The dog was hungry. I let her sleep inside.

I did the ring around the following day, telling Edna and Blue and the others what had happened, giving them the latest instalment. Blue wanted to know if he should visit. I told him no. By this stage he'd hooked up with a local girl – was she already his wife? I'm not sure, but he'd definitely hooked up with her, and maybe she was already pregnant? She must have been, because I think that's why I told him not to come. Kat remained a bit elusive. I don't think she'll shoot me for saying that. It is the truth, after all.

For my part, I visited the hospital once a week, and as I've said, every time, there was a new caseworker and I'd have to go through the whole story again. It didn't seem to me like the most efficient system, having all these young people popping in and out, trying to get on top of Fat's problems every week, but when I mentioned that, I was told, 'Oh, the system's so stretched.'

As to whether Fat was actually getting better, nobody seemed to be able to tell me. It didn't seem so, not to look at her. She was docile. She was tired. She was sometimes friendly. But she wasn't Fat. Something wasn't right. I wish

I had a better way to explain it, but really, that was it, she wasn't Fat, so I was pretty surprised, three months into Fat's stay there, when I got collared in the hallway by a matron-type of lady, who told me they were getting ready to move her out. I said, 'Move her where?' but this lady didn't seem to know. She said, 'We never keep anyone much past a few months on this ward. They stay two or three weeks, and then they move on.'

I said, 'Okay, but move on where?' On the one hand, I was thinking it would be good to get Fat closer to Forster so I could see her more often. But the lady didn't seem to know where she'd be going, only that she'd have to go.

'We need the beds,' she said.

I spoke to Edna about it. I said, 'They've got Fat on the move, but I don't get where she's going.' From what I understood, the institutions – the asylums, for want of a better word – had all closed back when I was a young man, but I wanted to be sure about it, so I asked a nurse at the hospital, who confirmed it, saying, 'And more's the pity.'

I said, 'Oh, come on, they were terrible places.' She said, 'Well, it's better than having the mentally impaired on the street, slicing each other open with broken bottles.' I had to agree with that.

Anyway, this matron-lady, she gave me some paperwork, and said I'd have to sign it. It was a form, under the Mental Health Act, that would make me Fat's guardian. I said, 'I'm already her father.' They said, 'Yes, but she's over 18. You need to be her legal guardian.' I said, 'And if I don't sign them?' They said, 'The State of NSW will become her guardian, and you won't have much say in what happens next.'

The matron told me, 'Legally speaking, once you've signed those papers, it's as if she's a child again. She'll be your ward, and you're her guardian, just like when she was small.'

I thought, well, that makes sense. Who else should take care of her if I didn't? I was happy to tell Fat about it, and when I did, she hugged me, like she used to hug me when she was little. Well, not quite. My arms can't get around her middle anymore.

I said, 'We'll get you better, Fat.'

Signing those forms seemed to trigger something in the system. The very next visit the matron saw me coming down the hall, plastic bag with grapes in it in one hand, carnations in the other, and she said, 'Have you come to take Donna-Faye?'

I said, 'Take her where?' She said, 'Take her home.' I didn't understand what she meant. Home? Nobody had said anything about home. But the matron said, 'She's got permission to leave. Her caseworker signed off on it.' Well, that could have meant anything. Which caseworker? When?

I thought, There must have been a mistake, or else somebody is kidding. Fat was still fairly heavily medicated at that point, liable to walk into walls and keep walking, if you see what I mean.

But the matron said, no, now that she had a guardian – that would be me – she could leave. I said, '*I'm* supposed to treat her?' and she laughed, and said, 'It's all done in the community now. It's so much cheaper and easier.' I thought, for who, but of course, I knew. Cheaper for governments. Cheaper for hospitals. Pretty difficult for us, as I suppose you know.

Anyway, the matron said a doctor would decide on the treatment for Fat, and she would have a chart with her medication on it and there would be people on hand to help me, if I ran into any trouble, and I should talk to her caseworker if I had any concerns, so I trotted down the hall to the caseworker's office. It was somebody new again. I said, 'Is this serious?' because it seemed to me that Fat was still a long way from being well. I said, 'I'm not sure this is right' and the caseworker said, 'Well, we need the bed.'

I said, 'Well, I'm not sure I can take care of her. I work full-time. She'd be home alone.'

The caseworker said, 'But didn't you agree to be the guardian?' And I said, 'Yes, but I still have to work.' In truth, work had been getting away from me. I'd been there a long time but people were starting to notice. I guess that explains part of why I agreed to what they came up with. The caseworker said, 'Well, there is one other option.' I was ready to hear it. She told me that a 'bed' had opened up – that's how they say it, they say a 'bed' not a 'spot' or a 'place' but a 'bed' – in one of the Department's units in regional NSW, and if we were quick, Fat might be able to get that bed.

I had, by that stage, learnt to talk the way they talked. I said, 'What kind of bed is this?' The caseworker said, 'The program is called Re-start.' All their programs have names like that.

I asked what it was about. She said there was a group of units where people could live while they were trying to get their lives back together. She said it was State-government funded, which is another word for 'free', and as I was finding out, anything that is free in mental health goes like hotcakes.

I said, 'And it's for people with mental health issues?' (See what I mean about my language, Your Honour? Nobody talks like that. Nobody says 'mental health issues'. But that's how they get you talking.)

The caseworker said, 'No, it's not.' Strictly speaking, it was for anyone but the mentally ill. It was for ex-crims coming out of prison, who needed to get onto their feet, or else it was for people coming out of rehab, who wanted to get away from their old suppliers, and it was for refugees who come to Australia with not much in the way of skills, not even English.

I said, 'I don't see how Fat fits into those categories.'

The caseworker said, 'She doesn't, but the bed is there, and it's funded and I'm willing to make a case to the health department that Fat qualifies because she needs to get away from Paul Haines.'

And in the end, that was what got me over the line, the idea that somebody understood what a loser he was, and that Fat needed to get away from him.

I should be clear: Haines had not been on the scene, not since Fat had entered the hospital. I had not seen him since that day he'd been stoned on the couch. He'd never even rung up to see what was going on. But Haines was an opportunist. I didn't doubt that he'd come sniffing around my place once he knew that Fat was there. It would be a power trip for him to get her home. Would she have gone with him? I hate to say this but probably, yes. So I said, 'Okay, let's get this Re-start underway.'

There were forms to fill out, before Fat could move. There were brochures, too. I looked through them. They had photographs of the units where Fat would live. I couldn't say how accurate they were, but in the pictures, they looked pretty good. They had aluminium security doors and fluorescent lights. They were that cream colour the government loves.

I said to the caseworker, 'Where are they?'

That's when she told me. That's when she floored me, actually. She said, 'They're in Tamworth.' Tamworth! Do you know where Tamworth is, Your Honour? Because I tell you, before all this happened, I'd never been there. I knew it as the country music town. I knew it as the place with a Big Guitar. I did not know the health department was sending mental health patients there.

I said, 'Why Tamworth?' The caseworker said, 'Oh, it's deliberate. It creates jobs, and it helps get people away from the city centres, where the problems are.'

I said, 'Fat doesn't know anybody in Tamworth' and the caseworker said, yes, that was the point. 'It's Re-start, remember. Donna-Faye will get a little unit to herself. Only the GP in town will know she's there.'

I was anxious about it. Where I was, outside Forster, it wasn't too difficult to pick up the New England Highway and end up in Tamworth but, as with the hospital, it would be hard to get there more than once a week.

The caseworker said, 'She won't be alone, though. There are other people in the same block of units.'

I said, 'Who lives there? Other nutters?' (Which, I suppose, shows that I didn't have the PC language quite right. The caseworker said, 'I thought we agreed, Med. We're not calling anyone nutters anymore.')

Then she said, 'No. Sudanese refugees. Families from Somalia and Sudanese people, most of them newly arrived in Australia, trying to find their feet.'

For the second time that day, she had me floored. It was not that Fat would be living with Sudanese – that was no big deal, they've got to live somewhere, don't they? But that we – Australia, I mean – were sending Sudanese people to *Tamworth*.

I said, 'Who's idea was that?' The caseworker, she said, 'Well, it's all part of the plan. Most of the new arrivals cannot read and write. They are illiterate in their own language. In some cases, they have never turned on a tap or flushed a toilet, or gone to a supermarket and used money. It takes some effort to assimilate them. The government spreads them around regional NSW, and Queensland, too, so everybody can help carry the burden.'

I thought, I wonder what the hell the Sudanese make of that? I had in mind a vision of them walking around barefoot across the Kalahari with baskets on their heads one minute, and then boot-scootin' around the Big Guitar in Tamworth the next.

The caseworker said, 'They keep pretty much to themselves but who knows, they might befriend Donna-Faye.' I wondered about that.

The first time I went to Tamworth, after Fat was moved there at the start of 2008, I saw a couple of Sudanese people walking down the road. They stood out on the landscape like you would not believe. They were the longest, tallest, blackest people I'd ever seen in my life, outside *National Geographic*, but with bright white eyes that were red around the rims, like they'd been crying.

The way they walked, it was like they were warriors. They were so upright it was as if they still had baskets on their heads. I wondered what they'd talk to Donna-Faye about.

I said to the caseworker – oh, yes, Fat had a caseworker in Tamworth, just like she did in Sydney, and it was never the same one – are they Muslim? I didn't think of it as a racist question. It hadn't been that long since the 9/11 attack, and then Bali had been blown up, and the war in Iraq was going on. Right or wrong, people were worried about Muslims, but the caseworker said, 'I have no idea.' That was bullshit, excuse my French. She just thought I was rude for asking. Maybe I was. Anyway, I found out for myself that most of them weren't Muslims. They were Christians. Not all of them. I did see a couple of the women, dressed up like pepper grinders, sort of shuffling down the street, and I thought, okay, they're not Christian, but some of the other women had crosses. I should also say that most of them were pretty good to me and to Fat, while she was there, and what happened between them and her . . . well, let's just say for now that it was obviously wrong, what they did, it was totally out of line, but it's not like we didn't do worse.

Fat's unit was nice enough. It had a bedroom, an ensuite bathroom and a microwave. The rent was $25 a week and it came straight out of her disability pension. I hadn't been happy about that – her being on the pension, I mean. I said, 'Nobody in our lot has ever been on the dole.' They said, 'It's not dole. It's disability pension' and they said Fat had to take it, otherwise she wouldn't have the ID number she needed to get into Re-start in the first place, and so we signed up for it.

I should also tell you, the times I went up to Tamworth before things went completely pear-shaped, Fat seemed pretty happy there. Like I've said, she wasn't Fat like before she went to the mental ward. Looking back, there were signs of what was going on inside. She would rock back and forward. She would whisper, or else she'd come over hard of hearing, and you'd have to shout. Sometimes she'd be suspicious of me for offering to help with some perfectly ordinary thing, like getting milk out of the little fridge. Her sense of distance was out. She'd go to put something on the bench, and she'd miss, and it would break on the floor. Silly things like that, they add up to a lot.

That said, the unit seemed a good place for her. She was free to come and go as she pleased. There were a few shops about where she could have a bit of a browse, and then, of course, she had her neighbours, the Sudanese. To me, that was interesting. They had a funny way of dressing – suit pants under dresses for the men – and they had barbecues out on the driveway, which smelled nice, but meant you couldn't park the car.

Under the Re-start rules, I couldn't stay in with Fat. She wasn't allowed visitors overnight, so when I went up, I'd set myself up at the pub. I knew from reading the Tamworth paper that the locals weren't too happy about having the Sudanese people there and nine times in 10, some bloke in the pub would end up telling me that the Sudanese were causing all kinds of problems. They were in court for driving off without paying for petrol, or driving without a licence, or they were taking over the computers at the local library.

Every bloke claimed to know a girl who had a friend who knew a nurse who worked at the Tamworth Hospital who was delivering babies to Sudanese girls who couldn't have been more than 12 or 13 years old. They'd tell you how the babies had to be cut out of the mothers' bellies because the mothers had been cut up and sewn shut and couldn't deliver a baby in the normal way.

People went on the internet and discovered that the camps in Kenya, where the Sudanese had been before they came to Australia, had TB. They wrote to the local newspapers, wanting to know whether the Australian government had screened for TB and they complained that the services that had been promised – the health services, the language services – were slow in coming.

One weekend I was there, the principal at one of the local schools was complaining that 'our kids' were suffering because the Sudanese kids couldn't read and write and needed so much help to catch up.

I can't say I had an opinion about the Sudanese people, not then. There was one thing I noticed, and it was that they did not necessarily get along. My idea had been, 'They're all from the same place, and they're all in the same boat now' and you'd think they'd be pulling together, but in fact they were warring with each other like you wouldn't believe. A bloke at the pub told me, 'It's all tribal. They're fighting battles that started 7000 years ago. Nobody even knows what it's about anymore.'

He said there wasn't a doubt in the world that some of the bad ones – he said the 'machete ones' – got through the system and ended up in Australia. He meant some of the ones that had done the chopping and the raping and the killing in the wars in Africa had made it through as refugees, when in fact they were the ones who sent people fleeing in the first place. I told him he had the wrong country. These people weren't from Rwanda.

There were other points of view. One bloke I met in the pub was the owner of the local meatworks. He was rapt to have the Sudanese, and if 1600 more were coming – that was the rumour – well, he'd have been even more rapt. He had jobs on the kill floor that he had never been able to fill.

'The Sudanese aren't squeamish,' he told me. 'They'll do anything.'

From memory, I was on my fifth visit to Tamworth when I realised that Fat and the Sudanese – well, they weren't actually keeping to themselves. I don't know why I thought they would be but still, I got the shock of my life when I put my head around the door in Fat's unit, and called out, 'Yoohoo, it's Dad' and from the corner of my eye, I saw a Sudanese guy, long as a ladder, taking off from Fat's kitchen, through the flyscreen door, and basically hurdling the back fence.

I said to Fat, 'What was that?' She said, 'That was Malok' and I said, 'And who's Malok?' She said, 'He's Malok.' She could be like that. Hard to pin down.

On the other hand, I wasn't born yesterday. It was clearly a bloke who didn't want to be seen, because otherwise why hurdle the fence? I said, 'Is that your friend, Fat?' and Fat said, 'That's Malok' – as I say, that was the way she was talking then, basically like a child – and I said, 'He doesn't look that old' and she said, 'He doesn't know how old he is' and I assumed she was confused about that, because who doesn't know how old they are? But I said, 'Well, that's nice, Fat, but I don't get why he had to run off?' and she said, 'He's Malok.'

Did I think they had some other kind of relationship, other than him sniffing around my girl, probably because she was chubby and exotic? No, I did not. I mean, Fat was still half-asleep most of the time, and Malok was a kid – a big kid, no doubt about that, but still a kid and he could barely string together a sentence in the English language.

I thought, I bet he comes here during the day, hoping to get a glimpse of Fat's leg, or something like that. Maybe the women he knows are the type that wear the hijabby robes. I thought, Maybe he's a snowdropper, taking her knickers off the line.

Certainly, I didn't think of him as somebody who was going to help upset the applecart in the way he did, and to be fair – I'm trying as hard as I can to be fair here – it wasn't his fault. Like I say, he was just a kid, a late-teen teenager with raging testosterone, and no idea how to handle it, and the women in his family, well, they lived by their own rules.

That said, I do remember, one time I was visiting Fat, trying to put a dryer onto the wall above the washing machine and I needed help. I'd gone to the next unit, and knocked on the door and when the African bloke answered, I'd mimed out what I needed – some of his height, basically, because he was a good two-foot taller than me – and he'd nodded and smiled and come over to Fat's, and helped me lift the dryer into place, and when we were out the front, job done, having a cold glass of beer, Malok walked by, as if to turn up her garden path, but then he saw me and he decided to keep walking, and the Sudanese bloke who'd been helping me pointed after him. He had a long, crooked finger, pink at the tip. He shook his head and said, 'No good, no good.' Now, you don't need to speak Swahili to get the message there, do you? He was saying, 'Keep your girl away from that one, he's bad news.'

Then, six months into the Tamworth Re-start experiment, a woman from the health department called me and said she had 'news'.

I said, 'What news?' and after a bit of umming and ahhing, she said, 'Well, basically Mr Atley, Donna-Faye is pregnant.'

I have to tell you, Your Honour, I was knocked on my

bottom. Winded. And, given what had happened with Seth, horrified.

I said, 'You are kidding, I hope?' I even thought, How? I mean, I know how it happens, but I still thought, How could they have *let* that happen? Wasn't the point of the Re-start program to keep Fat out of trouble? Hadn't she got to Tamworth after breaking down over the loss of Seth?

The caseworker was apologetic – to a point. That's another thing I've found about mental health. It's all good in theory, the treatments and the programs that they have, but when they go wrong, nobody takes responsibility. Nobody is to blame.

She said, 'Well, Donna-Faye's an adult' and I thought, She's an adult in your care! I said, 'I thought she was going to be *safe* in this program' and the caseworker, she said, 'Well, she's not *injured*. She's expecting a baby' . . . and then she cleared her throat, and I knew there was more coming.

She said, 'As Donna-Faye's guardian, there's something else you need to know.'

I said, 'Well, hit me with it.' What else could there possibly be?

She said, 'Well, it seems that the father of Donna-Faye's baby is the son of one of the local Sudanese.'

That took a minute to digest. I said, 'He's the son of one of the Sudanese?'

She said, 'That's what Donna-Faye has told us.'

I said, 'When you say, son . . .?'

She said, 'Yes, from what Donna-Faye has said, the father

is Malok Ibrahim, and if that's so, then Malok's not yet 18. He may not, in fact, be 17.'

Well, I thought, that's just peachy. That's just keen. Not a year after she'd lost Seth, Fat was pregnant. Not only that, the father was a Sudanese refugee. Not only that, he was a minor.

I shouldn't have got angry with the poor lady on the telephone. Believe me when I say I'm not normally the type to get angry, but on that occasion I did. I said, 'Do you people have any idea what you're doing? Heaven's above, the whole purpose of your program was to keep Fat safe.'

Part of my anger was grief, obviously. I mean, I knew even before they told me that there was no way that Fat would be allowed to *keep* the baby she was carrying. I knew that because of what people who used to hang out on our website told me. Not after what had happened to Seth, not after she'd been found wandering naked in the traffic, not after she'd caused a bus to run off the road, not after she'd been committed and was on medication, and living in assisted accommodation.

I called Edna and said, 'You mark my words, they'll come for this baby, just like they came for the last one.'

Edna said, 'Don't be silly, Med, people can't just up and take a baby from its mother.'

I said, 'Don't you read the news? They do it all the time' and it's true, Your Honour, you know it's true. I blame the media. It's the media that's made a crazy spectacle of child abuse. It's the media that carries on when somebody hurts a child, and now the Department has this weird power, where it can take any baby it wants. You have one baby taken away, they'll come for the next one, too. They won't run the risk that you'll hurt it.

I could hardly bear to face Fat with that news, but when the time came to explain it all to Fat, she didn't seem to care – care is not the right word, but it's the only one I can think of. She just said, 'Oh, okay.'

Did she understand? I doubt it. I mean, not long after we had that chat, a bloke came by to deliver a cradle, one he said he didn't need anymore. After he was gone, I had to say, 'Fat, you know they're not going to let you bring this baby home, don't you?' She nodded. She said, 'I know that, Dad' but when she thought I wasn't looking she went back to the cot, and fussed with sheets. To see her doing that hurt so much. I had to go outside.

Once the decision to take the baby from Fat had been made, the question became, who will take the baby? We didn't think the father – the boy, Malok – would be allowed to do it. He was in worse straits than Donna-Faye. He had no income and he couldn't read or write. As far as I knew, he didn't even have an Australian passport.

With the mother and the father ruled out, the Department turned to the next of kin, which basically meant me. I told the caseworker, I am Fat's guardian, and the grandfather, so the baby can come home with me, at least until Fat gets better. They ruled that out. They said, Med, you're too old. I knew straightaway that couldn't be the real reason. Plenty of grandparents have their kids to look after, don't they? Plenty of them are older than me. I said, 'What's the real reason?' They said, 'Well, Donna-Faye's had the test, and the baby is a girl.' I said, 'So the baby's a girl, and?' They said, 'Well, the Department doesn't usually place a baby girl with a single man.'

I said, 'You think I'm a child molester?' I said, 'You people have some strange ideas.' I cursed Pat. I thought, you ran off and left me with a baby and now you're gone, I'm not good enough to care for a baby. But there was no point arguing about it, obviously. Once the Department makes a decision, you can spend every cent you have fighting it, and good luck with how far you get. I said, 'What is the Department's plan?' I knew they'd have one. They always do.

They said, 'We are willing to assess other members of Donna-Faye's family, as potential guardians.' In English, that means I was supposed to come up with somebody in the family who would take the baby.

My first thought was Blue because, to me, Blue ticked all the boxes. He was still in his 30s, and he was married by then, and I'm pretty sure their eldest was already born. Blue's wife is Koori. Their children are coffee-coloured, like Fat's baby was obviously going to be coffee-coloured . . . but even as all this was going through my mind, I knew they'd never approve Blue. They'd take one look at his place out on the Ridge, the campsite with the drop toilet and the tank water and the tarps, and they'd scan around the neighbours – the fortune hunters, the dreamers – and the barefoot kids, and they'd say, 'Well, he doesn't meet our standards.'

There was something else, too, Blue had a record. I've never mentioned that to anyone. I don't see that it's anyone's business. I wouldn't mention it now, except I'm determined to be up-front. It's to do with something that happened a year or so after he moved to the Ridge, when he was young man, still a bit wet behind the ears.

The Ridge is one of those places where the men outnumber women. There weren't many girls about. If I know Blue, he wouldn't have made a habit of going to the knocking shop, but he did go one time, and a girl took his eye. She told him it was her first night. She hoped her first client would be a decent bloke. Was she making that up? I'd say it's odds on, but Blue gave her money and didn't have sex with her. Did he think he was in love? Maybe, or maybe it was like with the pups on the property, when he was boy. If there was an animal crying, he had to help. He told this girl, 'Come to my camp; I'll take care of you.' Of course she said yes, yes, but she needed some money to pay off her debt to the owner of the knocking shop, and the next night, when she didn't turn up at the camp and he went looking for her, where was she? At the knocking shop, with some other joker getting the 'It's my first night' routine. Blue got upset. They threw him out on his arse. When he tried to get back in, using a boot against the door, they called the cops, and for that, he got a record.

I thought, it sounds to me like the kind of record some men – good men – will always get. But I also knew that it would show up in the assessment – hookers, jail – and Blue would be a goner, at least as far as Fat's baby was concerned, and maybe the bureaucrats, who just love sniffing around, would start thinking about the state of his lodgings in relation to his own kids, too.

# I CAME TO SAY GOODBYE

That left me with one option: Kat.

Now, Your Honour, I hope that Kat will forgive me for saying this, but I hesitated before I put her name forward, the main concern being I wasn't sure she'd say yes. I mean, Kat's my firstborn, and she's my daughter, and of course I love her, and I'm proud of what she's achieved, but the truth is, I thought she'd say, 'I'm sorry, Dad, but I don't want anything to do with this mess.'

Kat had already moved back from New York by then. She did not come home to 'steal' Fat's baby, as some have said. Fat wasn't even pregnant when Kat came home. She'd bought a place in Hunters Hill and I'd actually been there once or twice. I'd felt like the poor cousin. Kat had developed posh taste. The house made you think you'd make it dirty just by putting your coat down. You had to take off your shoes to walk on the carpet. That was her husband, David. He's English. He's got a thing about shoes in the house. Anyway, the first time I'd gone there, it was tea she'd organised – a dinner party, she called it – and she had napkins folded in triangles, sticking out of the glasses. There were bowls with water and lemon in them. I knew they weren't for drinking. I knew they were for washing your fingers when you peeled the prawns, but there's nothing I like more than to pop a person's bubble. I picked up one of the bowls, and went to drink from it, pretending that I didn't know it was for my fingers. Kat's husband, David, he sort of leapt up, and said, 'No, Med!' and that sort of ruined the joke.

I tried to save the situation. I said, 'Oh, we're going to eat the prawns! I always thought of prawns as bait!' That didn't

209

go down too well, either. The night was sort of downhill from there.

The other thing, obviously, was that Kat and David still had no kids. Why that was, I'd never asked them. It was not my business to ask. Edna wanted to gossip about it. I told her there was no point gossiping with me; I didn't know anything. I figured they couldn't have kids. Otherwise, why wouldn't they have them? But when Edna said to Kat, 'Do you think you'll be having children?' Kat had said, 'Oh no, Auntie Edna, we're happy enough with Bella and George. They're like children to us.'

Bella and George were the dogs. The King Charles spaniels.

All that said, I was obviously going to phone Kat and at least put it to her to take Fat's baby before I was going to let welfare come and put the baby in a home with a stranger, and so that's what I did. I phoned up Kat and I explained the situation. I said, 'Fat's pregnant and they aren't going to let her keep the baby, which means somebody has to take it, or else it will end up in welfare; and not only that, the baby is going to be black.'

Well, Kat wasn't fazed about that part. The Atleys aren't racist. I don't believe most Australians are. She said, 'Another Aborigine? What are we, the Department of Reconciliation?' and she meant that in a nice way because Blue's wife was Koori, and I suppose that had been Kat's first impression, that Fat's baby must be part-Aborigine, too.

I said, 'No, no, Kat, the father's not Koori. The father's Sudanese. From what I know of him, he's black as night' and there was a bit of pause, while Kat absorbed that, and when her voice came down the line again, it was quieter than it had been, softer, more maternal.

She said, 'The father's Sudanese?' and I said, 'That's what they said' and went on to explain where Fat was living and how it had happened that she'd come into contact with the refugees. Kat listened to it all, and although she didn't say yes right away, there's no doubt in my mind that she was heading that way, because she kept saying, 'Wow' and, 'Wow again' and, well, I suppose I'm at the point now where I'm going to have to explain what happened to that little baby, but the more I think about doing it, the more I think I can't do it, and I hope you will forgive me, Your Honour, if I hand over to Kat now.

She's a brave girl, Kat. She's got a completely broken heart but she will do a good job of explaining it, I know she will.

# Chapter 16

## Kat Atley

YOUR HONOUR, MY NAME IS KA'AREN Atley and I was born in Forster Hospital in September 1970. My father, Med Atley, has asked me to assist him with a letter he is writing about my sister, Donna-Faye.

I understand that your court has been asked to decide what should happen to my sister's child. My father has some things he would like to bring to your attention in that regard, and he has asked me to put my side of the story to you, too. My father has allowed me to read what he's already written and I can see he's given you a good history of his marriage, and my childhood.

You will know that my mother left home when I was quite young, after which I went to boarding school and from there to Sydney University, to London, where I met my future husband, David Bennett, and then, in January 2001, we moved to New York. David and I were living in Manhattan in 2005 when Donna-Faye gave birth to Seth. I was pleased for my sister and David and I sent a small gift but to be honest, and I do want to be honest, we didn't see ourselves as having much to do with our nephew at that point, because we were living abroad, with no immediate plan to return to Australia.

Naturally, we were horrified when we heard, some 12 weeks later, that Seth had been taken to the John Hunter Hospital and that some kind of legal manoeuvre to remove him from my sister's care was underway. The details of that case were a mystery to me, until recently.

David and I returned to Sydney in 2008, in part because I had decided to start a family and I wanted to raise our children in Australia. We settled in Hunters Hill and I do remember inviting my father up to have a look at our new place. It was the first time I'd seen him in five years. I've read what he's written about that dinner we had and I agree, we were probably showing off a bit, but I believe my father was pleased to have us home. I enquired after Blue and Donna-Faye, and we talked about what had happened to Seth, and how Donna-Faye had moved to Tamworth to try to sort out the problems in her life.

I guess I'd been in Sydney for several months when my father called to tell me that Donna-Faye had again fallen pregnant and that somebody was going to have to take her baby.

I did not at first understand what he meant. Why would somebody have to take her baby? My father explained that the NSW Department of Community Services – DoCS, I believe they call themselves – had new powers that enabled them to swoop on parents who had already had one child removed from their care, and take any other children that came along.

I asked my father how Donna-Faye had reacted to that decision. From memory, he said, 'It didn't seem to register.'

He then asked me whether I'd take Donna-Faye's baby.

I did not immediately say yes. In fact, I hesitated for some time. Why did I hesitate? In part, I suppose, because David and I had not given up the dream of having a child of our own. It's true what my father has told you. I did not feel at all maternal in my 20s or even my early 30s. In fact, I was probably 37 years old before I heard the ticking of the biological clock and, then, as happens with so many people, I found I needed help. I did not conceive naturally. A friend recommended an IVF clinic in Sydney. We went through the process once, and it failed us. David was eager to try again but I was fairly certain that IVF wasn't for me. I hadn't responded well to medication or to the disappointment and yet, when my father called and said, 'Your sister is pregnant, and somebody needs to take the baby' – well, I had to decide whether I was willing to forgo another attempt at IVF to raise not my own but my sister's child.

We decided to take the first step in the process, and register as foster carers. The fact that we had to do that surprised me. I am, after all, Donna-Faye's sister. It's hardly unusual for sisters to take in each other's children. In some cultures, it's commonplace.

Nevertheless, the Department said I would have to be assessed. There was a great deal of paperwork to complete. I had to obtain references from friends and my employer. Both David and I had to do a police check, and of course, there had to be two copies of everything, verified by a Justice of the Peace. I am an organised person, but it was difficult for me to keep track of everything we needed. I can't imagine what it might be like to navigate the process if you were not a lawyer.

Once the paperwork was filed, David and I were asked to attend a parenting class at the Department's offices in Parramatta. We put our hearts and souls into preparing for it, reading books on child rearing and so forth, and I was surprised to find that the Department's approach was somewhat less organised. The class was held in a small room with a piece of A4 paper Blu-Tacked on the wall that said, 'Parenting Class.' When I put my head around the door, I saw people sitting in little school chairs. The aim of the class seemed to be to memorise what was being written on the whiteboard by a rather bored supervisor, and then complete a multiple-choice test. At the end of it, we got a certificate, which then had to be photocopied, and for reasons that escaped me, had to be sent back to the Department that had, in fact, issued it.

The next step involved a personal interview in our home. By that stage, I had arranged to fly Donna-Faye to Sydney from Tamworth. She was staying in our spare room. She was receiving treatment for her mental illness. The medication made her drowsy. I don't doubt that the pregnancy also sapped her energy. She was often vague, or tired, and she did sometimes behave quite strangely, by which I mean she'd become convinced that something awful was about to happen, and she'd become furtive and quiet, and I'd have to coax her out of her room. She certainly had in mind that people were watching her, perhaps even watching the house. I assured her that the Department – the welfare, she called them – did not have the resources to park a car outside the house to watch her 24 hours a day, although I'm not certain that she believed me.

I suppose people do wonder whether we talked about Seth and if we didn't, why we didn't, but it was difficult to talk to Donna-Faye in a serious way. She could sometimes talk for hours, and make no sense at all.

The main thing was, she was swelling beautifully.

It was while Donna-Faye was living with me that she decided, after watching an episode of *Days of Our Lives*, that she was going to call her little girl Savannah. I thought the name was absolutely gorgeous.

I managed to book Donna-Faye into the Eastern Private Hospital to have her baby. I'd heard nightmare stories about regional hospitals – the shortage of doctors, women giving birth in toilets and so on – and I didn't want Donna-Faye or her baby to be at any risk at all.

When I mentioned to the Department that Donna-Faye was staying with me, the social worker flew off the handle. She said it was 'presumptuous' of me to have Donna-Faye move in because I hadn't yet been assessed as a foster carer. She said it would place pressure on Donna-Faye to relinquish her daughter to me. I asked what on earth I was supposed to do, send Donna-Faye onto the street? Leave her in Tamworth, where she was alone? She was my sister, after all.

The social worker said I had caused a problem because Donna-Faye wasn't going to be allowed to live with her baby after she was born, and yet she was living with me. She said she would now have to find accommodation for Donna-Faye somewhere in Sydney. It wouldn't be easy. David and I offered to find a place for her, and cover the rent, but she said that could be construed as a bribe.

David was quite upset about that. 'How do the minds of these people work?' he said.

In any case, the social worker told me that Donna-Faye absolutely could not be present during our assessment interview, so I drove her out to the shopping centre to see a movie, and when she came back, she told me she felt certain that DoCS had been there, pretending to be ushers in the cinema. I had to tell her I didn't think so.

I knew that David would struggle with the assessment interview. Being English, he cannot bear to have people poking into his life. I had warned him against trying to attempt jokes with mid-level Australian bureaucrats. They take themselves extremely seriously and have no qualms at all about abusing their position to punish you.

I could see he took an instant dislike to the social worker, in her layered robes, with her wild hair. Her first questions were benign: how old are you, and what do you do for a living, and so forth?

Then she asked how we intended to preserve Savannah's heritage and encourage her positive identity as a part-Sudanese child?

David said, 'Well, she'll be black. That's not really something we can hide from her, is it?'

She asked whether we'd take Savannah to Sudan when she got older.

David said, 'I suppose that depends whether the war's still on.'

She asked how we'd explain Savannah's colouring to people. David said, 'We'll tell them to mind their own business.' What you are supposed to say, obviously, is: 'We'll encourage Savannah to be proud of her heritage.'

Towards the end of the interview, there was a brief discussion about Malok, and whether we'd 'support' a relationship with him. I said, yes, of course. I also said we were eager to offer Savannah a secure home in an area where there were many good schools. I explained that we would be able to provide for her but the social worker wanted to know was how I'd encourage Savannah's identity as a 'mixed-race' child.

After she'd gone, David said, 'She wants the baby to grow up with Sudanese people.' He said, 'She wanted us to say we'd teach her to walk down to the village well and get the bath water. Face it, Kat, we aren't black enough. We don't eat goat. That's what she was getting at.'

We were disappointed with her report when it came. Those things we had imagined as working in our favour were cast in a negative light. Much was made of the affluent neighbourhood in which we lived, and how it wasn't racially diverse.

I sent a copy of it, by email, to my father. He described it perfectly when he said, 'It's a load of horse manure. She's saying, "You think because you're loaded you can put your hand up and you'll get this exotic baby."'

I spoke to our lawyer that afternoon. I told him that the report was negative, that it said that Savannah should be placed with 'culturally appropriate carers' who would 'encourage her identity as a Sudanese child'. In short, it said Savannah would be better off with strangers than with David and me.

Donna-Faye came with us to court. The judge spent some time talking directly to her. She said, 'Ms Atley, do you understand that you are subject to a pre-birth notification?' and Donna-Faye said, 'No.' The judge continued, 'It means that the Department isn't prepared to let you care for your baby after it's born, because of your mental health' and Donna-Faye said, 'I've been on the psych ward but I'm not there now.'

The judge said, 'Do you understand what will happen to your baby after it's born?' Donna-Faye said, 'You mean when they take it away?' and the strange thing was, she didn't look unhappy about having to say that. She simply said it like she hoped it was the right answer.

The judge said, 'That's correct, and you know that your sister, Ka'aren Atley, and her husband, David, are keen to take your baby in?' and Donna-Faye nodded, and said,

'Oh yes, that would be good' and the judge said, 'But the Department thinks it might be better to place your baby with Sudanese carers?' and Donna-Faye said, 'Oh yes, that would be good, too.' The judge seemed confused. She said, 'Very well.'

The Department's lawyer argued that it would be in Savannah's best interests that she be raised with knowledge of her Sudanese culture. There was a lengthy discussion about whether it was possible for Sudanese children to properly appreciate their culture if they were not immersed in it.

To our great relief, the judge said, 'I'm sorry, but the Department's plan to place this baby with some unknown carers in some unknown area, for some unknown reason, makes no sense to me.' She said, 'When Savannah is born, she should be placed in the care of Ka'aren Atley and her husband, David Bennett.' She said we needed to ensure that Donna-Faye and Malok stayed involved in Savannah's life and she told the Department to draw up a schedule that we'd all follow, to make sure that happened. I sensed that representatives of the Department were unhappy with the ruling, but it's the judge that has the last word.

We left the court feeling pleased with the outcome. There was a little coffee shop in the court complex, and we went there to celebrate. I ordered a cappuccino, and Donna-Faye said, 'Oh, I want one too' and I had to remind her she was pregnant. I ordered her some tea.

I said, 'That was a great outcome for us, Donna-Faye. We've won.'

She said, 'We did.'

At the time, I didn't take that as a question, but perhaps it was one.

A week or so later, we took Donna-Faye and my father, who was also practically living with us, to the Eastern Private, for a tour. I remember Dad saying, 'It looks like a bloody Hyatt' and compared to casualty at Forster General, I suppose it does. There was a marble counter, and flowers on a pedestal in reception.

I had explained the situation to the hospital on the telephone: my sister, by then very pregnant, was booked into the hospital but my husband, David, and I would be assuming care of the child, Savannah, when she was born. They sent out a matron to meet us. Wanting to do the right thing, she gave Donna-Faye a welcome gift. She said, 'It's a show bag.' It had the hospital menu in it, and the famous Eastern Private bear – a white bear, with a medical cross on his vest.

Donna-Faye said, 'If I don't keep the baby, do I still get to keep the bear?' The matron looked embarrassed, and she laughed, and she said, 'Oh, I'm sure we can find another bear' which, in a way, made things worse.

A week or so later, we were there again, this time to check Donna-Faye in for the caesarean. I remember walking down the hall, Donna-Faye in front, as wide as the hall, my father beside her, just as round, with his rough beard and a short-sleeved shirt over his shorts.

Behind us there were two social workers, and Malok. The Department was so determined to have him involved in the process, whether he wanted to be involved or not, that they had sent a government car, at goodness-knows-what expense, up to Tamworth to collect him and bring him back to Sydney so he could be at the hospital when Savannah was born. I was pleased to see him. He was obviously going to be an important part of our lives. I went to embrace him. He hurtled backward so fast he crashed into a wall. He looked absolutely terrified, and not only of me.

In any case, off we went, down the hall, towards Donna-Faye's suite. She veered off course only once, to look at an enormous bear, slumped in the corner of a room so filled with flowers it looked like a florist.

'Look what they gave this lady for her baby!' she said. Then she looked at her Eastern Private bear, like she'd somehow been short-changed.

If Donna-Faye was doing some stickybeaking, it's fair to say some nurses were, too. I don't blame them. We were a curiosity. There was Donna-Faye, five-foot-nothing, round as a beach ball and white as a glove, and next to her, gangly Malok, long as licorice.

Donna-Faye's suite was the last along the corridor. The matron settled Donna-Faye onto the edge of her bed. She was so round, she had to keep her knees apart. She had been carrying the menu since we'd picked it up a week earlier. Now she said, 'Can I order anything?' and the matron said, 'Yes, of course you may' and Fat got to it, ticking yes to barramundi, and yes to crème brulee, and yes to prawn cocktails, and yes to crackers and cheese. My father took a seat in the recliner. He said, 'I'll take care of what she doesn't eat. I'm starving.'

The matron said, 'I'm going to give you a little something to keep you calm' and put some pills into Donna-Faye's hand, and then passed her a glass of water. She said, 'The doctor will be along shortly' and left the room. Donna-Faye lay down and closed her eyes. David switched on the flat screen. Somebody called Mel and Kochie were doing a morning show. I filled out some of the paperwork for Donna-Faye, and handed it to my father to sign. He was still her legal guardian.

After a while, two orderlies came for Donna-Faye. They helped her onto a trolley and wheeled her down the hall. We all followed. They stripped back her nightie, and exposed her belly and painted anaesthetic on it. They covered her skin with stickers that were connected to wires connected to machines. I felt so anxious I could hardly breathe. Over and again, I said, 'Are you okay, Donna-Faye? Are you okay?'

Who can say what she knew at that point?

David was his gentle best. He said, 'Step back, honey. Let them do what they have to do.' The orderly said, 'Oh, it'll be hours yet. The doctor hasn't even arrived. We're just moving her closer to the business end of the ward.'

David said, 'I'm going to go for a walk around.' He can't bear waiting. He told me later that he stumbled upon Malok in the hall. The poor boy had refused to go into the room where Donna-Faye was lying like a flattened seal, stained yellow and naked.

'He was standing like a broom against the wall,' David said. 'Jet black with a blue hairnet, looking like he'd rather be anywhere else, with those social worker witches hunched up in the chairs beside him.'

My father went walkabout for a while, too. He found a tearoom and made himself a cuppa. He got talking to one of the nurses, saying, 'My daughter's having a baby today.'

The nurse said, 'Well, congratulations.'

Dad said, 'I actually have to be in there for the birth. I'm the legal guardian. So I saw her born, and now I'll see her give birth.'

Dad was very proud of that.

The nurse looked a bit confused, so he gave her the short history. He was Donna-Faye's father, but also her guardian, and when the baby arrived, it wouldn't go home with Donna-Faye, but with her sister, Kat, and so on . . .

The nurse said, 'Oh, yes, I did hear about that one. She's on today, is she?' and they fell into a conversation. I'm sure I can guess how it would have gone. Dad would have asked how much it cost to have a baby in the Eastern Private and the nurse would have said, 'Oh, 10 grand' and my father would have done one of his long whistles and said, 'That's more than my car's worth'. At some point, the nurse apparently said, 'Why do you call your daughter fat? She's not fat, she's pregnant!'

My father said, 'No, we called her Fat before she was pregnant.'

The nurse said, 'Was she fat before?' and it's true, I suppose, that we were all so used to it in the family we'd forgotten how it must have sounded to people who didn't know Donna-Faye.

The nurse also wanted to know why Donna-Faye wasn't allowed to keep Savannah with her after she was born. Dad had to explain that Fat – Donna-Faye – had a mental illness. I know my father. He would have waited for the nurse to look horrified, and being a nurse, she wouldn't have been at all horrified. She said, 'Don't be embarrassed. So many people go though the same thing.' She told him stories about hospitals where she'd worked in Moree, where the mothers 'don't make a peep' when welfare comes for their babies.

'They accept it,' she said. 'They are told the government knows best.'

Dad wandered back after that, as did David. We waited some more. Donna-Faye was flat-out, ready to be sliced open. Nurses were buzzing about, excited by the prospect of delivering Savannah.

Finally the doctor arrived, and Donna-Faye was wheeled into a delivery suite. I stood to Donna-Faye's left, behind her head, holding her hand. The anaesthetist rolled her onto her side, and inserted the needle for the epidural, and then rolled her back onto her back. He looked at his watch, and after a minute or so passed, he started scratching at her belly, and pinching her skin, saying, 'Can you feel that? What about that?' When it was clear that Donna-Faye couldn't feel anything at all, he nodded to the obstetrician, who picked up a scalpel, and sliced Donna-Faye across the top of her shaved pubic area. The knife went through like butter.

From where I was standing, I could see the surgeon's blue gloves reaching deep into Donna-Faye's belly. There was a fair amount of blood, and then, up from the muck, came

Savannah. She was covered in mucus, and her pink mouth was open. She was waving her fists like she was furious, and she was trying hard to find her voice so she could scream.

I thought, She is so beautiful.

That's not just me saying that. Every news report has said how beautiful Savannah was. She had rusty spirals all over her head, and her skin was the colour of a blood plum.

I don't need to tell you that I fell in love with her. Of course I fell in love with her.

There was a bit to do after the birth. I suppose there always is. The obstetrician had to close up Donna-Faye; Savannah had to be bathed, and weighed. I looked for a place where I'd be out of the way, and when I turned, I saw that the two social workers that had brought Malok to the hospital had entered the room and were waving their pink and yellow documents about. They were saying they were the legal guardians of the newborn and they wanted access.

A young nurse stepped forward. Dad told me later it was the one he'd had a cuppa with. She put her hands up and said, 'Please, you can't be in here.' She tried to guide them towards the rubber doors. The doctor who had been trying to stitch Donna-Faye was saying, 'Leave! Leave!' Savannah was hiccuping, and then wailing. Malok was standing mute and confused, near the door. It was, in other words, quite a commotion.

Only Donna-Faye stayed calm. Never mind that she was lying there with her entrails still out, she simply accepted the chaos going on around her, just as she'd accepted the pregnancy, accepted that she was being cut open to give birth, accepted there was a baby in the room she wasn't allowed to hold.

David wasn't calm. He used his chest to back the social workers out of the room. I reached into my bag to find a mobile telephone. I was threatening to call our lawyer. That got me hustled out of the room, too. The social workers kept saying, 'the court says we're the legal guardians' and I suppose they were quite right about that.

We had thought, when we won the battle to have Savannah come home with us, that it meant we could take her home straightaway. We were floored when the Department told us it didn't work that way. Actually, was it my imagination, or did they seem to be delighted that it did not work that way? Two social workers told us there was paperwork to complete, before a child was handed from the Department's care to permanent care. The arrangement had to be sanctioned by the court. We said, 'But the court has already ruled on this. We are Savannah's permanent carers, for the rest of her life.'

They said, 'Yes, but the decision was made before Savannah was born. Now the court needs to see her birth certificate, and your birth certificate, and Donna-Faye's, and the agreement that the Department has drawn up, and all of that has to be stamped and approved, and until it is, Savannah remains in our care.'

It was a ridiculous system, obviously. We tried to argue with them. We said, 'What is the point of taking her from us, when she will end up back with us?' Because what made it worse was that Savannah wouldn't be allowed to stay in hospital with Donna-Faye during that time, and she wouldn't be allowed to stay with us, either. When I asked why not, the Department said Donna-Faye has been stripped of her parental rights. She is not the child's guardian, and you aren't either, not until the paperwork goes through. Technically, she's a ward of the State until you get your papers stamped.

They seemed so smug about it.

I was quite enraged. I said, 'So what on earth is supposed to happen to her? She's nobody's child, is that what you're saying?'

They said, 'No, she's in the care of the Minister, which means we will be placing her in foster care until all the paperwork is in order.'

I could hardly believe it. It seemed wrong to me – so wrong! – to take a baby girl from her biological mother and place her with a stranger, for what? Four days? Five days? A week? That time is so important. Those days are when the baby really bonds with a caregiver. So the Department had designed a system to allow Savannah to bond with somebody else, whom she'd never see again, and to break her bond with me, who would be her mother, for the rest of her life.

David said we'd take the matter to court, but courts being what they are, there was just no time. Our own barrister said, 'We'll never get in there in time. By the time you get a hearing, it will be time for you to take Savannah. Do you think you can bear it?'

I didn't think I could. Imagine it: your baby taken from the hospital, and gone God knows where? Because you've got no right to know. They won't divulge the name of the foster carer to you. They say, 'Oh, no, we can't do that. It's a privacy issue.' I was shouting at them. I said, 'How can we be sure that they are taking care of her?' The lady on the phone said, 'We have a procedure for registering all our carers' and so on, and on, as if that would comfort me, and, 'they have had police checks' which made my hair stand on end and, 'they have experience caring for newborns' which made it sound like a procession of babies going through there, like a sausage factory.

We argued our heads off, but it made no difference. We said it was ridiculous and cruel. The conversations got quite heated and once I had seen Savannah, and held Savannah, and smelled Savannah, I could not imagine handing her over to the care of people who seemed, to me, obsessed with rules and power, and not with the welfare of our little girl. But the Department said, 'The rules are the rules. Savannah cannot go home with you until the placement is certified by the court, and she cannot stay in the hospital because she is not sick. She will have to stay with registered carers.'

'I told them, yes, but who? Where? I wasn't entitled to know any of these things, and Donna-Faye wasn't told either. It took an enormous amount of wrangling simply to get the Department to say the couple were 'very nice' and lived 'north of the Bridge' and that's all they would say, and they intended to take her on the day of her birth.

I will always thank God for the intervention of the nursing staff, in particular the matron who was on duty that day. She point blank told them there was nobody there to accept their documents and organise the transfer, and they would have to come back, not the next day but the day after. Oh, they tried to insist, saying it was a contempt of court to ignore the order, but the matron, in her white shoes, stood firm. She said, 'I'm sorry, there is nobody here to authorise it, and you cannot take a baby from the ward without the hospital's permission.'

'I was in awe, hearing her stand up to them. Social workers can be frightening. Later, she told me she simply couldn't let a newborn infant, still with a crusted umbilical cord, an infant who hadn't yet started nursing, leave the hospital. It would be abuse, is what she said. I said, 'Child abuse?' and she said, 'Not only child abuse. Abuse of the mother.'

I felt a stab through the heart when she said that. I shouldn't have, but I did. Donna-Faye was Savannah's mother. It's just that I already felt that I was, too.

In any case, it was because of that proud matron that David, Donna-Faye and I were able to spend the first days of Savannah's life with Savannah, in the hospital. David slept in the armchair. Savannah slept in her Perspex cot, the one that doubled as a baby bath. Donna-Faye had the bed. I slept on the floor.

We took turns to change Savannah, and to hold Savannah and rock Savannah, to bathe and burp Savannah. When I say we, I mean, David and me, and Dad, too, when he was in visiting, which was all the time.

We'd look at each other and say, 'I can't believe she's here.' Again, I mean David and I would say that. Donna-Faye seemed not to know that Savannah was there, at least not all the time.

I attended most of the classes for new mothers. Donna-Faye didn't want to do it. I don't mean she objected. She simply showed no interest. Perhaps she was exhausted? She certainly seemed to sleep a lot. Meanwhile, I knew I had much to learn. I knew it from the first day I held Savannah and she started to cry and I thought, Okay, who do I hand her to? And it dawned on me, to nobody. It was up to me to comfort her.

There were practical things I needed to learn, too. How hot was too hot, for bath water? How cold was too cold? I went to the classes, and listened intently. A nurse showed us – me, and the other new mums, plenty of them still swelled from pregnancy, looking like they hadn't yet given birth, and all of us so tired – how to put a drop of water on the inside of our wrists, to test the temperature before we put our babies in the bath.

She taught me how to hold Savannah so her head wouldn't fall back, and how to cup water in my hands, to scoop over her. I was worried about her umbilical cord, dry and dark like a burnt match. The nurse taught me how to bathe the velvet skin around it, and told me that one day, I'd go to take Savannah from the cot, and it would be gone, stuck to her nappy, maybe, or else somewhere in her bed, and if I was lucky, I'd find it, but plenty of people didn't.

I saw other mothers at the newborn classes. They were besotted with their newborns, and as confused as me, and sometimes, I saw them sneaking a glimpse at Savannah. Maybe they were thinking, How does that work? White mother, white father, chocolate-coloured baby? They'd talk about their birth stories – they were still in robes, most of them, with cotton slippers on their swollen feet – and I was there in pants and a sweater, not joining in.

None of them came out and said, 'What's going on?' The ward wasn't like that, it was filled with women feeling tender, special, blessed. One or two of the new mums did come by and peek into our cot, and said, 'She's gorgeous' or 'She's beautiful' and I knew they were speaking the truth.

Of course the social workers came back, just as they'd promised to do. They came back twice, actually. The first time they said they had a legal right to examine Savannah and took her from the room. I had to bite the inside of cheeks to stop myself from screaming.

When they came back the next time, it was for our little girl. I thought I wouldn't be able to stand it. We had to watch while those witches from the Department marched in, all smug, scooped her up and carried her away. I could have torn flesh from their backs. David had to keep a hand wrapped around the fabric on the back of my jacket, to keep me anchored me to the floor.

I went home with David that night and I was on the couch, crying into his lap, when the telephone rang, and it was a woman whose voice I didn't recognise. It was a gentle and pleasant voice. She told me she had Savannah in her care, and straightaway I knew it was true. I asked her how on earth she had tracked us down, and she said, 'Oh, all the information is always on the paperwork and I always call the mother. It seems so stupid not to.'

I could have kissed her. Had she been in the room with me, and not on the telephone, I would have kissed her. I said, 'Oh, thank you so much, it means the world to me that you have called.' I said, 'How is she? Is she alright?' And then I had to say; 'I've got to tell you, I'm not the mother. My sister is the biological mother' but she said, 'Oh, I know very well the circumstances. You are the mother. Now, I want you to know that Savannah is beautiful, and she's safe, so you dry your tears and go to bed and the week will go by in no time.'

The week did not fly by. It was extremely difficult, that first week, to think of anything other than Savannah, knowing that she was sleeping elsewhere, and not really knowing where. Try to put yourself in that position. Every minute of every day, thinking: Where is she now? What is she doing? Is she hungry? How long does it take them to get to her when she cries? Do they change her often enough? Have they washed the jumpsuit I dressed her in? Is there anything left around her that still smells of me, still reminds her of me?

Does she miss me? Does she even remember me?

There were times when I sobbed so hard, and David held me so tightly, that I thought my ribs might break, or else his ribs would break, and I remember saying to him, 'Hold me harder, tighter, hold me' because that's what I wanted. I wanted my ribs to crack, so my heart could explode.

Donna-Faye hadn't come home with us. We paid for her to stay in the hospital for five days, to recover from her operation. It seemed to me that she was happy there. I went to visit her every day. Each time – and this amused me – she would take the menu and order everything on it, saying she was ordering for me. She would order steak and salad and two desserts and champagne and cheese. Her tray would come and she would work her way through the food, methodically, deliberately, happily.

One day I said to her, 'Donna-Faye, do you want to talk about Savannah?' Her cheeks were filled with cheesecake. She opened her mouth as if to say something but then kept chewing and smiling. Eventually, she wiped the back of her hand over the back of her mouth and said, 'No, she's gone now.'

I said, 'We're going to take great care of her. You can see her whenever you want.'

She stabbed her fork back in her cake and shook her head and said, 'She won't come back. They don't, you know.'

# Chapter 17

## Kat Atley

As it turned out, Savannah wasn't apart from us for a week. It was only four days in the end, before the paper work was signed and stamped, and our lawyers rushed it to the court house, where it was quickly received, and then, with what seemed like great reluctance, we were given the address of the couple who lived 'north of the Bridge' – in Manly, as it turned out – and who had been caring for our little girl.

We drove around there, too quickly, hearts thumping, and when David pulled into the drive, he nearly ran through the front window, and had to stamp his foot down on the brake, and we could not untangle ourselves from our seatbelts fast enough.

I will never forget that foster carer's kindness. Her name, from memory, was Mrs Waite. She had blown up four or five pink balloons, and hung them over the front door, so we'd know we were at the right place. One of the balloons was heart-shaped, and it said, 'It's a girl!'

I started to cry. Mrs Waite must have heard our car pull into the drive, because their door opened just as mine did, and as I fell toward her, she was falling toward me, down the pathway, with Savannah in her arms.

The first thing I thought was, you've grown so much! In just four days, I'd missed so much of her development, and I felt so jealous. But Mrs Waite held me and we held Savannah together, like a three-person sandwich, and David put his arms around the bunch of us, and led us toward the front door, arms entwined, walking sideways, like crabs, and then we were inside, and Mrs Waite was presenting us with an album that documented every day of Savannah's life, every day that she'd spent with them, and she told me what Savannah had been doing, and where she had been sleeping. She gave me a print of her foot that they'd made from a clay set, and a card with Savannah's newborn handprint on it, with the words: 'Savannah Atley, aged: two days' in gold pen, along the frame, and she told me she'd made sure that the blanket I'd given Savannah – the one I'd held to my chest and rubbed with my hands – had been with her in her crib, and with her in her pram.

'There's not a day she hasn't been able to smell you,' she said. 'Trust me, you've been with her in spirit, every day.'

We thanked her profusely. We held Savannah close to

our hearts. And then it was time to leave, and to start our new life with our little girl. More than anything, we wanted to do it without interference. We knew, and I think everybody knows, that we all would have managed so much better if we'd just been allowed to find our way, including a way for Savannah to know her natural parents.

The Department was adamant that it not be that way. Shortly after Donna-Faye was discharged from Eastern Private, and a day or so after Savannah spent her first night in her wicker crib at the foot of the bed I shared with David, the Department turned up with what amounted to a roster.

It set out the times that Savannah would spend with Donna-Faye, at an apartment in Darlinghurst they had found for her, and the time she was required to spend with Malok, who was still living in the unit in Tamworth, where he'd met Donna-Faye.

The first time I saw the roster, it made me cry. It seemed to have been drawn up by people who did not have children. There was no allowance for Savannah, and her routine. On Wednesday afternoons, at precisely 1 pm, I was required to drop her at Anglicare's Family Contact Centre, where Donna-Faye would be waiting, for a supervised contact visit.

No allowance was made for the fact that Savannah might be napping, or that she might not have had her feed, or that she might have a temperature. Then, too, no allowance was made for me, and how I needed to know what she was doing in that hour. I had no idea how to fill that time. I remember once thinking, Well, Kat, what did you do before she came along?, and I honestly couldn't remember. It was like she had always been with me.

I could hear her when she wasn't there, too.

I'd be rinsing a cup to put in the dishwasher and she'd coo. I'd put down my cup and go to her cot, and of course, she wouldn't be there, she'd be with Donna-Faye, 20 kilometres away.

I still hear that sound, even now.

Perhaps I always will.

Before the contact regimen started, we endured two, or perhaps three, meetings with the Department.

On the first occasion, David and I, and Savannah, were all required to be present so we could be 'observed' interacting with each other. It was entirely uncomfortable. The social worker sat in a chair with a clipboard, making notes. David and I had no idea what we were supposed to do, so we played peek-a-boo and when Savannah got bored with that, David let her rattle his keys.

Later, when I was able to read the report – our lawyer made sure I got to read all the reports – I saw the social worker had made fairly obvious remarks, about Savannah being able to make eye-contact, and hold up her own head.

On another accasion, a psychologist asked me to go through Savannah's routine. I explained that I had taken a year off work. My days were devoted to Savannah and, to some extent, David's were, too. We woke up each morning, wondering what she'd conquer next. All parents think their children are brilliant, but she really was brilliant. She'd learn so much in one day. David would go to work, and come home at night, and he'd say she was unrecognisable, that's how much she'd picked up.

I remember the first time she smiled at me.

It means so much, that first smile.

I'd been running around, doing all the things you have to do for a newborn, and it's often thankless, and then you get this wonderful smile, and suddenly the effort is all worthwhile.

I remember when she first held up her own head. I didn't have to cup her under the head anymore. Her neck had grown strong. She could look around.

She liked to grab at things.

I had to make sure I always had something for her to grab, or else she'd grab my pendant, and pull on it.

She'd grab my nose. My earrings. My earlobes.

It wasn't long before she was out of the Baby Bjorn. She was obviously going to be a tall girl, like her father. We turned her around, and had her facing out for a while – people said you could keep a baby in a sling like that, until they were six months old – but, to be honest, it was easier to get her out of the Baby Bjorn and into a stroller, because otherwise, it took forever to get anywhere. People would see David coming, his lovely English face and Savannah, cocoa-coloured, with her tight curls and her pink fists under his chin, and they'd have to stop and make remarks.

Most people were wonderful.

They'd assume we'd adopted her, and they'd say well-meaning things, like, 'Oh, what a brave thing' and, 'Did it take very long? It's so expensive, and it takes so long!' And depending on how we felt, we'd either answer them, or not, or agree with them, or say, 'No, she's our daughter' and let them deal with that.

We didn't mind the attention, but it did take a very long time to get anywhere.

It was the same when David let her ride on his shoulders. Once she had some control over herself, David would put her up, and she'd take big fistfuls of his hair, and use it like handles, to hang on. It was agony for him. He'd try to take her hands in his, and move them off his hair, but then she'd stick her fingers in his ears, or else in his eyes, and he'd find himself blinded.

We didn't do an enormous number of big outings. There were things we planned to do, like take Savannah back to England to meet David's family, and to New York, to meet our old friends. A girlfriend in Manhattan had sent some lovely things over, and I'd gone mad with the camera, taking photographs and uploading them onto Savannah's own website, charting her every move, and I was keen to show her off in person, too, but I wasn't yet ready to experiment with plane travel. I know that some parents do it. We thought, she's had such a journey already. Let's give her time, to become attached and secure.

One thing we did do, just before we lost Savannah, was catch the ferry to Taronga Zoo.

It was an incredibly hot day. I probably didn't know enough about what a baby needs, and what a baby can stand, during a day's outing. It would have been enough to visit the zoo but we thought she'd enjoy the ferry and the train, too.

# I CAME TO SAY GOODBYE

I don't know whether it was all the smells – the hay, the poo – or the monkeys screeching and carrying on – or too much moving around, into the train, onto the ferry, up the hill, but she really didn't like it. We'd hoped to be able to say, 'Look at the elephant! Look at the orang-utan!' but she was in David's arms, shaking her head, burying her face in his chest, hiding in his shirt and he was trying to peel her off, and say, 'Look, Savannah!' and she'd shake her head again and make it clear she didn't want anything to do with it. And then, after an hour or so, when we'd completely given up, taken refuge at the picnic tables, and she was in her stroller and taking her bottle, I had opened the lid on a little Tupperware container and had given her a chunk of melon to suck on, and a seagull – a plain seagull, white and grey with pink legs – came by, picking at hot chips people had left on the ground, and that's what she liked. She became all animated at that. She dropped her bottle and was pointing and making a noise that sounded like 'Qwa, Qwa'.

David and I were laughing and thinking, why did we pack up the stroller and organise all the nappies and bottles and cloths and changes of clothes, and come across town and stand in the heat and pay the entry fee, so she could get excited about a seagull? But that's what happens, isn't it? It's the small things they enjoy. It was the same at home. We could give her a lovely toy from Seed, or Fisher Price, something with all the bells and whistles, and she'd want the plastic mixing bowl to put on her head. Friends would bring gifts, and she'd tear at the paper with both palms, rip it to pieces, and ignore the present. I'd get so embarrassed!

She'd suck on an old wooden spoon for hours, and throw the teething ring down, and never look at it again.

David was often the first to reach her cot in the morning. He was great like that; he knew I'd been up in the night, feeding and changing. He'd rug her up and wander down to the water's edge to see the boats. He'd get a takeaway coffee and come home at around 7 am and I'd pop Savannah in her high chair, and try to spoon some mush into her, and I'd play with her until it came time for her morning nap. I'd put her down, and I'd think, well, Kat, try to catch up on some sleep, but of course I never did. There was so much to do! Beds to change, nappies to throw out, bottles to sterilise, maybe try to fit in a shower. Sometimes I'd scold myself, because I used to think, what is it that new mothers do all day? and now I was finding out.

Before I knew it, it would be noon, and Savannah would be awake, and wanting a bottle. She'd cry in her cot and kick off her blankets – that's another thing I'll never forget, how much she hated having blankets on her, how she'd always kick herself free, no matter how tightly she was swaddled – and I'd have to put her on my hip, and get the teat of the bottle into her mouth before the tears came. I didn't like to see her cry. The bubbles of milk, white against her lips, I liked to see.

Depending on what day it was, we'd spend the afternoon going out and about. Rockin' and rollin', David called it. Rockin' about town. Savannah would go in her stroller and we'd head out to a baby group or the toy library or to a local cafe to meet up with other mums.

It doesn't sound like much, but I was completely content. Savannah was a gorgeous, happy baby, and I was very much in love with her.

I don't say that parts of it weren't hard. It was hard to adjust to a new routine centred around a tiny baby. I missed my sleep! I missed being able to have a shower and go to the toilet in peace. I worried that Savannah would get bored with just me to play with all day. I'm sure you've heard things like that before. All parents say the same things. I suppose that's why, just before Savannah died, I had in mind enrolling her in a childcare centre, a few steps from our front door. There was a little boy there, adopted from China. His mother had seen me coming and going with Savannah and she'd stopped me one day and we'd had one of those conversations that new mothers have out on the street, just pouring our hearts out to each other, sharing our frustrations, declaring that we'd never been so much in love.

We agreed that it would be good for her boy, Xhou, and for Savannah, to be together at creche, just one day a week, so they would grow up knowing that everybody is different.

I'm so glad now that I never got around to arranging that day in creche.

It might have meant that I missed a day with Savannah. I couldn't bear to know I'd given up any time with her, voluntarily.

I know I have to tell you now what happened. I know that is why my father has given me this section to write.

I know I've been pushing away the moment when I'm going to have to write it down.

It's still so hard.

In July 2009 Savannah was five months old. She was due for her fourth visit with Malok, in Tamworth. If the contact visits with Donna-Faye were difficult, then the contact with Malok was torture. He had returned to Tamworth after the birth. The Department had found him a job in the kill room at the meat-works. From what I gather, he worked hard at it. He turned up on time. He finished every shift. His boss was pleased with him. He was entitled to see his daughter one Saturday a month, including overnight.

The Department offered to do what they called 'the transfer' meaning they wanted to pick Savannah up from her home with us, and drive her, in one of their dinky little three-door hatchbacks, to the airport, for the flight to Tamworth. A social worker would accompany her, and stay overnight, and then fly back with her the following day.

David was agog. 'What must it cost?' he said.

It didn't matter what it cost. We would not do things that way. I could not have allowed Savannah to travel on a plane without me. What if something happened to her? We said, no, thank you very much. We will manage it, and we did. Once a month, we flew with Savannah to Tamworth. I remember the first time, when she was just four weeks old, she was so small the air hostess had to fold back her blankets to properly see her face, and when she did, she said, 'Oh, divine. Did you adopt her?'

I answered honestly. I said no, she's mine.

I don't recall that Malok ever met us at the airport. Maybe he still wasn't old enough to drive? I know only that he didn't drive. He walked everywhere. He walked to work. He walked home. He walked around Tamworth. We'd sometimes see him striding along the freeway as we were heading into town. And he was almost never alone.

Before our first visit, I'd asked the Department if I could stay with Savannah, while she had her contact visit with Malok. I thought she was too young to be separated from me, and that Malok was too immature to handle a baby. They denied the request, of course. They said it was 'important for Savannah to come to know her identity as a part-Sudanese girl by being immersed in their culture'. They said there was a 'power imbalance' between David and I, on one hand, and Malok and his family, on the other.

'There is something wrong with people who think like that,' said David, when he read their report. 'Does it never occur to them that we all love Savannah, and that we all want to be part of her life? That instead of putting up barriers between us, they might encourage us to learn to love each other?'

Given that we couldn't stay with Malok and his family in Tamworth, David and I organised a room at the local Best Western. I called the staff ahead of our first visit and explained that we'd be coming monthly, and asked if we could have the same room, because we'd have a little baby with us.

The staff at the Best Western were fantastic about it. They made a fuss of Savannah but then, so did everyone. She was a special girl. It seemed to me that she generated love and happiness wherever she went.

It isn't easy to travel with an infant. We had to buy a travel cot. It had to go on as oversized baggage and was always the last thing to come off the plane. Then I'd make David unwrap it and unpack it and make sure it hadn't been damaged before Savannah could go in it.

I'd have Savannah in my arms or David would have her in the Baby Bjorn, against his chest. We'd have her nappies and her bottles, her formula and her clothes – something for hot weather, and something for cold weather, something in case it rained, something in case she threw up, or got dirty, and on it went.

The first time we had to hand Savannah over, it broke my heart. The exchange took place in the Department's offices, in Tamworth. Malok was there with a Departmental worker and some members of his extended family. I'd been led to believe that his mother wasn't in Australia, and nor was his father, and it was possible, actually, that they'd been killed in the war.

He lived with aunts, uncles, cousins, and others, all of whom were referred to as his kin, and I understood from the reading we'd done that 'family' meant something different to him. It wasn't brothers, sisters, parents. It was a range of people, all of whom were due the respect he'd pay his parents.

They took Savannah away, and we had expected to pick her up from the Department's office on Sunday but the social worker rang and said, 'No, it's okay, you can pick her up from Malok's unit', and so, from then on, we'd drop her at Malok's, and we'd pick her up from there, too.

So what happened during our last visit to Tamworth? We boarded the plane on the Friday, as we had always done.

# I CAME TO SAY GOODBYE

We picked up the hire car and checked into the Best Western. The staff fussed over Savannah, saying how lovely she was, how big she was getting.

Savannah slept well, and she was up with the birds. We had breakfast in the hotel. David put Savannah in her Baby Bjorn. She was almost, but not quite, too big for it. We walked hand-in-hand from the motel to the unit where Malok lived.

Malok was there, but he wasn't dressed for a weekend with Savannah. He was wearing white overalls, like he was ready for work. We knew that he sometimes worked a Saturday shift. Why we still had to deliver Savannah to him when he'd be at work most of the day, I can't tell you, except that the Department insisted that it was important for Savannah to know her 'extended Sudanese family' and their 'culture'.

Malok took Savannah from us. He looked pleased to see her. He always did. He kissed her on top of the head. He handed her to a woman, who was presumably an aunt or a cousin. David and I said our goodbyes, and went back to the Best Western to wait out our day and night away from her.

And while we were gone, they cut her.

They cut her.

From the moment we went to pick her up on the Sunday morning, after the long Saturday night without her, I knew that something was terribly, horribly wrong.

The unit was full of people. It was always full of people, but this time, it was really filled to its capacity, and it was still early. We were never late. There were dozens of women and a strange sense of heightened excitement in the room.

There was a great deal of food about. The smell of spices, and of food cooking, was overwhelming, and Malok, he seemed to be the centre of the festivities.

When David and I came to the door, women came towards us with their arms outstretched. They guided us in. We were confused. We were bewildered. We smiled back at them. We couldn't figure out what all this was about. I was looking around for Savannah and somebody – a woman, I think, although I don't precisely remember – said something that set the other women off, and suddenly the room was full of screamingly happy women, like colourful birds; squawking, smiling, laughing and nodding. I could not understand what was going on, only that Malok was grinning at me, showing enormous white teeth, and then he was handing Savannah to me, presenting her like a gift, nodding, smiling, like she was somehow different from the day before, and then a group of women rushed forward, and it seemed they wanted to kiss me, and kiss Savannah, and I felt extremely uncomfortable. I wanted to get out of there.

I held Savannah close. I looked into her face. She seemed normal enough. She wasn't crying. She wasn't clingy. She was just as she always was: delightful. It wasn't until I put her down on the hotel bed to change her nappy that I could see what they'd done.

There wasn't a great deal of blood, but there was blood.

There wasn't a gaping wound. There weren't any wire stitches or deep cuts but there was a scratch, a sore, on the tip of her private parts.

I screamed for David.

He must have thought I'd uncovered a knife wound, because I was screaming, they've cut her, they've cut her, they've cut her, and the motel staff came running and people from the room next door came running, too.

I held Savannah close to my chest, her bare bottom on my arm, and I was rushing this way, and that way, wild with grief, wild with anger. I couldn't think straight. I couldn't think what to do. It was David who said, we've got to get her to the hospital, and it was David who somehow managed to find the keys and get us into the car and get the car started. I couldn't bear to put Savannah into the baby seat. I held her on my lap, tighter than I'd ever held anything. I kept my lips pressed upon her head. Tears were rolling down my face and it was making Savannah cry, but I couldn't stop.

We pushed into the waiting room, pushed past other people that were waiting, and forced ourselves on the staff.

The doctor we saw in Tamworth that day was brilliant. He was sympathetic and capable, and caring, and lovely. He bathed Savannah gently so we could see exactly what had gone on, and he told us it was the tiniest, tiniest pinprick, the size of a bee sting, just enough to satisfy local custom, nowhere near enough to demand stitches.

Look, he said, it's not even bleeding anymore. Look, you can hardly even see it.

The hospital telephoned a Sudanese support worker, to counsel us. There were half-a-dozen of them in Tamworth and their job, it seemed, was to liaise between the refugees and the wider community, arranging such things as accommodation and work visas and immunisations, and to talk to the white community about Sudanese customs. And so, while I held my beautiful daughter and sobbed into her hair, this woman, who was herself Sudanese, talked to me about 'the culture' in Sudan. She said the local community had been told not to do what they had done to Savannah. They had been told that it was banned here, totally banned, punishable by law, but it was hard to make them stop. She said some women had taken to doing a little pinprick on baby girls, quickly and discreetly, before anybody noticed, to try to keep the practice going on some limited scale. They seemed to be hoping that the white community, our community, would turn a blind eye to it because it wasn't done with sharp stones, it wasn't the whole flesh cut away. I didn't want to hear any of it. I'm ashamed to say I lost my patience. I shouted at the counsellor. I said, 'How can you even think this is alright?' She told me, 'It's not alright.' She told me it wouldn't have been Malok, he likely wouldn't have even known about it until it was done. She told me it's the women who do it, because it is women who want it, who expect it and the men are kept out of it. Probably the first Malok knew of it was when he came in from the kill floor to the big celebration.

She said that what had been done to Savannah was 'very minor' and it could have been 'much worse'. They could have cut all of her parts away, sewn her completely shut and made it impossible for her to urinate, or when the time came, to menstruate. The way she said it, it was like she was pleased with the progress she'd made, having girls not butchered, just stabbed a bit. She said that what had happened to Savannah was proof that the message was getting through. The community knew they weren't allowed to do these things and so they were trying to hide what they were doing. They weren't cutting girls anymore, now they were just pricking them.

I thought, They just prick them! They take a dirty sewing needle, and they prick them and make them bleed, and they think it's normal, it's acceptable, and it's necessary. They don't do it on a dirt floor. They don't do it with a piece of stone. But they still do it, and then they celebrate.

David was saying, 'I can't believe I'm hearing this. My daughter has been butchered and you seem to think that's fine.' The support worker said, 'Please, calm down.' She hadn't been butchered. She had been scratched, and maybe we should consider what it meant. Savannah had a white mother – two white mothers, she said – and despite this, she had been accepted into her community! And wasn't that marvellous? And it wasn't a cut, it was a scratch, a prick, and it was still required in some cultures, and really, there was no harm done, no sewing, no infection, all healed up already, and who were we to judge?

I told this woman straight. I said, 'I do not care for your analysis. I do not care for your political correctness. I look at you and I assume, since you are a working woman, that you are a feminist, and it seems to me that feminists have long been on the right side in this debate, and now it seems to me that you are on the side of child abuse, and dressing it up as culture, and tradition.'

I said I was taking Savannah out of the hospital that instant, and I was putting her on the plane to Sydney, where

I would report the matter to police. I said I would push with all my might to ensure that charges were laid. When I walked out with Savannah, I did not look back.

David called our personal GP – Savannah's GP – from the airport, to alert him to the situation and, God bless him, he was not at all caught up in the rights of people to practise their culture. He was as concerned – as alarmed, as horrified – as we were, and he agreed to meet us at Sydney Children's Hospital, where he could examine Savannah.

We did not telephone the Department. In my view, it was partly the Department's fault that this had happened, because clearly, the people that Savannah was being left with did not understand Australian law.

We also called our lawyer. We told him what had happened and, as with our GP, as with any normal person, he could hardly believe it. He told us he would go to the NSW Supreme Court and request an emergency hearing, and he would make sure that Malok's right to see Savannah was severely curtailed, so much so that he wouldn't be able to see her, except in Sydney, with supervision. I asked him when and he said immediately. He acted so fast that the Department really had to scramble. They got a call from the NSW Supreme Court saying an action was underway, and they had to rush to get somebody there.

I understand from our lawyer that they argued pretty passionately in favour of the status quo, which, frankly, made me sick. They argued that it wasn't clear what had happened to Savannah; that nobody could be sure who was involved; that the police would have to investigate; that charges would have to be laid; that cultural practices had to be taken into account; that it was important to Savannah to have ongoing contact with her Sudanese family, all the stuff we'd heard so many times, but the judge didn't muck around. He said, 'The child returns to the care of Ka'aren Atley and David Bennett, with no further contact with Malok Ibrahim, not while this is being sorted out', and we were fairly certain, from the way he said it, that there would be no further contact, not unsupervised, not ever.

David and Savannah and I waited at the hospital while the hearing was underway. You'll know, I suppose, that it was the last time we spent any time with Savannah. She was, by then, a little under five months old and she was beautiful.

She was in the room they call the Pandas, with five other infants. Not newborns. The newborns were down the hall in Joeys. She was with other children who'd been injured somehow. One boy had both legs in a cast that came up to his chest. Another had a bandage over his eye. Someone had drawn a skull and crossbones on it. He looked like a little pirate.

At some point, David went downstairs and bought a stuffed giraffe from the flower shop near the kiosk. Savannah hadn't liked it as much as we'd thought. Maybe it scared her a little. We put it on the windowsill. She was keen to play with David's keys, though. She put them in her mouth, and when I took them from her, she cried. She was playing like normal, in other words.

We chatted with the couple that were sitting near the next cot. Their child had taken a tumble. They were anxious.

They asked us what was wrong with Savannah. I said that it seemed like she had a urinary tract infection. I wasn't about to broadcast the facts to the world.

The verdict – the decision, they call it – came in around 6 pm. Our lawyer said we were free to take Savannah home. We wouldn't need to worry about the contact orders. Everything was suspended. Savannah would stay with us while the court had another look at what was best for her.

I closed up the phone, and started pulling Savannah's things together but then our GP came by and said it would be best for her to stay another night.

I wasn't at all keen. The cut – the pinprick – you could hardly even see it anymore. But our GP said it was in a sensitive place, and the catheter they'd inserted to draw urine away from the area while they examined her had only just been removed, and she'd have to wear a nappy, and the nappy would get wet, and he was worried about infection.

He said, 'Look, I don't want to worry you. It's healed perfectly, I'm sure of that. There won't be any scarring. I can't see any problems, longer term.' But still, he said, it was probably wise for Savannah to stay on the ward for one night. It wouldn't do any harm.

And so we went home. We went home to our empty house in Hunters Hill, and we sat in silence on the couch, and then, at a loss as to what to do, I got up, and went into the kitchen, and began restacking Savannah's baby food. I went through her plastic bowls, and her curved spoons, washing and wiping them. I wiped the high chair down. I folded her bibs and eventually, I curled up on the floor of her room, holding her blanket, and at some point, I must have fallen sleep.

It must have been early – I'd say 3 am, maybe earlier than that – when we heard a knock on the door, and David, who had fallen asleep in the lounge, went to open it and it was Donna-Faye.

People have asked me, how did she look? She looked much she always looked, somewhat vague and disoriented, weary, confused. I must have looked a bit disoriented myself. I'd slept on the floor in my clothes, and I'd been brought to the door, when it was still dark outside. I was concerned to see Donna-Faye there, not only because it was 3 am, but also because it seemed that she had driven to our house in an old Corolla, and I wasn't aware that she could drive, or had access to a car.

I said, 'Well hello, Donna-Faye', and I stepped back to welcome her into the house. I was thinking to myself: Does she know what had happened to Savannah in Tamworth? I'm not really sure. I don't really know. We hadn't told her. We hadn't even told Dad, not yet. The court knew, and the Department knew, so maybe Donna-Faye did know. Somebody must have said something, because she said, 'She's gone back into hospital?'

Just like that, 'She's gone back into hospital?' like, 'She's gone to the milk bar?' There was no concern in her voice.

I said, 'Yes' and I stepped further back into the hall to let her in, but Donna-Faye didn't step forward. She didn't say, 'Well, what happened to her? Did she hit her head or take a tumble? Does she have a cold? Why is she in the hospital?'

She simply stood, holding a large, stuffed toy, an incredibly ugly, purple dinosaur thing, one of those toys that doesn't come from a toy shop, but from a fete or a show, the kind of thing that people win when they put balls into the mouths of clowns, and it wasn't new. There were small balls of polystyrene popping out through a broken seam under the toy's arm, so perhaps it was something she'd picked up at a fete one day, years earlier, during a break in her pony shows. She held it towards me. She said, 'Can you give her this?'

I took the animal and, straightaway, it started leaking white balls, lighter than air, on the runner in the hall. I said, 'Come in, Donna, don't stand there on the porch.'

She said, 'I'm okay. I just wanted to make sure you got this to give to Savannah.'

I said – and maybe this was the wrong thing to say – I said, 'It's gorgeous, Donna, but I'm not sure it's right for Savannah. Look, it's leaking. She might swallow one of these balls.'

She said, 'You could fix it up.'

I said, 'I could get that done, yes.'

She continued to stand there for a moment, and then she said, 'Well, bye.'

I said, 'Do you know what happened?' because at that point, I still wasn't sure that Donna-Faye really knew what happened. She hadn't even said, 'Is my baby alright?' Behind me, David said, 'Ka'aren, careful' but Donna-Faye merely shrugged and said, 'I suppose it's just what happens.'

Now, what does that mean?

# I CAME TO SAY GOODBYE

*I suppose it's just what happens?*

Maybe to Donna-Faye, that made sense. She had babies, and they went into hospital, and she didn't see them again.

Maybe by then, in the steel grip of her madness, she thought that's what happened to everybody's baby.

I said, 'Are you sure you won't come in, Donna?'

She said, 'I better get on. Just, if you can get it fixed and give it to Savannah, will you?'

I said, 'Well, Donna, I'll certainly try.'

She nodded and turned away and walked back to the Corolla. She opened the driver's door, and she got in the car. I turned and went inside to raise my eyebrows at David and show him the purple toy she'd brought. I heard the engine start and then, just before she should have pulled away, Donna-Faye got out of the car again, and came back onto the porch and knocked for a second time.

I opened up. I was confused. I saw that Donna-Faye's car was still running, and that the driver's door was open and the headlights were on, and it was surreal, so early in the morning to hear such noises, and see such things.

I said, 'Well, hello again. Are you coming in?'

She said, 'No.'

I said, 'Did you forget something?'

She said, 'I came to say goodbye.'

Now, as I've said, it wasn't unusual for Donna-Faye to get muddled. I knew that she was on some kind of medication . . . on all sorts of medication. She had been taking it when she lived with us. She had already said bye and now here she was again, not a minute later, saying, Bye.

I said, 'Okay, well then, bye, Fat.'
She said, 'Okay. Bye.'
And she was gone.

# Chapter 18

## Kat Atley

THE FIRST PERSON TO TELL ME that Savannah was missing wasn't the police, and it wasn't the Department. I heard it at six in the morning on 702 on the ABC, along with every other person in Sydney.

An announcer broke into the program to say, 'Police are searching for a baby that has apparently gone missing from Sydney Children's Hospital in Parramatta.' That was all; there was no more than that. 'Police are searching for a baby that has apparently gone missing from Sydney Children's Hospital in Parramatta.'

People have asked me how I knew it was Savannah. I don't know, except that I knew. I knew that instant, that very second, that it had to be Savannah, and just as my heart

261

was racing towards the back of my throat, just as my stomach turned towards the floor, the telephone rang, and it was the police.

They didn't need to tell me to drive to Donna-Faye's. I was half-dressed. I had on one shoe. David was in the driveway. I had the mobile telephone in one hand, and the dogs were yapping after me. David was turning the keys over in his hands, trying to get one into the ignition.

I was talking – shouting, crying – at the police on the phone. I was saying, 'How long has she been gone? Are you sure it was my sister?' My mind was turning over the possibilities, shuffling through them like so many black Tarot cards. I forced those thoughts back. I thought, No, no, she's fine, she'll be at the apartment. She's just gone and lost her mind again.

David was racing towards her apartment when the second report came over the radio, 'Baby thrown from The Gap.'

*Baby thrown from The Gap.*

*Baby thrown from The Gap.*

Even now, when I close my eyes and I hear those words, it's like an axe going through my heart.

*Baby thrown from The Gap.*

It was like the world exploded. Before we could think, before we could even go into shock, there were police around the car. How they got there, I cannot say. I do not know. Did they track us by our mobile? By our licence plate? David says we stopped dead in the middle of the road but I don't remember that. All I know is that they were suddenly there, alongside us, roaring with us towards The Gap, all of us, thinking, No, no, no, no, no.

When I look back now, I can see the blue lights going. I don't remember sirens but surely there were sirens. I was praying, no, no, no, and please, God, don't let it be too late, but of course it was.

It was too late.

The CCTV at the hospital shows what happened. Donna-Faye walked through the front revolving door in her slippers and her robe. The time of her arrival can be seen at the bottom of the screen. It was four o'clock in the morning. She walked down the hall, past where the matron was playing Solitaire. She walked through the Joeys, into the Pandas, and lifted Savannah out of her cot, and put her in the shopping bag. She left the way she came, except with the bag now hanging heavily from her hand, and the stuffed giraffe sticking up, through the handles.

There isn't much footage from the car park. We know that Donna-Faye put Savannah in the baby seat in the back of the Corolla and turned left onto Parramatta Road and it seems that she arrived at The Gap just as the day was dawning. There is a carpark near the main, wooden viewing platform. Donna-Faye stopped there, parked her car, and sat for a while.

There were two American tourists, cameras around their necks, and they saw her sitting, and they saw her get out of the car, unclip the capsule and walk out to the viewing platform. She didn't say anything to anyone. She didn't look upset. She simply stood for several minutes and then, before either of the Americans could say: 'Don't!' or 'No!' or 'Stop!' she stepped forward, lifted the baby capsule over the barrier, and calmly dropped it over the edge.

# Chapter 19

## Med Atley

KAT HAS GIVEN YOU THE DETAILS of what happened to Savannah, Your Honour. I'm grateful to her for that. I wouldn't have been able to do it.

I want to tell you what happened afterwards. Media were like flies around a carcass for a while, just all over the property. I was tempted, sometimes, to go out and fire the shotgun, just to clear the air.

What they wanted, I couldn't tell you. To know what happened, I suppose, like I'm supposed to explain it? How could you explain it?

One woman, I won't say which one, but a famous one, she came personally to the door. She put a note underneath, handwritten, so I've got her signature. She said she'd guarantee me privacy, she'd guarantee she'd get the rest of them off the lawn if I just agreed to talk to her. She'd make sure the rest of them went away.

She didn't mention money, but money was implied. She said the deal we'd do, it would be between me and her personally. It would be sensitive. It would give the Atley family an opportunity to explain. I thought to myself, Explain what? That Donna-Faye put my granddaughter over the cliff?

I'm not stupid. I knew she didn't actually want an explanation. She wanted ratings.

She wasn't the only one who tried it on. Some reporters brought flowers, and left them on the porch with 'Deepest Condolences from Channel Blah Blah' and mobile numbers to call.

The cops who came to the property told me: you don't have to say anything. They said, 'If it's any consolation, the Sudanese community up in Tamworth are being harassed to death as well.' You wouldn't have known it from the coverage but most of the refugees we get in Australia aren't into the mutilation thing. They wouldn't dream of doing to anyone what was done to Savannah, before Donna-Faye put her over The Gap. It's not part of their culture. They had spokesmen out, trying to make that clear, that part of the reason they wanted their girls raised here was to get away from that kind of thing, but of course, the media – and some White Power, Neo-Nazi types – harassed them anyway.

Newspaper columnists were churning other stuff out, on family law, on courts, on welfare, on post-natal depression, on whether The Gap ought to be fenced. They dragged out people whose kids had jumped off The Gap, committed suicide, to say a fence was long overdue. They dragged out the mayor of Tamworth to say the meatworks wouldn't operate if it weren't for the Sudanese. They got a picture of Savannah off Kat's Facebook, and showed it over and over again.

They talked about what could have been done to save Savannah, too. That was the most hurtful part. You can see from the footage how hard the cops tried. One guy was hanging from a helicopter, really hanging, face down in the water, being dunked like a tea bag, trying to get her.

I've seen the footage where, on the fifth or sixth attempt, he grasps the handle. You can hear a cheer go up, which shows how badly people wanted to put things right. But he shook his head and signalled no to the people up on top of the cliff. Savannah wasn't in the capsule. The straps that were meant to hold her down had been torn away. Then somebody pointed further out and the camera zoomed in. You could see her little body, rising and falling on the waves.

So I felt pretty cross with the media that said the rescue crews could have done more, or been quicker or whatever.

The cops told me to ignore it all. They said there'd only be a couple of events where I'd have to endure being in the public eye, one of which was the funeral, but that was alright. I understood that people wanted to be at the funeral, and people who couldn't get there would want to see it on the TV.

Blue and his wife, Claudette, and their new baby, Amy, and her daughter, Indiana, from before she met Blue, came down for it, and Kat and David drove out. The cemetery isn't at Forster, it's across the bridge, at Tuncurry. Through the window of the hire car, I saw that somebody had painted a sign that said, 'So Inocent!' A few of the shopkeepers had closed their doors, shut up shop, so they could walk with us from the gravel car park to the place where we buried Savannah.

David carried Savannah's coffin in his arms.

There was no particular religion to the service. We didn't bother with the Catholic mass. Some local schoolkids, in short shorts and college blazers, belted out a song on a drum kit, with electric guitars. It was a rock song that maybe meant something to them, and nothing to me, but that was alright. Young people need to grieve.

Most of the blokes from the Shire turned up, as did girls I hadn't seen since primary school, now grown up with children of their own. There were girls who had been to school with Donna-Faye too. I couldn't believe how many of them turned up, even though a lot of them would have felt sick about what Donna-Faye had done.

I hadn't known to expect Malok and his family, but you could hardly miss it when they arrived. The media people, who had been standing back, and trying to be respectful, leapt forward, and the cameras, the flashes went nuts – click-click-click-click – and I thought for a moment that perhaps a celebrity was arriving. The Prime Minister, maybe. He'd been on the news, saying how tragic it all was. But it wasn't him.

It was Malok, with eight or 10 of his family members, all of them absolutely grief-stricken, with tears pouring down their night-black faces. I stood up, and they came to me and one of the women – a real large woman, with coloured material knotted around her head – opened her arms, and I collapsed against her skin, and her breast heaved and wobbled against me.

That was the photograph that appeared in the newspaper the next day. The old bloke in the bad suit with the scruffy beard, and the enormous Sudanese lady, holding each other and crying. They put it under the headline, 'United in Grief.'

I remember the Mayor – technically my boss, I suppose – said a few words. It was pretty hot. Sunscreen was dripping off his face. Towards the end of the service, the Salvation Army captain got up, and signalled to the little school children, in boater hats and bobby socks, to get up from the floor and come over, hand-in-hand, and fill Kat's lap with paper butterflies.

The American couple from The Gap – the ones that had seen Fat and Savannah – came up afterwards and put yellow roses in Kat's arms, too. They were from Texas, and I suppose that meant something to them. The man said, 'I'm sorry for your loss' and I said, 'Well, that's kind of you.'

We went back to the house after the funeral. Kat and David stayed the night, as did Blue, and the little ones. It was terrific to have them there. You could grab them when they passed by, and sort of breathe them in. Claudette was really good about the baby. She let people have a hold, let us pass her round like a parcel, and cry a bit on her. Only me and Kat couldn't really do it.

Edna stayed with us, too. We pulled the mattresses off the beds – Blue's mattress, and Kat's that had become Donna-Faye's – and put them on the lounge room floor, around the TV, and we slept like that, on the floor.

People brought food to the door. We let them leave it.

Then Edna went home, and Blue took the girls, and Kat and David left, too, and I was alone again.

I had bad nightmares for a while. I'd be thinking, No, no, no, no, not that, not Savannah, I've got to get to her, and then, of course, I'd wake up, and I'd be swamped by the knowledge it was too late.

It happened when I was wide awake, too. I'd be holding the kettle or putting a pot into the microwave or driving the car down to the mailbox and I'd remember, she's gone, and I'd have to stop, and bow my head down, and then I'd have to cry.

# Chapter 20

## Med Atley

THE SECOND TIME WE HAD TO face the media was when Fat got committed to the mental hospital, which happened instead of her going to Silverwater, which is the jail.

Kat helped out with that. She was hurting a lot but she had her QC put up the argument, on the day that we lost Savannah, that Fat was obviously not of sound mind.

The QC found a bed at a clinic in Sydney, the kind of place that takes TV presenters and rugby players who need to pull themselves together in private. The QC said Fat should go there while the psychiatrists figured out whether she was well enough to face a trial.

From the street, the clinic looks like a big old Victorian mansion. It's got the iron lace balcony and the lawns and the heavy gates.

I don't know who tipped off the media but they were outside on the day Donna-Faye got taken in. They must have thought it was a big story. They had white vans with satellite dishes and make-up tents for the news anchors.

They got the ambulance driving through the gates. It parked on the gravel in front of the main entrance and the back doors swung open and Donna-Faye stepped out and walked the length of the car park in the pouring rain. If you watch that footage, you can see she does nothing to stop herself from getting wet. She doesn't hold up an umbrella and nobody holds one over her. She doesn't duck her head. She walks up the drive with police on either side of her, and her nightie gets drenched and sticks to her body and it's practically at the point where it's completely see-through when they finally get her onto the porch and through the front door.

We sent Edna in with her. Nobody knew Edna from Adam so she wasn't likely to be harassed. I couldn't go because they kept saying I was a witness. Kat couldn't go because she might be a witness, too. So Edna went and Edna told me the whole staff was standing in the foyer, waiting for Donna-Faye.

A nurse opened the heavy front door and helped Donna-Faye through it, and it was the same nurse that saw that it wasn't only rain that was making my girl so wet. Donna-Faye had wet her pants.

The nurse took her by the elbow and helped her over to a chair. Edna said it was one of those chairs with the padding on the arms and the carving on the back, where you'd never imagine seating somebody who had wet themselves, and who was soaked, besides, but the nurse didn't make a move to protect the chair, she sat Donna-Faye down, and put a blanket over her knees and said, 'We'll get you dried off, don't you worry.'

Edna told me that Donna-Faye wasn't crying. She was standing there, bewildered, and then she was sitting down in her wet nightie, and her knees were white, and her hair was plastered down over her face, and Edna was thinking, She must be freezing, and they came with a blanket.

The registrar came out of his office. He strode towards the chair, and he looked into Donna-Faye's face and he said, 'Miss Atley?' but Donna-Faye didn't answer. She was still shivering. The registrar got down on his knees to bring himself eye to eye and he said, 'Donna-Faye?' and Donna-Faye looked up, and looked around, and she must have seen where she was sitting, on this chair that looked like a throne, in wet clothes, with wet hair, with a whole lot of people standing around, wearing white canvas pants and rubber-soled shoes.

There was a reception desk with a huge spray of flowers. There were signs telling people not to use their mobile phones. Donna-Faye seemed to be taking it all in and it seemed to dawn on her that she was in a hospital, and that's when she spoke. She said something like, 'That's right' or else, 'Alright.'

Edna got down on her old knees, too, because it was the first time Fat had really said anything, and she said, 'Fat? It's Auntie Edna here. What did you say, love?' and

Donna-Faye, she said, 'That's right, I'm meant to be here' which didn't really make any sense, except of course, she was absolutely right. She's absolutely where she's meant to be, and maybe where she should have been all along.

Anyway, just as the whole mess started with a bang, it stopped. The media, I mean. They stopped coming. I was grateful. It gave me time to get my thoughts together.

The cops came by to tell me there was no chance that Fat would face charges. One of them said, 'They'd have to be kidding' and I've got to say, I'm no expert, but it does seem to me that Fat's not all there anymore, so what would be the point?

And if she was all there, if she did know what she'd done, well, it's not like anyone could punish her anymore than she'd punish herself.

About a week or so after Savannah's funeral, after Fat went into the clinic, a nice woman from there came around to talk to me, and she stayed for about a week, sleeping on the couch, which was obviously well beyond the call of duty. I don't know for sure if David paid for it, but I'd say David paid for it.

The lady told me I could talk to her about Savannah and about Fat, instead of talking to the media, which some people seem to do just so they can talk it out.

I told her straight. 'This is my fault. I didn't raise her right.'

I told her about Fat's mum walking out – no sign of Pat through all this by the way. It was all over the news, all around the world, but not a word form Pat, which tells you all you need to know about her level of care – and I told her that I never made the fact that Pat walked too much of a big deal, and maybe I should have made a big deal of it, got the counsellor out or something, but people didn't do that much then and Fat was only two at the time.

I told her how I sort of missed that Fat was growing up from girl to woman, and that the first signs of it – the Chinaman at the front door – scared me half to death.

I told her about that Haines idiot, and how I'd always believed that Haines grabbed Seth that night when Fat was at work and gave him a shake to shut him up, or flung him down to keep him quiet, and I was dead scared that if I talked to Fat about that, if I'd really pinned her down and made her spit it out, well, I'd have had to do something about it, which would have meant confronting Haines and how I didn't have the stomach for it, because I knew, back then, in a battle of wills between me and Haines, I'd lose Fat. She'd have sided with him.

That's what girls do, when it comes down to Dad versus some loser boyfriend, and I didn't want to lose her. I wanted to keep her close and maybe that's because I thought my best chance to save her was to somehow stay in her life, and maybe it also means that I wouldn't have been able to stand to lose Pat, and then to lose my little girl, too.

I talked about what Fat must have been thinking that day, up at The Gap. She wasn't thinking straight, that's for sure.

The lady said there's no use turning that over in your mind. She wasn't herself. I said you mean she was crazy and she nodded and said, 'What she did was crazy' and it was nice to finally hear somebody say that.

After she went back to her office, or her home, or wherever it was she normally worked, I was alone again, and some people might tell you that I started to drink and maybe I did drink more than I should have done.

For a while there, I drank every night. I smoked more than I do now, and I suppose that's significant, too. Smoking killed my father, remember, and I remember thinking, I hope it kills me, too.

One night I got so drunk I set the bed on fire, and I was angry when I woke up in clouds of black smoke, the place stinking to high heaven. Not angry that I had a fair bit of cleaning to do. I was angry that the bed hadn't taken the house up, with me in it.

My mindset, basically, was, 'I can't live with this' and so it made sense. 'Kill yourself, Med. Don't do it in a way that's going to traumatise the family, already torn to bits. Don't leave a corpse hanging from the Hills Hoist for some poor bastard to cut down. Don't blow your head off with a shotgun and probably miss and end up a vegetable. Do it in a slow, acceptable way, like men have done for a hundred years. Smoke and drink yourself to death.'

Well, I didn't die, obviously. It seems to me now that people don't die when they want to die. Edna says it's God that keeps them going because he loves us. I told her, if that's so, he's got a strange way of showing how much he loves us. Edna said no, he's letting you find the edge of your rage and when you do, you'll take a step back from it and I suppose that turned out to be true, because the day did come when I decided I'd quit drinking so much, and put a padlock on the bar fridge and thought, okay, enough with that.

I tried to go back to the Shire but the pressure of it was a bit much. People are kind, but it seems like they always want to know things that I can't explain.

One example, a lady in the lift at work might say, 'Oh, I heard what happened. I'm so sorry' and I'd say thank you and then she might say something like, 'Did she have a breakdown?'

I'd think, Well, her mum walked out when she was a toddler, and her old man tried to raise her and manages to bugger it up. She hooks up with Haines and tries to be a mum and he sends her to work. At some point, she would have figured out that it was Haines who hurt Seth but she doesn't dob him in. Why, I don't know. Too scared, maybe? Couldn't prove it, maybe?

Welfare steps in but they don't help her. They don't support her. Then she gets pregnant again and she's made to feel ashamed of that.

Straightaway, everyone says, Oh, this can't be happening. You can't have this baby. Look at what happened to your first one. No, no, we'll have to take this baby off you.

Then Savannah is born and is thriving and happy but she's not allowed to live with her mum, who gets shoved to one side.

All that stuff coming down on her, it must have been hard.

People have said to me, 'What was she thinking?'

She *wasn't* thinking. I look at her now, and I can see that. She wasn't thinking at all.

But how do you say all that to a woman in a lift?

It was too hard, so I quit work. I was pretty near to retirement anyway. I never wanted to work past 60.

What I've done since I left the Shire is fix this place up.

I started by digging trenches. Don't ask me why. Digging felt right. The pain across the shoulders. The effort I had to put in. The sweat that poured out. I needed all of that.

Then I had to put something in the trenches. I mean, what's a trench with nothing in it? So I laid some pipes for an irrigation system. I put down some topsoil. I planted. I cleared crap that had built up over the years. The transformation, I've got to tell you, it looks good, and it gave me something else to think about. I might go to bed, thinking, First thing, Med, get that part for the tractor, and believe me, that was an improvement on what I'd been thinking for months, which was this: Savannah. Savannah. Savannah.

Savannahsavannahsavannahsavannahsavannahsavannah.

I remember the first day I realised I'd just thought about her, meaning I hadn't been thinking about her until that point on that day, and I felt guilty, but I suppose if that hadn't happened, if I hadn't been able to pull myself together about it, I wouldn't be sitting here now, writing this letter.

Which brings me to the point of it. I mean, why am I writing all this down?

Well, basically, Your Honour, because there's been quite a bit said about my family – about me, and Pat, and Kat, and Blue – and some of it's fair enough and some of it's not.

Now, I don't know what kind of family you've got, Your Honour, but if you're like every judge you see on TV, I'm guessing you are married, with grown-up kids, who ended up teaching you more than you taught them.

If you're around my age, you'll also know what I know, which is that family is the only thing that matters.

I'm raving now, but lately it's been driving me mad. I'll go to the bowls club or to the RSL, and I'll hear people talking about their families, and they'll be saying things like, 'Oh, my sister-in-law, I just can't stand her' or else, 'My mother's husband, he's hopeless' or else, 'My brother and me, we used to be close but we fell out, haven't spoken for years.'

You know what I think of saying to them?

I think of saying, 'Goddamn it, that's your family you're talking about there, and if family means anything to you, make up. You don't have to see each other every day, but know this, they're all you've got. Don't abandon anyone, and don't let anyone abandon you.'

I think of saying to them, 'The time will come, you'll get a knock on the door, and it'll be a cousin, or a brother-in-law, or an uncle, and they'll say, "I've done the wrong thing. I've gambled all the money. I've signed a false cheque. I've had an affair. I've robbed a bank, or seduced the neighbour's wife," and do you know what I'd say to that? I'd say, come on in. I'll make up the bed. Because that's what family is. People get born, they carry your name, and you're supposed to take care of them.

And so I guess what I'm asking you, Your Honour, is whether you're going to let me do that – whether you're going to let me take care of my own.

I know what it means. It means you're going to have to

forgive me. Not just me, but all of us – forgive Kat, and David, and Blue, and me.

We know what people think of us. They think some of us are crazy and the rest of us insane, and those of us who aren't either of those things still manage to make a complete hash of things.

They think we haven't supported each other in the way we ought to have done, and I wouldn't be surprised if you thought that too. I wouldn't be at all surprised to hear you say, 'I've got no sympathy for that Atley mob.'

Well, I hear you, and I'm saying, fair enough. We made a hash of things. All of us did, and we know it. But that was then, and this is now, and what we're saying now is, can you forgive us? Not because we deserve to be forgiven. We know we don't deserve it, so don't do it for us. Do it for Seth. That's what we're asking you, forgive us for Seth, because Seth, he needs us.

# Chapter 21

## Kat Atley

I'VE NOW READ MY FATHER'S LETTER in its entirety, Your Honour, and he's asked me whether there is anything I'd add.

I suppose I'd say only this. There was a time, and it shames me to admit this, when David and I probably wouldn't have thought of adopting a disabled child. We would have been concerned about the effect it would have on our lives, and on our freedom to work and to travel, and so forth.

I won't lie and say that if we'd been asked to take Seth when he first got injured, those things would have mattered to us, and perhaps we would have said we really couldn't do it, we don't feel capable.

Things are obviously different now. My sister had two children; I haven't been lucky enough to have any.

Both of Donna-Faye's children were removed from her care. I do not believe there was ever any evidence that she posed a risk to either of them. It seems to me that she was driven to do what she did precisely because her children were being taken away from her, for reasons she couldn't understand.

I know something of her pain. I do not want to overstep, but I think it's fair to say that Donna-Faye and I will forever be bonded by the loss of Savannah.

Savannah was the love of my life.

I've no reason to believe that she was not the love of Donna-Faye's life, too.

There was an afternoon, six or seven weeks after Savannah died, when David opened the door on Savannah's nursery. We took a deep breath. We began moving things, one stuffed toy at a time. I went through Savannah's drawers. I folded each jumpsuit, each singlet, each sock, each hat.

We dismantled the cot. I took the adhesive turtle mural off the wall. I took down the teddy clock. I folded the plaster cast of her hands into bubble wrap.

We put most things in the back of David's car, and drove them to a storage shed. I could not bear to donate them. Who would take Savannah's clothes? Who would dress their own baby in a jumpsuit from a child that died? No mother would do it. We locked her things away. We pay the rent on a storage unit we have never visited.

Perhaps one day we will.

It isn't only Savannah that is no longer with us, obviously.

# I CAME TO SAY GOODBYE

We've lost Donna-Faye too. We are permitted to see her once a month for an hour. What she knows of those visits, I cannot tell you. I leave too exhausted to enquire.

I have obsessed about what I might have done to save Donna-Faye from her madness, before it was too late.

My father has told you that long before Savannah was born, Donna-Faye wasn't well. I knew that she'd been taken into care in Sydney, and placed under supervision in Tamworth. Why didn't I do something?

The only answer I can come up with is this one: I was obsessed, at that time, with myself. I was obsessed with getting out of the fishing town where I was raised and creating for myself a life that more closely resembled that of the girls with whom I boarded.

I was obsessed with getting up the ladder. In the process, I abandoned my sister. Of course I couldn't see how badly things would turn out, but that's the fact of the matter and finally, I can face it.

It seems to me that had I been available to Fat, and to my father when they needed us, in the courts, and when the first calamities occurred, I would have known what to do. I would have been able to find people that would have cracked open Donna-Faye's faith in Paul Haines, and forced him to admit what he'd done to Seth.

We would have found a way to keep Seth at home.

What I did instead was sit back and listen, or half-listen, on the telephone, from 16,000 kilometres away.

It's no excuse to say I was away. That was a choice I made, to stay abroad when I was needed at home.

In any case, we did not know, Your Honour, that there was anything we could do for Seth, not until now. I realise that's another failing of ours – how could we not know? – but we had always assumed that the decision taken by the court, way back when, to take Seth away from Fat meant that we, too, were cut out of his life.

Also, for as long as I can remember – from the day I first heard that Seth had gone into hospital – we were told that he was dying. Any day now, he'd die. But it never happened. Of course, we could and should have stepped up and said, 'Well, as long as he's alive, we'd like to be in his life' but we did not do that.

Perhaps we thought it was none of our business? More likely, we thought we don't want to make this our business.

Now, of course, with all that has happened – Savannah gone, and Donna-Faye, too, and our hearts completely broken – we are told that Seth is going to be put into State care, into foster homes, apparently because nobody in his family has ever been to see him, and therefore, nobody wants him.

Well, it isn't true, Your Honour.

We do want him. In fact, we need him. I realise that's going to be a problem for some of the people who come to your court. They are going to say, once again, it's all about the Atley family and what they want and what they need and maybe there's some truth to that. We do need him. But we also want him, any way he comes.

# Chapter 22

## Violet Bowen

Dear Judge Judd,

I am writing to you for one reason and one reason only, and that is to thank you. I'm sure you don't hear those words very often so allow me to say it again. Thank you!

What you have done is important. What you have done is special.

I better explain who I am. For two years now, I have been a volunteer at Sydney Aged Care, and Seth Atley-Haines – Seth Atley, if you don't mind me giving him the name by which he should be known – has been one of the children in my care.

Several weeks ago, I had the enormous pleasure to introduce Seth Atley to a member of his family. For a very long time, I thought that would never happen.

I hoped it would happen and I prayed it would happen but as time when on, I admit, I started to think, do they even care about this boy? Now I see, of course they do, and they always did.

When I think about how close they came to losing him – how close he came to losing them! – well, it gives me the shivers.

I have been visiting Seth at least once a week since he was moved from intensive care to the old people's home or, as they call them now, the aged care facility.

Now, before I get to how a beautiful little boy like Seth ended up in an aged care facility, let me tell you how I ended up there, caring for little children!

While I'm at it, may I also say that we need more volunteers to visit children who live in aged care facilities?

I want people to know how rewarding it is, to make a difference in a child's life, especially a disabled child. People feel a bit daunted – they say, oh, I wouldn't know what to do – but let me assure you, it's doesn't matter how old you are – I'm 72 years young myself – or whether you have any particular skills, we can always use an extra pair of hands.

But back to how I got here. I was married at age 21. I am Catholic and my husband was Catholic too. We both thought I would soon fall pregnant – it wasn't discussed, we simply expected it – and it took three years. That was awkward, because in those days, the pressure was on. A baby followed the wedding. My mother wondered what on earth I was doing. We were just at the stage where we were thinking about seeing a doctor when I fell in.

# I CAME TO SAY GOODBYE

Well, I was fit as a fiddle for the whole pregnancy, and I was actually outside, in my apron, picking apricots from the trees, when my waters broke. I went into the local hospital, but the baby wouldn't come. Now, in those days, they put a little something under your nose and whiffed you off, and I don't remember my son being born, and I didn't see anybody take him out of the room, but I do think that I put my head up and said, 'Is everything alright?' and somebody said, 'The baby . . .' and I don't recall the rest. I was under the ether.

Later that day, my husband called for the priest, and when the priest came, I said, 'Have you come to baptise the baby?' And he said, 'The baby is dead.'

Now, don't get upset. It happened to women in those days. I wasn't the only one. My husband came into the hospital and left with the undertaker, and they buried the baby, and I was never told where, and that was the way things were done.

I came out of hospital, and I saw my doctor and I said, 'Am I to blame?' and he said, 'Certainly not' but some other mothers in the town, they crossed the streets with their prams when they saw me.

It was another three years before the next son arrived, and then two girls, and another boy, and then another girl, so in the end, I was blessed, and now I can say I have six children, five living, and nine grandchildren (and one on the way).

After 51 years of marriage, my husband died. I thought, Violet, you've got time on your hands and you're fit and well, you go out there and see what you can do to help. I'd been used to volunteering. I'd done the tuckshop at the children's school. I'd taken Guides, until that fell out of favour.

On the community wall at Coles, I saw a note that said the Probus Club was looking for volunteers to visit sick children that lived on wards among the elderly.

I thought to myself, why on earth are there sick children living on wards with the elderly? I went along to a meeting and they said there are many children who have a disability, who can't stay at home with their parents, and there is nowhere for them to go.

The lady from the aged care told us, 'These children really do need residential care' but there aren't any homes, not anymore, and the only places that have the staff to lift them in and out of bed and take proper care of them are the aged care facilities.

I'm sure I don't need to tell you this, Your Honour, but I think it's not right. It's not right, but that's the way it is.

I signed up for the training course. The first time I went out to the aged care facility to meet the children – well, I fell in love, didn't I? There were six of them, sitting in those wheelchairs with the high backs and the head rests, and one had an oxygen tank and half had colostomy bags.

They couldn't walk, obviously. They had spina bifida or cerebral palsy and some other conditions – you give up trying to remember the names of some of the things they've got – and some were blind. There was no question of them being able to go to the toilet on their own, or anything else. They needed full-time care.

# I CAME TO SAY GOODBYE

In any case, each of us new volunteers was assigned a child to visit and I got Seth, and I don't need to tell you this, but he was adorable. Adorable! He was three years old when we met – he's now five – with hair as white as a butler's glove, and his skin was very white, too. I suppose he'd never been outdoors all that much.

He had a very large head, and at first I thought, oh, perhaps he's one of the children with encephalitis – the water on the brain that swells up the forehead – but the nurse, she said, no, actually, his head isn't that big. It only looked big because his body was small. He hadn't been exercised.

Like the other children, Seth didn't stand up, and so he was often in his padded chair, which seemed a shame to me. Imagine spending all your time on your bottom, or in your bed? Seth's not got a broken spine. He might stand one day and he might even walk. But in the meantime, I spoke to my son about it, and he had an idea. He got a plastic baby walker, the type with the seat built in, and he removed the wheels, so it wouldn't slide about, and we put it in the boot of the car and drove it out to the aged-care facility, and my son picked up Seth and threaded his legs through the leg holes and Seth was standing! Not really standing. The nappy part took the weight of him, but he looked like he was standing, his little white legs were straight down for once, and it seemed to me that he was thrilled to bits! He went to clap his hands and missed – he always misses! – but he definitely went to clap.

There were dials and mirrors and spinning barrels on the walker, and Seth, although they say he's blind, can see a bit.

I've held up a balloon, I've moved it slowly across the room, and his eyes will follow it.

He felt around and he made the barrel spin, and he flipped the mirror back and forward. You could see he was enjoying it.

It isn't the role of volunteers to ask too many questions, but of course we're all very curious about why the different children are in the aged care centre, and of course, Seth had the sad story. He wasn't born the way he is, something happened to him when he was a baby. The nurses told me his father shook him, but nobody could ever prove it.

I thought, oh, poor Seth, you poor mite. I don't deny that it made me love him even more.

The nurse, she said, 'They thought he'd be a vegetable' but it was clear to me that he wasn't a vegetable, not at all! Oh no, Seth knows what's going on. He's got real potential.

From time to time, doctors come by and they try to get Seth to make sounds, or play some games – Hands on Shoulders, Hands on Heads, or Simon Says – and they mark their clipboards, saying he can't do it, and that's true, he hasn't quite got the hang of it, but that's not to say he doesn't enjoy it. He enjoys it, and in fact there's quite a lot that he enjoys. In my view, you've just got to be a little patient with him.

For example, the hospital has got chickens in a coop in the grounds, and before I became Seth's volunteer, he wasn't allowed to be in the group of children who were wheeled down there to collect the eggs.

I wondered why that was and the nurse didn't seem to know so I wheeled him out there and put a warm egg in his hands, and he nodded and smiled, bobbing that big head of his, all the way back to the hospital kitchen, and he did not break that egg, which to me was quite amazing, because Seth doesn't have much control over his limbs. He can jerk about quite a bit when he's upset, but he did not break that egg.

If I had to say why it was that others hadn't tried a few new tricks with Seth, I'd say it's because there's no doubt the staff are run off their feet, but also, it's true, Seth was crying a lot when I first met him. Some visits, he would cry the whole time, just cry and cry, and I'd have to rock him and pat him, and he'd make the most wretched noises and fight with me, and leave me with bruises but I didn't give up on him.

It was my daughter who had the idea to soothe him with music. Music soothes the savage beast! She donated a little iPod – the AldiPod we call it, because it's not one of the expensive ones, it's the Aldi one – and she put music onto it, and she bought soft earphones, and Seth can sit with that on, singing like a bird. Not words, nothing melodic, not in time to the music, but he will wave his hands about like he's the conductor of a little orchestra, and he'll make a sound like a penny whistle, long and sweet and high.

As to feeding him, well, Seth doesn't feed himself, but he's not tube-fed either. Some of the children have the tube into the stomach, but Seth can take food orally and so, now he's more content and used to me, I take his bottle – he's got his own special mix – and hold it for him to drink, and sometimes – not every time, but sometimes – Seth will put his hand out, and feel around, and put his hand on the bottle while I'm feeding him.

I have to say, I've long been of the view that given what he can do – as opposed to what he can't do – Seth shouldn't be in the nursing home. I always believed that he would just do so much better if he was at home with somebody, and part of a proper family.

The problem, of course, was there was nowhere for him to go. His mother couldn't take him, and of course, you can't just adopt a child like Seth out, can you?

I was genuinely starting to worry about how he'd fare as he got older, and started to understand more about where he was, when his mother, his poor mother, did what she did.

I won't say anything more about that. Like everybody, I read about it in the paper and we volunteers, we were told that Seth was the brother of the baby that had gone over The Gap, and it was almost too much for me. I held Seth that day. I held him under my chin, and rocked and patted him, thinking, 'Haven't you suffered enough?' And then, of course, his mother got committed, and I guess that's when I understood, she really isn't going to be able to come back for him.

Once she'd been committed, of course, the courts could revisit the problem of Seth. While she was alive and well, there was always a chance that he'd be restored to her care. Now that can't happen, so they decided to see if they could try to place him with another family, and I was just on the verge of putting my own hand up, to say that with my daughters and the others, we could manage, and we'd be delighted, when his own family turned up.

# I CAME TO SAY GOODBYE

Can you imagine it? Out of the blue, there they were.

Why they hadn't visited before, I didn't really understand, except that the grandpa – Med his name is, odd name for a man, I know – he told me that the family thought they were banned from seeing Seth. He told me that his daughter, Donna-Faye, was banned from all contact, and he assumed that the ban covered him too, and it was only recently that a lawyer told them, no, he could have applied to the court to see Seth, and probably, he would have been allowed to see Seth from the get-go.

But courts and rules, not everybody understands them, do they?

Then, of course, he got the letter from you, Judge Judd, saying an order was to be made, to make Seth a permanent ward of the State, and did he have any objection?

Did he have any objection!

Well, you know very well, he had an objection! I've seen what he wrote to you. He couldn't be more honest.

I want to tell you now about the first day Med came onto the ward, after he'd got permission to start rebuilding the bond that will make Seth part of his own family again.

Seth and I, we weren't actually on the ward. I'd taken him out to the trellis, where the jasmine grows, and we were sitting on the bench there, listening to birdsong.

All morning, I'd been saying to him, 'Well, Seth, today's the day!' because of course, I'd been given notice that they were coming, and perhaps it's my faith in God, but I knew it would work out well for him

I had Seth's bottle, and I was preparing to take Seth onto

my lap, to put his head back like a baby and give him a good feed, when I saw them. There were two young people – Ka'aren (I call her Kat, now) and her husband, David, and then Blue Paul and two children, Amy and Indiana.

Then, too, there was another man, not as old as me, but not young. Bald on top with a big old beard, and kind of sad-looking.

I thought, that must be grandpa. I was holding Seth on my lap, supporting his head. They walked over and I could see they were nervous as anything. They stood at some distance and I said, 'Hello! Please, come and sit down' and waved them forward, and made room for them on the bench.

The grandpa, he was first to sit down. I tilted Seth forward a little, and said, 'Here you are. This is Seth.'

He said, 'Hello, Seth.'

Blue was crying, and then Kat, she started crying, too.

The little ones didn't seem to know what to make of it all. I noticed they were dressed in their best. They had shiny shoes and bobby socks and dresses, and they were niggling and shoving at each other, the way children do when they are trying so hard to be good.

I smiled at Med, and encouraged him closer. I held up Seth's bottle. I said, 'Would you like to feed him?'

He said, 'Is that alright?'

I said, 'Of course it's alright' and I lifted Seth, who was bobbing about and smiling his big head off, and put him on Med's lap, and showed Med how to support his head and to keep his legs from getting tangled over themselves. I gave him Seth's bottle. I said, 'Here' and showed him how the teat went into Seth's mouth, just like with a newborn baby, and I said, 'Don't worry about him, he's a good eater.'

And he was very good at it, the grandpa was. He held that child securely, and Seth, although he started off looking at him a little uncertainly, and looking over at me, and back at him, he started to slurp away, and better than that, do you know what he did? He started feeling his way around the bottle, feeling for the grandpa's hand, and when he found it, he stopped, and he put his little hand over the grandpa's hand, and he kept it there.

The grandpa, his eyes just filled with tears.

I said, 'He likes you.'

The grandpa, he said, 'Do you think he does?'

I looked at him. I said, 'Of course he does. You're his grandaddy.'

He said, 'Well, I like him too.'

And that was the day that I truly knew what a good decision you'd made, Your Honour, because that was the day that I knew for certain, Seth was going home.

Read on for an extract from *Ghost Child*,
Available in March 2014

*The past is always close behind...*
On 11 November 1982, police were called to a housing
estate an hour west of Melbourne. In the lounge room of
an otherwise ordinary brick veneer home, they found a five-
year-old boy lying on the carpet. His arms were by his sides,
his palms flat. The paramedics could see no obvious signs of
trauma other than an almost imperceptible indentation to the
boy's skull, but he died the next day.

The boy's mother said a man had attacked her son on the
way back from the shops, but few people were surprised when
she and her boyfriend went to prison for the crime. Police
declared themselves satisfied that justice had been done. And
yet, for years, rumours swept the estate and clung like cobwebs
to the long-vacant house: there had been a cover-up. The real
perpetrator, at least according to local gossip, was the boy's six-
year-old sister, Lauren . . .

'A gripping debut novel . . . Taut writing helps ratchet up the
tension between the voices of each of the people involved,
until all the layers are stripped away to finally reveal the truth'
– *Australian Women's Weekly*

# Prologue

On 11 November 1982, Victorian police were called to a home on the Barrett housing estate, an hour west of Melbourne. In the lounge room of an otherwise ordinary brick-veneer home, they found a five-year-old boy lying still and silent on the carpet. His arms were by his sides, his palms flat.

There were no obvious signs of trauma. The boy was neither bruised nor bleeding, but when paramedics turned him gently onto his side they found an almost imperceptible indentation in his skull, as broad as a man's hand and as shallow as a soap dish.

The boy's mother told police her son had been walking through the schoolyard with one of his younger brothers when they were approached by a man who wanted the change in their pockets. The brothers refused to hand over the money so the man knocked the older boy to the ground and began to kick and punch him.

The younger boy ran home to raise the alarm. Their mother carried the injured boy home in her arms. She called an ambulance, but nothing could be done.

The story made the front page of *The Sun* newspaper in Melbourne and the TV news.

Police made a public appeal for witnesses but, in truth, nobody really believed the mother's version of events. The Barrett Estate was poor but no one was bashing children for loose change – not then. Ultimately, the mother and her boyfriend were called in for questioning. Police believed that one of them – possibly both – was involved in the boy's death.

There was a great deal of interest in the case, but when it finally came to court, the Chief Justice closed the hearing. The verdict would be released; so, too, would any sentence that was handed down. But the events leading up to the little boy's death would remain a mystery.

Few people were surprised to hear that the boy's mother and her boyfriend went to prison for the crime. Police declared themselves satisfied with the result, saying there was no doubt justice had been done. And yet for years rumours swept the Barrett Estate, passing from neighbour to neighbour and clinging like cobwebs to the long-vacant house: there had been a cover-up. The real perpetrator, at least according to local gossip, was the boy's six-year-old sister, Lauren.

# Lauren Cameron

When a young woman lives by herself, it's assumed she must be lonely. I'd say the opposite is true. In fact, if anybody had asked me what it was like when I first started living on my own, I would have said, 'It was perfect.' I was completely alone – I had no close friends, and nobody I called family – and that was precisely what I wanted.

The place I moved into was basically a shed, and it was built on a battle-axe block behind somebody else's house. The property itself was on Sydney's northern beaches. There was a family living in the main house, the one that fronted the beach. They owned the block and, like many Sydneysiders who had beachside property in the 1980s, they decided to make the most of it by carving a driveway down the side, building a granny flat out the back and renting it to me.

After the first meeting, when they gave me the keys and we talked about the rent, I had nothing whatsoever to do with them. They were a family – a mum, a dad and two teenage kids – living in the main house, and I was the boarder. I could get to my place without bothering them. I just walked down the driveway, opened my door and I was home. I had my own toilet, shower and enough of a kitchen, so there was no reason to go knocking.

Before I moved in, I bought four things. The most expensive was a queen-size sheet set in a leopard-skin print, with two pillowcases. I bought a box of black crockery, with dinner plates shaped like hexagons. I had this idea, then, that I might one day have close friends who could come over for dinner. I also bought a new steam iron and ironing-board, these last things because it was a condition of my employment that my uniform be straight and clean.

I still remember the first morning I woke in my own place. I was seventeen years old. I padded into the kitchen in my moccasins, put the kettle on the stove top, and pressed the red button to make the flame ignite. I took the plastic cover off the new ironing-board and scrunched it into a ball. I was fiddling underneath the board, trying to find the lever that makes the legs stick out, when the kettle began to whistle itself into hysterics. I put the ironing-board down and took a cup from the crockery set, removing some of the cardboard that had been packed around it, and made a cup of tea – hot and sugary, with the bag taken out, not left in – and I thought to myself, 'This is just like playing house! I'm okay here. Things are going to be fine.'

When the family told the neighbours they'd rented out the granny flat, they probably wanted to know whether I was going to cause trouble – whether I was going to bring boys home and make a racket. But the answer was no, I was not. I amused myself in the granny flat by learning new and humble domestic tasks: sweeping the floor with a straw broom; bending to collect the mess in a dustpan and brush; buying garbage bags with two handles that tied at the top. My idea of a good night was to eat Tim Tams in bed and to smoke cigarettes on the porch, although only after I saw the lights in the main house go out.

The owners would have said, 'Oh, she's the perfect tenant, like a mouse, so quiet, you never even know she's there.'

From time to time, I'd bump into the mum – not my mum, but the mum who lived in the main house. I'd be heading out to work and she'd be on the nature strip, getting shopping bags out of the boot of her car or something, and she'd smile at me – probably because everybody approves of hospital staff – and I'd smile back at her.

I didn't see much of the dad. Perhaps he'd decided that there was nothing to be gained from getting too close to the girl who lived in his shed. I had nothing much to do with the children, either. I was closer in age to them than to their parents, but really, what did we have in common? They came out from time to time, to jump on the trampoline and to sit under the pirate flag in the old tree house, but we rarely spoke.

I'd taken a job as a nurse's aide in a city hospital, and I'm sure my co-workers at first understood why I lived alone. I was new to Sydney so it made sense, at least in the beginning, that I wouldn't have many friends. After I'd settled, though, they must have wondered why I continued to live in a granny flat when I could easily have shared a city apartment with one of the other aides. The noticeboard at work often had handwritten signs tacked up, advertising rooms for rent. 'Outgoing girl wanted to share FUN FLAT!' one of the ads said. The truth is, the things the other girls wanted to do – going to nightclubs, drinking Fluffy Ducks and Orgasms and Harvey Wallbangers – didn't sound like fun to me.

Of course, I wasn't famous then, far from it. I was just the quiet girl, the churchy girl that lived alone, prayed in the hospital chapel, and never socialised. I'm sure they all got a shock when photographs of me started appearing in newspapers, just as I'm sure the family I boarded with got a shock when journalists swarmed the granny flat, waving microphones on sticks.

I got a bit of a shock myself. I took refuge in my bed, hiding under the leopard-skin sheets, trying to fight the urge to *run*. Because, really, run where? There was nowhere to go.

I don't know how long I would have stayed under the covers if Harley hadn't turned up. He walked down the side drive, past the windows of the main house. I heard the mum rap on the glass. 'Hey, you,' she said. 'Off our property!'

Harley said, 'I'm not with the media. I'm Harley Cashman. Lauren's my sister.'

She would have been startled. For one thing, the mum knew me not as Lauren Cashman but as Lauren *Cameron,* which was the name I'd given her when I moved in. She didn't know I had a brother, either. I'd told them what I used to tell everyone: 'I have no family.'

Harley knocked at my door and when I didn't answer, I heard him push it open. I didn't stir but I could feel warm sunshine pour across my bed.

Harley said, 'Mate, what *are* you doing? Everyone's looking for you.'

I didn't respond so he pulled back the doona and said, 'Lauren, seriously, this is ridiculous. Get up.'

I felt so frightened and overwhelmed that I wasn't sure that I could. I said to Harley, 'I can't.'

He said, 'Sure you can.'

We went on like that for a while, him saying, 'Come on, Lauren,' and me saying, 'Just go away, Harley,' until he said, 'Okay, look, I'm not going to hang around here forever. If you want me gone, I'm gone.'

It was then that I realised I didn't want him to go, not without me, not ever again. I rose from the bed, untangling myself from the sheets, and said, 'Okay, all right.'

'That's right,' he said. 'Get up, and let's get you out of here.'

I was wearing only a T-shirt and a pair of knickers.

'You're going to need to get dressed,' he said, and started picking up some clothes I'd flung onto the floor. Compared with him – with anyone – I was tiny. He held up a pair of my pants and said, 'How do you even get one leg in here?'

I snatched them away and went into the bathroom to dress myself.

'Good on you,' he said when I emerged. 'Now, let's go.'

He ushered me to the door and we left the granny flat together, me with a jumper over my head in case there was a photographer still lurking, trying to get a picture. He'd parked his car on the nature strip. I couldn't see anything because the jumper was over my face so he guided me into the passenger seat. It was only once we'd started moving, once I was sure we were clear of the suburban streets and onto a freeway, that I took the jumper off, and said, 'Where are we going?'

Harley said, 'I've decided that you should meet the folks.'

I said, '*Whose* folks?'

He said, 'Mum is gonna love you.'

I thought, '*Your* mum. Not mine.'

I rolled the jumper into a ball and put it on the floor near my feet. I said, 'She doesn't even *know* me, Harley.'

He said, 'Mate, you're my *sister*. What more is there to know?'

I didn't answer. What more was there to know? What do any of us know? We think we know the basic facts about our lives: those are my parents and these are my siblings and this is my story, at least as I've come to tell it. But, really, how much of it is true?

# Detective Senior Sergeant Brian Muggeridge

When I first met Lauren Cameron her name was not Lauren Cameron, it was Lauren Cashman. I don't know when she changed it, although I've got a pretty good idea why.

Lauren likes to tell people that she has no parents and no siblings. It isn't true. When I first met her she had a mother, a sister, and not one but two brothers, and all of them were called Cashman.

I met them on the evening of 11 November 1982. I remember the date because it was Remembrance Day and I'd been on parade since dawn with the old Diggers at the Cenotaph on the Barrett Estate. I was hoping to knock off early, but then I got a call to go out to the Cashman place on DeCastella Drive. A mum had called triple-O, screaming that her kid had been bashed, and

11

although a young constable was on her way to the scene, a more senior police officer was going to be needed.

The Cashmans lived in a Commission house – quite a few of the neighbours later made a point of telling me that when I went around taking statements from them. They said, 'Those people, they don't own here. It's Housing Commission. They're just renting.'

What did they mean by that? Not that the family was poor. There were plenty of poor people on the Barrett Estate. I don't mean down-and-outs. We had quite a few old-age pensioners and a few single mums on the estate, but in those days, most people worked. We had labourers, hairdressers, panel beaters, and a good bunch of guys down at Barrett Glass. Nobody was flush. At a guess, the highest earner on the estate would have been the school principal, on something like $45,000 a year. It was a 'working-class' estate in the proper sense of the word: people worked, although not for much.

So no, the neighbours didn't mean 'poor'. They meant something else, something that in those days was harder to define. These days, we wouldn't hesitate. We'd say the mother was a bludger with four kids under six to three different blokes, none of whom were on the scene.

Anyway, I drove up to the house as fast as I could. I was in one of those white Commodores they gave coppers in those days. The idea was to give us the speed and the muscle we'd need to catch the crooks. Trouble

12

was, every bloke under thirty on the Barrett Estate had a white Commodore, and they souped them up to make them go faster. There were a couple of Commodores already parked in the driveway of the Cashman house when I got there. At first I thought they were both police cars, but on second glance it was pretty obvious that one of them wasn't. The suspension had been lowered – in those days we used a beer can to check, and there was no way you'd get a VB under this car – plus the windows had been tinted. No, this one wasn't a police car. This car belonged either to a man who lived in the house, or to a man who at least visited often enough to feel comfortable parking in the drive.

The ambulance was already there and I saw the paramedics leap from it and move like lightning across the lawn, the white soles of their shoes flashing. I got out of the car and made my way up the path, expecting to find the house in a state of chaos. I mean, that's quite normal, isn't it? If a kid has come a cropper and the parents have had to call an ambulance, well, you can expect a lot of noise. The parents will be screaming and crying and it's my job to get them to settle down, so we can start figuring out what happened. But there was no panic in Lauren's house.

The mother, Lisa, was in the kitchen with the young female police constable. Lisa was pale and extremely thin, a chain-smoker, with hair that had been frizzed and dyed red so many times you couldn't tell what colour it originally was. She was twenty-six years old, but she had that worn-down look that women get when they've fallen pregnant for the first time at a young age. If I was to hold up a picture of her alongside pictures of today's twenty-six-year-old girls, fresh from university and still giggly, you'd have said she was forty.

Anyway, Lisa was standing in the kitchen when I arrived, holding herself up against the laminate bench and chewing the skin around her thumb. Like I say, I expected some kind of frenzy, but I got the feeling she was just plain irritated, like here was something she really didn't need; all these people in uniform in her house, it pissed her off.

In the lounge room a big bloke – a near-naked bloke – was holding this kid up under the arms like a puppet, trying to make his feet grip the carpet. It was hopeless. The kid's legs kept buckling, and his head was lolling about on his neck.

I could see what the big fella was trying to do. He was trying to make the boy stand up, but I could see that wasn't going to happen. The kid was all floppy and he had those 'sunset eyes' you get when the brain is gone, with the eyeballs not focused and the lids half-closed. The paramedics were trying to intervene. They weren't shouting at him, but they were talking loudly, saying, 'Please, put the boy down.'

There were other kids in the house: a boy of about three, and a girl who was still a toddler, both of them in the lounge room, all curious and afraid. And then there was Lauren. She's wasn't in the lounge room. She was in the hall. How did she look? Well, what can I say? In the looks department, she was blessed. She had buck teeth and freckles across her nose, and she was wearing a T-shirt that had some kind of cartoon animal on the front. She could have been anybody's little Aussie rug rat except that, like all the other kids in the house, she had this extraordinary white hair. I don't mean white-blonde, like some kids have, I mean white-white, like a Samoyed dog. It was curled all around her face and cascaded down her back, so long that she probably would have been able to sit on it. She had white eyelashes, and white eyebrows, too, but she wasn't albino – that would be going too far. No, she was more like a ghost. And it wasn't just the hair that made me think that. It was the way she was hovering in the hallway, like she was trying to decide whether it was all right to come and look at what was going on.

The first words I heard out of Lisa's mouth were: 'Get up.' I've got to say, it struck me as strange. The big bloke had let the boy fall to the floor and the paramedics were leaning over him, and I'd say it should have been obvious to anyone that the boy was in no position to stand up, but that's what the mother said. She came out from the kitchen, broke into the huddle around him, and said, 'Jacob, get up.'

'Is he dead?' Those were the first words I heard from

Lauren. She'd come creeping down the hall, wanting to get a good look.

'Don't be stupid, Lauren,' her mother said. 'Go get the heater.'

Again, it was such a strange thing to say. This was November, remember, so it was as good as summer in Melbourne. We'd been sweating out by the Cenotaph. Some of the school kids who'd been standing to attention while the band played, they'd actually fainted. Lauren didn't argue with her mother, though. She went off down the hall and came back with a portable heater. It was three orange bars in an aluminium shell, and it was covered in dust, but Lisa took it from her and plugged it in, and within seconds the whole house was filled with smoke from the dust on the elements. That didn't stop the mother, though. She put the thing close to Jacob's head, and his white hair began to steam. I realised his hair must have been damp.

The paramedics were working like crazy. One of the paramedics said, 'Please, get it out of the way,' and the other said, 'What's the boy's name? How old is he?'

'He's five,' said Lisa. 'He's Jake. Jacob.'

The paramedic said, 'We're going to have to get him to hospital.'

'Jesus,' said Lisa. 'I ain't got ambulance cover.'

I think that's when I stepped in. I'm pretty sure my first words would have been, 'Hello. I'm Detective Senior Sergeant Brian Muggeridge, Barrett CIB.'

16

Nobody paid any attention. One of the paramedics was trying to fit an oxygen mask over the boy's face, and the other was kicking the heater out of the way while trying to get the wheels out from under a stretcher, so they could get Jake off the floor and out the door.

'You won't need cover,' said the paramedic.

'You'll need to come with us,' said the other.

I said, 'Hang on, I'm just going to need a few seconds here.'

Lisa glared at me and then turned her back, so I went over to the copper in the kitchen and said, 'What you got?'

The young constable must have been a new recruit because her shirt was still sharp across the creases. By that time I'd been a copper for about eight years, I suppose, and maybe it was starting to show. My father had been in the force and he'd told me, 'The pay's lousy but at least you get to retire at fifty-five.' That appealed to me. All I could see myself doing as a young fella was working long enough to buy a boat and spend my retirement fishing. What I didn't know then was what I'd have to go through to get to retirement age. The human misery, it was already wearing me down.

The new recruit told me the mother had sent her boys to the shops for cigarettes. Jacob, who was five, and Harley, who was three, were on their way home when a man came up and told them to hand over the change. They refused, and so the man started roughing them up, knocking them to the ground and kicking them. The younger boy, Harley, managed to break away, run home and raise the alarm. Lisa had followed him back to the school grounds and found Jacob lying there, unconscious. She carried him home in her arms.

I thought, 'No.'

I can't tell you exactly how or why I knew the story wasn't true. Instinct, maybe. I'll admit that I was swayed by the condition of the house. It was slumped on its foundations as if the burden of housing so many fractured families had taken a toll on the frame.

I don't know whether Lisa had been listening to the constable who gave me these details, but when I moved again towards her, to try to ask a few questions, she got pretty agitated. She said, 'I gotta go with Jake,' and she came into the kitchen and started gathering cigarettes and other things off the kitchen bench. She had a Glomesh purse and a set of house keys with a plastic tag hanging off the ring that said 'Never Mind The Dog, Beware the Bitch Who Lives Here!' She stuffed those things into her handbag, and then she opened the fridge and took out a baby's bottle filled with orange cordial, which she gave to her boyfriend, saying, 'Make sure you give this to Hayley.'

The boyfriend said, 'Do you want me to come?'

She said, 'You stay here.'

I noticed straightaway that there was no tenderness

in the exchange. I mean, you might expect this guy to be comforting Lisa a bit at this stage, or at least to be saying, 'Don't worry, he'll be fine,' or something, given that they were obviously an item, but that wasn't what was happening. It made me wonder how long they'd actually been together, or even known each other. Later, we'd find out they'd been together six weeks.

I thought to myself, 'Did he do it?' Look, I know that sounds biased against blokes, but how many times had I been to a situation where a kid was out cold and the de facto was the one who'd done it?

The paramedics looked ready to leave and were starting to push Jake out toward the ambulance. Lisa was obviously going to have to go with them, but getting her out the door was going to be no simple matter because by now the media was all over the lawn. In those days, reporters had access to police scanners. They can't do it any more, not with mobile phones and scrambled messages and so forth, but in those days we basically had CB radios, and it wasn't illegal, not then, to intercept what you heard on the two-way system. So they would have heard the call – a child had been beaten on the Barrett Estate; paramedics required – and they'd have followed the ambulance to the house, and now they were outside, waiting to hear what had gone on so they could write it up for the next day's papers.

They wouldn't interfere with the paramedics. They'd be allowed to make their way to the ambulance, to get the boy inside, but Lisa . . . well, she wasn't injured, so they'd see her as fair game.

I said to Lisa, 'I'm going to have to help you get past the press. They'll be shouting questions at you but you just stick with me and I'll get you though.'

She was nodding her head and gripping her bag. We went out the front door and I tried to help her into the back of the ambulance, but she tripped and we had to make a second go of it, which gave the snappers plenty of time to get a picture. I thought she'd immediately fuss over the boy when she got inside, but she didn't. Instead, she looked out through the glass doors of the ambulance, towards the flashes from the cameras and the bobbing, fuzzy microphones, and she was wearing a very strange expression. If I had to put a name to it, I'd say she was thrilled.

I made a note of the time. The call to triple-O had been placed at around 5.40 p.m. and now it was getting toward 7 p.m. The deadline for the newspaper reporters was 10 p.m., at the absolute latest, and the photographers were at least an hour from their darkrooms in Melbourne's CBD, so it was clear that they'd soon have to get moving if they were going to get this story in the paper. I knew from experience, though, that they'd probably wait for a statement from the cops before they'd move. Lisa was shouting things at them through the glass doors of the ambulance, things like: 'They ought to lock 'em up and throw away the key!'

They knew they had a story – a good story – and now it was up to me to give the thing some context.

The other thing they'd want, of course, was a picture of Jake, not only of him going into the ambulance but a nice portrait, something good and clear, that they could whack on the front page. I scanned the pack, looking for somebody I recognised, and straightaway saw a guy from *The Sun* I remembered from some other job. I signalled to him to come forward, into the house, telling him I'd give him a photograph that he could share with the others. We stepped through the front door and walked straight into the boyfriend. He was standing in the lounge room, his massive legs and chest still bare, just looking like a stunned mullet, taking up all the space.

I said, 'I'm Detective Muggeridge. You're . . . ?

He said, 'Peter Tabone.'

I said, 'Right, Mr Tabone, can you help me here? I need a photograph of Jacob that I can give to the press, something we can copy for the newspapers.'

By way of an answer, he said, 'He's not my kid.'

I'd already figured that for myself, so I let it go and scanned the room, and immediately saw a portrait – a bright, white-and-blue portrait of four children – in a cardboard frame on the mantelpiece. I picked it up and said, 'Are these the children? Which one is Jake?'

Unaccountably, Peter brightened.

'I paid for that,' he said. 'Pretty all right, isn't it? Pretty good, actually.'

21

He seemed not to understand the seriousness of the situation. We weren't here to *admire* the photo; we were here to find Jake's attacker. Again, I said, 'Which one is Jake?'

Peter considered the photograph for a moment, then pointed and said, 'That one.'

Jake was seated in the middle of the group. Like all of them, he was wearing blue jeans and a white T-shirt, and he was flanked on both sides by siblings. Behind them was a cloudy background: not dull-cloudy, but a bright blue background with white clouds. I handed the photograph to the *Sun* photographer, who laid it down on the kitchen bench and said, 'Thanks, mate. We appreciate this.' He lifted up his camera and began photographing it. That was the easiest way to get a copy in those days, before digital prints and email, you'd just copy a photograph with your own camera, develop it in the darkroom, and send it by courier to colleagues from rival papers. The copies would be in colour, but in the newspaper they'd turn out black and white, which was a pity, because the thing that was most striking about the kids, the thing that any witness was likely to remember, was the hair.

Peter seemed very interested in the photographer and his gear, but he didn't seem too happy about his portrait being copied. He said, 'Why do they need a picture?'

I said, 'If anybody sees this picture, they might

remember seeing Jake on the way to the shops and they might remember something suspicious, and that's going to help us catch the culprit.'

Peter said, 'Yeah, okay, but remember, *I* paid for that picture.'

The photographer looked up, surprised. Was Peter suggesting that he should pay for the right to copy it? The photographer let it go. I remember thinking, 'These guys aren't bad. The press gets a bad rap but they've got a job to do and, on this occasion, that meant getting a picture, any picture of the kid, so people could look at it and say, "What a cute kid! How could anybody hurt a child like that? What's the world coming to?"'

When the *Sun* guy was done, I put the portrait back on the mantelpiece and went outside. The press was waiting for me, waiting for some kind of official comment to go with their stories. I stood in the forest of microphones and said, 'As you have no doubt gathered, we have a serious incident on our hands here.'

They nodded and waited.

'We've got a five-year-old boy who was sent to the shops with his brother, and it appears that they've been set upon by a man who has bashed him, possibly for the change they were carrying.'

I paused to give them time to write this down.

'I think you'll agree that's a cowardly crime, to beat an innocent boy, a five-year-old boy,' I continued.

'We are appealing for witnesses to come forward. We ask anyone who might have seen anything suspicious to please call Crime Stoppers. I think you've all got the number.'

One reporter said, 'Can we speak to the parents?' and I said no. Another reporter wanted to know what kind of injury the boy had suffered. I said, 'That's obviously a matter for the specialists. At this stage it's unclear, but I think I'm safe in saying that the young lad is in quite a bad way.'

They wanted to know the boy's name and I told them: Jacob Cashman. They wanted to know how to spell Jacob – was it Jakob or Jacob or, who knows these days, Jaycub? – and I confirmed it: It was J-A-C-O-B, Jacob. Jacob John Cashman. Referring to notes taken by the new recruit, I added: 'Born 1 August, 1977. He's five.'

'He's what?' The reporters hadn't heard me. Daylight was fading and the cockatoos that made their nests in Barrett's gum trees had taken flight. They were swooping and screaming, apparently furious.

I repeated myself, louder this time. I said, 'Five. The young boy, the victim, he's five.' And somehow, those words brought silence upon all of us.

I turned and went back through the front door. The boyfriend, Peter, had turned on the TV and the children were watching, of all things, *The Love Boat*. They didn't turn to look at me. There was a day coming when they'd have to face up to what happened in that house on DeCastella Drive, but it wouldn't be that day and, likely, not for years, so I let them go on watching.